MICHIKUSA HOUSE

MICHIKUSA HOUSE

a Novel

EMILY GRANDY

HOMEBOUND PUBLICATIONS
BERKSHIRE MOUNTAINS, MASS.

HOMEBOUND PUBLICATIONS

WWW.HOMEBOUND PUBLICATIONS.COM

© 2023 TEXT AND ILLUSTRATIONS BY EMILY GRANDY

All Rights Reserved
Published in 2023 by Wayfarer Books,
A Division of Homebound Publications
Interior Design by Connor L. Wolfe
Cover Design by Stephanie Shafer
Interior Illustrations by Emily Grandy

TRADE PAPERBACK. 978-1-953340603
EBOOK 978-1-953340-55-9

10 9 8 7 6 5 4 3 2 1

Look for our titles in paperback, ebook, and audiobook wherever books are sold. Wholesale offerings for retailers available through Ingram.

Homebound Publications is committed to ecological stewardship. We greatly value the natural environment and invest in conservation. For each book purchased in our online store we plant one tree.

PO Box 1601, Northampton, MA 01060

| 860.574.5847 | info@homeboundpublications.com |

HOMEBOUNDPUBLICATIONS.COM & WAYFARERBOOKS.ORG

For Andrew

PROLOGUE

There was a time, a few years ago now, when I lived in a house without mirrors. For thirteen months, it was as if I could see nothing of myself below chest height, what little could fit inside the frame of a handheld compact I used to insert my contact lenses. How strange, I thought, to see only features disembodied. Wavy chestnut hair, set to frizz by summer's mugginess. A pair of large blue-grey eyes the color of river stones. I had been sent overseas to stay with a friend of my mother's, an artist she'd known since college who had a studio on Japan's Kyushu Island, somewhere in Oita Prefecture. It wasn't that the old place didn't have any mirrors but that my mother requested they be stowed away. The idea was that I should "live in the real world for a few minutes." Meaning that I should stop thinking about myself, fixating on my body, how it looked, and how it felt to live inside it. "You need to do something useful with your hands, Winona," she had said, my mother the ceramicist. "Something tactile." Her advice for anything that ailed, from menstrual cramps to existential afflictions.

In that respect, her friend Shoko—Mrs. Hanada, a woman thirty years my senior who had solidified over time thanks to long hours of manual labor on the farm and at her ceramics wheel—functioned as the ideal mentor. And her property, Michikusa House, was the model classroom. The word *mi-chi-ku-sa*, written either as みちくさ or 道草 in Japanese, translates to something like "grass by the wayside," but its meaning runs deeper than that. Michikusa implies dawdling, traveling to wherever you're going without haste. That's exactly how I remember it. A place to slow down. A place for rest and recovery. Or, in my case, rehabilitation.

It started as a straightforward arrangement. I had already taken some medical leave and regained the weight the doctors advised, but still hadn't found an appetite. Or, for that matter, a purpose, a reason to get better. A change in scenery was recommended. Being in the financial bracket that permitted extensive travel, my parents arranged the whole thing. Thirteen months in the Japanese *satoyama*, a small mountain village so remote it didn't even have a convenience store. Shoko accommodated each of my mother's careful requests. No mirrors. Supervised meals. Plenty of fresh mountain air, puttering around in the garden, and good home cooking. What none of us expected, me least of all, was that I would emerge fully transformed.

Whenever I reflect on my time at Michikusa House, I picture the farm and gardens as they were in autumn when I first arrived. A lush palette of crimson, ochre, and bronze. The aged farmhouse, with its blue clay roof tiles and elegant sliding doors, sat behind a low stone wall. Leading to it was a road so infrequently used it was caped in moss and overhung with fronds of feathery grass. Mountains hugged close on every side, so big they functioned like a shoji screen, blocking the view, receding only when I looked up at the sky. After the leaves fell, we plucked sweet persimmons from gnarled, skeletal trees. Then the winter solstice passed, marking an incremental shift toward light and renewal. At the end of a humid summer, those long grasses overhanging the roadside turned to straw and dropped their seeds once more. Time, which had dawdled all summer and into autumn, snapped back into high gear with the urgency of the overslept as frost made its first entrance, and I prepared for my homebound journey.

When I returned to my parents' house, to that familiar Midwest college town, I arrived just in time for Thanksgiving. Over pumpkin pie, my mother commented on my "healthy glow" and newly muscled figure, aspects of myself I had scarcely considered in Japan, without the aid of a mirror. Or, for that matter, anyone to impress. Apart from Shoko and her husband, there was only one other full-time resident at Michikusa House that year. His name was Jun Nakashima, and the only way to impress him was in the kitchen.

I had never known anyone with a passion for food before, whose familiarity with ingredients surpassed his intimacy with other humans. That is to say, Jun Nakashima was an outstanding cook. He had the most refined, discerning palate of anyone I had ever met. Jun always said he would rather eat at home than suffer a disappointing meal at a restaurant, and he found most restaurants disappointing. Though, I should add one disclaimer: he did enjoy guessing ingredients that went into making dishes, even those he disfavored. This turned out to be an easy challenge at Michikusa House, even for me, where foods laid upon the table resembled their original forms: grilled fish, boiled *satsumaimo*, pickled radish, miso soup with floating seaweed tendrils, steamed white rice. Meals served at Michikusa House made the shortest of journeys. They began, like a story, right outside the front door. Edibles plucked from the soil or lifted from the stream that ambled past the farm made only a quick stopover in the kitchen before settling in attractive configurations on the low *chabudai* table in the Hanada's sitting room. Apart from *shoyu, mirin,* and *sake,* very few flavor additions were required; the plants and fish alone were that tasteful. This fact, Jun said to me more than once, solidified his goal: to cultivate the best, most superior flavors in foods. He'd had a hunch that good food did not arise solely from the kitchen but began its life in good soil, be it farmland, mountaintop, or river bottom. What, then, contributed most to the quality of that soil and, by extension, to exquisite taste, I asked him? It was that question, Jun said, that inspired him. Gave him a purpose. I envied that about Jun, that he had found propulsion outside the daily tasks required for survival. Whether he ever accomplished his goal, however, I can't say.

Shortly after my residency at Michikusa House ended, Jun Nakashima slipped out of existence, as if he had been hoovered into the vacuum of space like so much stardust. In the age of digital communication, it should have been easy to locate him, to stay in touch even over very long distances, half a world away. That didn't happen, though not for want of trying on my part. I discovered Jun's mobile number was no longer in service. The email address he had given me bounced back every message I sent. Apart from an outdated Facebook account, Jun had no social media presence I could find. I even tried contacting him the old-fashioned way, writing to his parents' address in Rendaiji. Unless they understood my sloppy Japanese penmanship, it's unlikely he ever received it. I gave up trying to reach him after six months—half the amount of time we had spent getting to know one another. If he wanted to talk to me, I told myself, he would find a way. Sadly, he never did.

Without a person to attach them to, I cling to random facts and disembodied details about Jun's life. For instance, I know that before he came to Michikusa House, Jun had dropped out of college, like I had, though in his case, Jun had been attending a well-known international culinary school in Sydney. Before that, he lived in the Rendaiji neighborhood of Nishi-ku, one of the five wards of Kumamoto. His parents' house overlooked the Tsuboi River, the raised Shinkansen bullet train track, and the Kagoshima line train depot, which drew trainspotters to the neighborhood with noticeable regularity. Across the street from his house, a Buddhist temple claimed a corner lot, and beside it sat a stocked fishing hole where fathers gathered on weekends with their children to sample the art of snagging and luring in a catch. The neighborhood, Jun said, was both too loud and too quiet. Yet, to my Midwest mind, it sounded colorful and curious, a place I hoped to visit one day. I admitted this to him once, and my fluttering heart was rewarded with his signature cockeyed grin, a cheeky, mischievous sort of affection. "Maybe one day, Win-chan," Jun had said.

In Jun's company, I found I was no longer myself—or rather, I was no longer an echo of the person I once was, no longer obsessing over the reflection of such intimate details as the curvature of my upper arms or the concavity of my abdomen. With Jun, I became a seed ready to dive toward sunlight and, at last, finally, breathe. But then, how can someone about whom I know so much, who animates my fondest memories, just evaporate? I know the answer, of course, because it's my fault Jun disappeared. At least, I blame myself for it.

Truth be told, it wasn't all sunshine and gushing roses at Michikusa House. The beastly summer heat, weighed down by air so humid you could carve it out with a garden spade. Layers of earth—soil from the garden, clay from the studio—clinging perpetually to the undersides of my fingernails. Nowhere to go and no way to get there—not on my own, not without a Japanese driver's license. The infernal language barrier. The long-held secrets. That scolding from Shoko. The fight with Jun. The static silence that followed.

There have been times when I've tried to leave Michikusa House behind, convinced I shouldn't look back so much. Then there came a point when I just stopped resisting. I'm in a different place now, further ahead than I once was, but that doesn't mean I can discredit Shoko's patience or Jun's passion, how they tugged me out of the miserable fog where I had been dwelling for so many years. After all, the two of them taught me everything that matters, how to go on living.

CHAPTER 1

When I wake, still weary and unseeing, it's to the sound of whirring, grinding, leaf-blowing equipment. A rare autumn thunderstorm surged through last night, robbing me of sleep and claiming plenty of maple and oak limbs in the process, if the level of chainsaw noise is any indication. Despite it being Sunday, the groundskeepers at the cemetery next to my studio are hard at work. I had hoped for a casual lie-in, a day of rest and recovery after a torturous week of classes, coursework, and late nights at the medical library, but no such luck is to be had, evidently.

Outside, the noise dies away. Someone shouts garbled instructions. I check the time then roll out of bed. After putting in my contacts and running through my morning bathroom rituals, I put the kettle on. When the tea's ready, I take my phone, mug, and a wool shawl onto the balcony. I spy the groundskeepers on the far side of the stone barrier that separates my dead-end street from the sprawling, historic plot. They're tidying up the last fallen branches, by the looks of it. The scattered leaves appear iridescent, glittering with damp. I sit down in the creaky wicker chair, the shawl wrapped around my shoulders. Last night's rain notwithstanding, the day feels crisp and cool, like crystallized sugar candy you could snap off in shards. I'm grateful for my east-facing view. The morning light folds across my lap like a blanket. A gentle breeze tinkles the *furin* wind chime I still haven't taken down, a relic of hot, sticky summer days long since passed, and of promises that will never be fulfilled. It was a gift to me, that wind chime. My only souvenir from my stay in Japan. I should pack it away, along with the rest of my memories of that place. But the motivation doesn't rise to meet the demand, as if stowing the *furin* might dissolve those treasured mental images. I stay where I am and sip my tea, realizing this is the first Sunday I've spent on my own in…well, quite a while. Maybe that's why my mind's wandering more than usual. When I'm alone, my thoughts tend to retrace events from the past.

These days, I'm not often alone. I have a full class schedule, work at the library, then Liam drives up to spend weekends at my place. His apartment is about a century newer than mine and more polished, but I don't own a car and don't need one when everything from campus to the co-op grocer's is within walking distance. This weekend, however, Liam's stuck in Toronto on a rare business trip. The fact I still don't entirely understand what he does—something with nuclear energy systems, work he's not allowed to talk about—speaks to one of several imbalances in our relationship. The fact I'm revisiting—working on completing an undergraduate degree while he's out earning six figures, speaks to another.

As I'm thinking this, my phone buzzes. A message from Liam.

"Hey Win, I got an earlier flight back. You free? I'll stop by." I reply with a thumbs up, saying I'll just be here, working on my essay—shorthand for looking at a blank screen. *"Great. See you in 30-35 mins,"* he responds, adding a single, pink-hearted flourish.

I should shower, make myself presentable. I offer the remainder of my tea to the sink drain and reorient my laptop on the table alongside a stack of under-utilized and over-priced textbooks. I'll deal with the essay later.

I choose a record, something Diana Ross, a powerful

selection I can harmonize with. The clothes I'm wearing, along with those that have hung over the back of the chair all week, go into the hamper. Under the running water, Diana's words are indecipherable, the beat and melody barely audible, but the music is transcendent. I need her deliverance. When faced with the mirror image of this nude body, it still appears distorted in the glass. Two years of therapy and those old superhighways aimed at self-criticism were never deconstructed. I feign indifference.

I'm toweling off my hair when I hear footsteps rattling the staircase—the old fire escape that leads to my studio apartment. I open the door before he knocks. Unsurprised by the greeting, Liam steps over the threshold lugging a paper bag, its bottom sagging dangerously, threatening to rip.

"Hey, Win," he says, pulling me into a one-armed hug, setting the bag on the nearest countertop. The button-up shirt, though no longer constrained by a necktie or suit jacket, describes a rigid, weekdays-only silhouette I'm unaccustomed to seeing on him. A heavy five o'clock shadow serves to chisel his jawline in sculpture-like precision. "You okay?"

"Fine, yeah," I say, taking a step back. "You?"

"Beat." Liam pours a glass of water and chugs the whole thing, leaning over the sink. He refuses to use public restrooms, which means consuming food or liquids before or during travel is not an option. Whether dehydration and dips in blood sugar are worth the tradeoff is, in my view, debatable. "Sorry I couldn't be here yesterday."

"I've had enough to keep me occupied," I say, gesturing toward the laptop, the essay I'm struggling to craft.

"I brought lunch," he says. "And stuff for Claymore. Mom sent a bag of cat food her guys won't eat and some toys he'll probably never play with, but there you go. It's been sitting in my trunk all weekend."

"Oh. Okay. Thanks," I say, wishing I'd been offered some say in our meal plans. Wishing he'd asked, rather than presumed. I know this thought is uncharitable, especially given that I had planned on eating last night's leftovers alone. Alone, unless you count Claymore, Liam's brother's recently abandoned psychotic cat.

"How's he doing?"

"Clay? I hardly see him. I think he's tunneled into the attic somehow. But the bowl empties, the box fills, and the couch is becoming increasingly shredded, so I think it's safe to assume he's still lurking around. Oh, and I heard him doing that yowling thing in the middle of the night. I swear, I nearly pissed the bed the first time. I thought there was a ghost in the attic."

"I warned you. He's a beast."

"Hopefully, he'll settle down once he gets used to the place," I say, as Liam finishes a second glass of water. "Wish I could lure him out a bit more, though. I feel bad. I don't want him to be scared of me or of being here."

Liam looks to the ceiling, as if he's heard the cat crawling around overhead. "Least he didn't end up at the shelter. Better than he deserves, probably."

"He's not that bad. Your brother's just a terrible pet owner. Clay didn't have a chance. Who names their cat after a landmine, for god's sake?"

"Have you ever seen one? Claymores get propped up on four little legs before they detonate; looks bit like a cat, I guess. And, fun fact, the claymore landmine is actually named after a Scottish sword."

"That would be confusing if the two ever met on the battlefield." Before Mr. Encyclopedia can tell me how unlikely that would be, I head for the bathroom, the hair drier. "The point is," I say loudly over the rush of hot air, "explosive or not, your brother didn't do the poor little guy any favors. Like, ever."

Liam steps into view. Hovering in the doorway, he waits until I'm no longer inverted to say, "Well, Mom thanks you for taking him, and sent about twenty cans of cat food as a consolation prize."

"Have you heard from Mike since he left?" I ask, raking a comb through the messy mane that now reaches my shoulder blades.

Liam's brother, Mike, up and moved to Texas about a month ago, supposedly to become a rancher or some awful thing. Not the ranching part, per se, just the idea of somebody who's worked an assembly line his entire adult life spontaneously abandoning his rental unit, his belongings, and his cat for the sake of cattle. Or maybe it's more the promise of greener grasses and open pastures.

"Nope. Mom hasn't either."

"Poor Meredith. If I had a car, I'd go visit her more."

"I don't know what the hell he's thinking," Liam grumbles.

"We could drive over next weekend. I could cook dinner or something, if she wants."

"I'll mention it," Liam says in a way that makes me think he won't.

I remember the day Mike left because I spent most of that night listening to Liam gripe over the phone about "taking responsibility" and "acting like a grown-up", a talk he probably should've had with his brother, not me, but as an only child I'm hardly a fair judge. The next day, Saturday, Liam came to my place as usual, but—surprise!—he showed up with a blue plastic cat carrier and a brand new litter box full of pet paraphernalia. Liam couldn't take Clay because his apartment doesn't allow pets, nor did he want the responsibility of pet ownership—at least not of a volatile one. Nor did Liam's mom, Meredith, like the idea of introducing a wild card into her clowder of elderly felines. Liam offered to pay the pet fees and vet bills if I agreed to take Mike's reject. That, or the shelter—and we all know how that typically ends, especially for misbehaved and unfriendly little gremlins. Sure, I had my coursework and a job to think about. Also, I'd never owned a cat before. Still, I couldn't be the one responsible for sentencing the poor thing to death just because his treatment and upbringing conditioned him into bad habits. I spent the remainder of that weekend in a dizzying frenzy of online videos and tutorials outlining the many intricacies of cat care, from play schedules to grooming to diet specifications, completely ignoring my partner in the process.

"You finish that paper yet?" Liam asks, nodding toward the laptop.

"What do you think?" I tie my hair back, then disengage from the mirror. "I swear, it's like these people—this professor, especially, is trying to reduce human nutrition down to a dataset you can plot on a spreadsheet." I cross the room and slap the laptop closed, frustrated, embarrassed by the blank page.

"Sounds like somebody's got a chip on her shoulder."

"You think so?" I explode, then catch myself. He's only teasing. Liam knows the whole story. He was there.

We started dating, officially, in high school, around the same time I began dabbling in the art of weight loss under the guise of self-improvement or, possibly, invoking drama to avoid seeming ordinary, ugly, or forgettable. After graduation, he witnessed the transformation that made me almost unrecognizable: the turning inward, the emotional detachment. Starving. After all, there were jeans to fit into, a tragic aesthetic to apply like mascara. Like everyone else, he became "concerned." When the time came, he supported the decision—made on my behalf—to step away from college. Take some "time off." Meaning outpatient rehab. During the lengthy recovery that followed, while I struggled to adapt to life without a crutch—the purging, the isolation—Liam stood by me, uncomplaining. Afterward, when I went to Japan, even then, he always called to check in, see if I was doing okay.

After a beat of surprise, he asks, "You doing okay?"

"I don't know." I fold my arms, an act that feels defensive. "I'm second-guessing myself a lot. Like I can't trust my own judgment, you know?"

"How so?"

"Returning to school. I thought it was the right move."

"It was," he assures me. "You got better. You're much healthier now. It was time to start over, finish your degree," he says, as if life were an equation. If you plug in the right tasks and the right milestones, then out pops success. A plus B equals C. He would feel that way. That formula worked for him.

"Right," I concede, "but I wanted to go this route because I thought that by doing this nutrition course, I could help other people avoid what I went through."

"Yeah. You'll be certified to do that after—"

"That's not what I meant," I interject. "It's not about the certification."

"Then what's the problem?" he asks.

"The problem is, this degree isn't about helping people. We haven't talked at all about why people develop disordered eating habits to begin with. It's all about, like, molecular chemistry, which is not—" I stop talking, seeing confusion draw Liam's brows into a frown.

"Didn't you read the course descriptions?" he asks, as if my answer either way could help matters now.

"I don't remember," I huff. Ever since my recovery, I've struggled with recall, as if wrecking my physical health wasn't enough. Sometimes I'll search for a word only to bury it deeper in a twisted jumble. Certain memories, the ones I cling to hardest, those stand out clearly, but others have faded so significantly it's as if they never happened. In school, where memorization tends to matter more than critical thinking and application of content, I've become all but useless. To make matters worse, it didn't used to be this way. I used to be as academically able, and as capable, as Liam. Mr. and Mrs. Encyclopedia.

"All I know is," I continue, "I genuinely thought we would have, you know, like, a farming rotation. I mean, that's where 'nutrition' starts, right?" I picture Michikusa House, its charming kitchen garden, all those herbs, the plump, ripe vegetables. "Did I not ask about that when we toured the campus? See what I mean, though, why I'm second-guessing myself? Something's off. It's probably just me."

"You're not, you know, falling back into old habits, are you?"

"Relapsing" is the word he's looking for but he can't say it. And no, I'm not. I haven't relapsed in, what, four years? Almost five? "No. I'm fine," I assure him.

"Maybe you should drop the library job," he says. "You don't need to overwork yourself or start stressing about stuff. I can help if you need anything."

"It's two nights a week."

He nods, acquiescent. "I'm just glad you didn't end up doing the grounds crew thing over there." He indicates the cemetery, where the crew is wrapping up the last of their leaf-blowing activities, moving their particolored pile towards the bed of a truck parked nearby.

"You were right. It would've been too much. Too many hours," I agree, though I miss getting up close and personal with earth, like I did in Japan. I miss holding a seed the size of a grain of sand in my palm, watching the miracle of seasonal rebirth as it sprouts and matures into something edible. I miss growing my own food. Though I grew up in a small Midwest town that closely abutted complete rural wilderness, I didn't learn to name wildflowers and songbirds or, for that matter, learn to poke holes in the dirt and help things grow until I spent time at Michikusa House, half a world away. Under the tutelage of Shoko Hanada, I became convinced the two—personal well-being and wilderness, wildness—are interwoven in an untieable knot. When care is given on both sides, the benefits are reciprocal. Yet, strangely, this institution of higher education, where I've invested a whole year's worth of time and money learning about "nutrition," marches to a different, more abstract tune. One I'm out of sync with.

"I could use a walk," I say. "Cemetery?"

"Sure. Just let me change first. I've got clothes in the car."

*   *   *

Liam's hand slips into mine as we pass underneath boughs of maple, each papery leaf the color of a Chinese lantern. How can anyone find cemeteries unsettling? This one, especially, is so peaceful. Quiet and serene. A place I wouldn't mind spending eternity, resting under a blanket of earth. In fact, it was this historic cemetery that solidified my choice in apartments. I toured units during high summer in advance of my academic re-start date. I knew at once that I wanted to spend my days overlooking these lush gardens from that second-story balcony. I wanted to roll out of bed and see sprawling flower beds, gnarled trees, winding paths, and crumbling monuments blanketed in jade-green lichen—rare finds in this neighborhood along otherwise urban streets. The landlord let me have it for a steal. It's usually his last property to go, he told me; no one likes living near a cemetery. I, apparently, am the exception.

I had interviewed for a job as a cemetery groundskeeper, but Liam talked me out of accepting the position when it was offered. Even when they vowed to accommodate my class schedule, Liam argued the time commitment would be too heavy to balance alongside my coursework. I took an evening shift at the medical library, instead, a few hours two nights a week. When the weather cooperates, I walk the cemetery's meandering paths for the fresh air and exercise. If I pass anyone, they're usually laying cut flowers, their vehicle parked nearby. Nobody seems to wander but me.

"I prefer this to school," I say, admitting it aloud, both to Liam and to myself.

"The trees look nice this time of year," he replies blandly, letting go of my hand, preferring his jacket pockets. It fits him well. Though being as tall and lean as a mannequin, almost everything looks good on him. I used to compare myself, my body, to his when we first started dating, wishing I could be that thin, androgynously so. Funny, to think that at one time, I believed nothing in the world mattered more than my pant size. So much wasted effort and narcissistic attention.

"That's not what I meant," I say. He waits for me to explain. "I'm sick of these classes. There's so much chemistry, and four classes on vitamin and mineral supplementation before I can graduate. We write essays on topics like 'metabolic dysregulation' and 'evaluating nutrition for consumers.' It's all so abstracted from the reality of eating."

"What would you prefer to write about?" His neutrality, the calm pool of his inner world, his rock-steady faith that he knows more than I do, it fuels the fire building in and around my belly. Why can't he rise up, be angry with me for a change? Yes, he is likely the smartest, most patient man I'm likely to meet, but his lifeless responses to my crises have, over time, worn me thin.

"The essay isn't the point," I say. "It's the curriculum."

"I don't get it. What's wrong with the curriculum? You said chemistry, vitamins, minerals…"

I want to throw something, though not necessarily at Liam. He's simply been cudgeled into worshiping the reductive research program. He sees the world as an engineering project, an object you can disassemble into its constituent parts which, once identified, can be fully understood. But reductionism only works for objects that can be cleanly separated; it's an impractical method to apply to organic, flowing, messy biology.

"Chemistry involves isolated processes," I say, "but nutrition starts with living, breathing things, processes that are in constant flux."

"Okay, so—?"

"So, if you want to study nutrition, you should be observing whole ecosystems, all the moving parts, over long periods."

"Sounds like Shoko talking again."

"So, what? She taught me everything. It's thanks to her I got well, here and here." I point to my gut, then my head. "It didn't happen in a clinic, I can tell you that much."

"Win, every student feels like their time is being wasted on things that aren't relevant to them at some point. Trust me, I've been there. I probably don't use half of what I learned at CMU, but that's not the point."

"Obviously—an education should reveal points of view and ideas you never would've come across otherwise."

"Right. An education—and the application of the scientific method in particular—it can free us of our preconceptions," he says, a little too pointedly.

"Or, on the flip side, it can stoke egos and make people feel like they already know everything there is to know, make them feel self-important."

"You think it's made me that way?" he asks. "Self-important?"

I consider the point I'm trying to make here, the deep layers I'm working hard to excavate. Overhead, a robin flits between branches, almost too small to notice at this distance but for the powerful, recognizable song. A call for love, a celebration of bounty? A discovery, a warning?

"What I'm saying is, science is limited in scope and spirit. It can take an awfully narrow view of things, but the reality is way more complex than—"

"So, you're saying your field is obsolete? That there's nothing you can learn from it, this program?"

"In its current format, yeah, it kind of is. Otherwise, people in this country wouldn't have disordered eating problems, if all we had to do was rely on experts to tell us what to do and what to eat." What will it take to make him understand? Is he even trying to? I want to shake him, throw him off balance, force him to wake up, and quit pressing the snooze button. "Now that I'm in it, it seems, I don't know, kind of dysfunctional. Science isn't perfect; it isn't even unbiased."

"No, humans are biased. Their methods are imperfect, their statistics can be manipulated, and their funding programs favor hot topics over less flashy research questions. But the scientific method at its core—"

"You know what I mean, Liam."

"—Hate to break it to you, Win, but it's the best method we've got for figuring anything out."

"There are other ways to learn about something." Speaking slowly, I explain that for the vast majority of human history, we had to learn from our surroundings and environment, from wisdom passed down through generations. "Hell, we even paid attention to our own bodies, for crying out loud."

He barely shrugs, the most noncommittal display imaginable. "What's your point?"

The point is there were no vitamin supplements, no microscopes revealing the chemical interactions that occur when we eat something. And there certainly were no grocery stores launching advertising campaigns. But I don't say any of this.

I stare at Liam, trying to locate the fountain that once outpoured so much delight in discovery. Through middle and high school, I fed off that zest, his passion for science and robotics, his love of invention. I recall his kindness, too, or his pity, maybe, for the quiet girl, his middle school science partner with no obvious friends. Eventually—inevitably, perhaps—casual proximity engendered attraction, in a physical sense. I grew increasingly fond of his narrow lankiness, those dark lashes, and that wildly curly mop of hair, characteristics he never fully outgrew. The spark that finally ignited our burgeoning romance, somewhere around sophomore year, remains murky in my memory. I remember relishing in the newness of his boyish affections, feeling secretly astonished that my body could be anything other than a casing, utterly forgettable. Once I discovered it could make another person beg and tremble, my body never went back to being wholly mine, simple and effortless. However, neither is a relationship ever simple and effortless. Love cannot persist entirely on enthusiasm.

"I honestly don't know what you're after, Win. I really don't."

"Maybe I would be better off working on a farm." At Michikusa House, I think recklessly. In Japan, at least, with Jun and Shoko, I felt deeply grounded in reality, not removed from it. The learning that took place there wasn't isolated from seasonal cycles or humble biology, nor was it obscured by the lenses of academia and commerce.

"You don't mean any farm, though, do you?" he says, reading me too easily.

"That experience changed how I think about everything. It changed…god, it changed how I live. That means something. I want to have that again."

"But you're here now. So, let's…try to think about how you can mimic what you liked so much."

The place, the work, the people. Jun.

Liam says, "Why not find an internship? Something hands-on, doing something outdoors. Then you could get credit toward your degree, at least."

"God, you sound like my mother."

"Well, did you ever consider she might be right? It was her idea for you to go abroad in the first place, remember?"

"Says the guy who told me not to take the groundskeeper job because it would be too many hours. How would I fit an internship on top of classes, coursework, and library hours?"

"Here, come sit."

He chooses a bench. I join him but leave a noticeable gap between us. He doesn't slide over to fill it. I stare straight ahead, taking in the grassy slope decorated with weathered monuments and evergreen shrubbery. It makes me feel better. No matter what happens in this lifetime or what we accomplish, learn, or acquire, we all end up in the same place.

"How about you drop the library thing? It's not like you need the spending money, right?" he says. "Your parents have you covered. We've all got your back."

I hug my arms around myself, a gesture that could easily be mistaken as an effort to withstand the cold. "But then the internship would be the only part I'm interested in. Like I said, I don't care about the classes. So why keep up the pretense?"

"Because you need those little letters after your name if you're ever going to get anywhere."

"Liam, I don't want to do this anymore." Admitting it aloud, I feel the weight tumble from my shoulders and the squeeze on my solar plexus slacken.

"Do what?" he asks.

Only then do I realize I've implied more than one ending. My institutional education for one, and potentially, quite possibly, our relationship for another. *Which did I mean*, I wonder? Honestly, I'm not sure. I can't imagine, literally cannot envision my future without Liam in it. The intrusive thought, the image of leaving him, the uncertainty it offers like a tantalizing alternative, frightens me.

As expected, Liam interprets my comment only insofar as it relates to my own prospects. "You mean you want to quit school...again?" He punctuates the last word as if to deliberately sting me.

I turn to face him. "You know why I dropped out last time. You of all people. So don't act like this is the same thing. This is a totally different problem...reason, whatever."

Jun would understand. Jun would have agreed with me that this course is a waste of time and a whole lot else.

I realize I'm considering the opinion of a man I haven't spoken to in two years, someone I knew only one-tenth the time

I've known Liam. Liam, the man I'm supposed to trust and admire above all others.

"Okay," he says. "Let's say you drop out." The 'again' is only implied this time. "You hate it here, you're learning nothing... then what? You think you can get a job without a degree?"

"I could, actually. Plenty of people do."

"Oh yeah?"

"Yeah, and it's kind of insulting to say otherwise. Plenty of people choose a path that doesn't involve a college degree. As I recall, your dad and your brother managed just fine."

"My dad did back-breaking manual labor right up until the day he died. Is that what you want?" Liam says, as if I'm a belligerent child throwing a tantrum.

"That work is necessary and valuable!"

"I've seen what that kind of work does to people, Win. That's why I busted my ass in school and put myself through college, precisely so I wouldn't end up like...you know what? Forget it."

"Why are you acting like this is your decision, like you know better than me what I should be doing? You're implying that I'll fail, be a failure, if I don't follow your version of what it means to have a successful life."

"No, Winona. What I think is that you don't know what it's like. You've never not had money to deal with problems when they arise. When you got sick, you took two years of medical leave. And yeah, I know it was necessary, because you literally could have died otherwise. But then you got to jet off to Japan for another year, for chrissake, and your parents supported you that entire time. You think it was like that for my dad when he got sick? Who had his back? You think anyone was there to pick my mom up after he died? Jesus, that's why I practically lived at your house through high school, remember? Because she was completely incapable of...goddammit."

We've both been stung. We retreat to opposite corners.

I hate arguing with him, disagreeing constantly. *Why can't this be easy anymore, you and me? What happened to us, the fun we used to have?* I will myself to be a nicer girlfriend and take his hand. The familiarity of it reassures me somewhat. Liam softens.

"I know you're smart and could do anything you put your mind to," he says, though the cliche fails to land, and we both know it. "Whatever you do, I'm going to care. Come here." He wraps an arm around my shoulder. "You've only just started your second year. The classes might improve, you could have better professors, ones whose beliefs align more with yours."

"I doubt it," I mutter.

"Okay," he sighs. "I hear what you're saying, and I can tell you're unhappy, but I've been thinking."

"About...?" His hesitation worries me. What *has* he been thinking? About ending things, like I suggested, or about new beginnings? God, is he going to propose, right here in the cemetery? My gut clenches.

"Why don't we move in together?"

"What?"

"Let's move in together. Let's just do it."

I don't know how to respond, not at first. This is not what I was expecting. "But you said it would be better to wait until I graduated. Your commute from here to work would be ridiculous."

"I know, but...screw it. We could cut our expenses in half sharing one place. I could help take care of things. It might alleviate some of the pressure on you. Plus, we'd get to spend every evening together. Would that make you happier?" He waits for my reaction. I sit very still. When I don't budge, he prompts, "What are you thinking?"

What am I thinking? The idea wasn't even in my wheelhouse of possibilities. He's right, though. My parents wouldn't have to front the rent for my apartment anymore. I could drop the library job; or find an internship doing something I'm actually interested in. Is that the outcome I wanted, though? Five minutes ago, I didn't even want to continue this program, full stop. I wanted to plan my exit. Then again, I'm not known for calculating the risks before jumping into—or out of—commitments.

Finally, I say, "Can I think on it a bit?"

I can tell this is not the response he hoped for, but I can't muster the effervescence he expects. Liam agrees. We rise and keep on walking.

CHAPTER 2

I think on it for three days, pondering Liam's proposition during in-between moments: between classes, between assignments, between resting my head on my pillow and falling asleep at night. I'm thinking of it now as I pass my favorite tree in the cemetery, an elegant Japanese maple shading a family mausoleum the size of a small house. Half the reason I love this tree, I think, is because it reminds me of that first vision I had of Michikusa House.

I remember I arrived late in the day, having spent the better part of the morning and afternoon dozing through a Shinkansen high-speed rail journey, shuffling me from Tokyo to Kitakyushu. Groggy and still suffering the ill-effects of jet lag, I somehow managed to navigate the interchange successfully without losing my suitcase or forgetting the gift for Shoko on the seat beside me. The connection ushered me, at last, to Tateishi, where I disembarked. Waiting outside the little station, suitcase propped at my side and gift box in hand, I remember first, oddly, spying not the dazzling mountain topography or the graceful clay rooftops of the neighboring homes, but the bright red vending machine placed right beside the depot's exit. I'd already enjoyed a small *ekiben* lunchbox on the train— "A uniquely Japanese experience one ought not to miss," according to my guidebook, an ill-advised purchase given how little sightseeing I would be doing—but what I craved was coffee. Even a canned one would do. I considered searching for the correct change but mustering the effort required to sift through the unfamiliar coins felt beyond me.

Thankfully, for my remaining strength was fading fast, Hideyuki Hanada appeared in his little green *keitora*, a mini pickup truck roughly half the size of the metal monsters I was accustomed to seeing back home. Perhaps I should have been more wary than I was—a young woman alone, accepting a ride from a stranger in a foreign country—but I wasn't in America anymore, where men owned guns and tended to point them at schoolchildren and churchgoers and work colleagues. Nor was Mr. Hanada a total stranger. His wife, Shoko, and my mother had remained good friends throughout the previous few decades, since well before I was born, ever since their college days. Shoko had been an exchange student in my mother's first freshman ceramics class. Their friendship grew from there, tended and cultivated like a precious, prize-winning rose. Eventually, they even traded places; my mother studied abroad for a semester in Toho Village, in Fukuoka Prefecture. There she stayed with Shoko's family, expert ceramicists in Koishiwara ware. Then, many years later, long after she got married, had a child, and became a professor at the same school she once attended, my mother returned to Japan. She spent my entire eighth grade year on sabbatical at Michikusa House, during which time she and Shoko collaborated on an intensive ceramics project. She returned not just with a delicate collection of pottery to show and sell, but also with photos: pictures of the old traditional house, the abundantly producing farm, the *noborigama* kiln, and the friendly-looking couple, Shoko and Hideyuki Hanada. So, in a way, I felt like I knew the man, my mother's oldest friend's husband, albeit only from a distance.

Being the only white girl—heck, the only person—outside the station, we made the connection easily. I bowed and in my rudimentary Japanese, supplemented by phrases I had memorized on the train, thanked him for meeting me. Unlike his wife, Mr. Hanada spoke no English, simply bowed then hefted my suitcase into the back of his little truck. Hanada-san seemed perfectly at ease maintaining our separate silences during that ambling drive from Tateishi Station. I was content to watch the autumn scenery breeze by, holding the wrapped gift box on my lap. The route took us past tidy homes with open verandas, manicured gardens, and terraced rice fields. Beyond this slim layer of civilization, evergreen-capped mountains leaned in protectively. I had never seen anything like it, accustomed as I was to the unwavering flatness of the American Midwest. The tree-covered undulations that shaped the horizon seemed plucked from another world.

As we began our ascent, the road swiftly narrowed to a single, dangerously thin lane and suddenly I understood the necessity of driving a vehicle as small as Hanada-san's. Up and up we drove, winding our way along slender switchbacks, roads made even narrower by dense groves of bamboo grass draped over both shoulders. Houses and fields finally gave themselves over completely to the ever-encroaching forest. Once in a great while, the trees would break their tight ranks to reveal a valley variegated by autumn leaves flecked with all the colors of a kabocha pumpkin and tree-ripened mulberries, of savory spices, of cumin, sage, and mustard seed. But before I could even muster what seemed an appropriate level of appreciation for such a sight, the trees knitted themselves back together again, as if afraid of revealing too much. Only occasionally did signs of human life peek at us through the branches—a parade of telephone poles here, a maintenance vehicle pulled to the side of the road there, a parking lot large enough to accommodate only a single van at a particularly scenic overlook. At one point, we swerved onto the barely-there, leaf-strewn shoulder to let another driver pass.

Hanada-san waved as if they knew each other. A few turns later, we were sloping downwards again, down toward the valley floor, this time passing fruit orchards and a Shinto shrine. We bypassed one town and then another before eventually turning onto a road I felt sure was a bike path, given its dimensions. The path was so buried in leaves I couldn't see pavement underneath. Clearly, no one drove this way, ever, and I feared we were lost. Hanada-san slowed and said something that sounded like "*inoshishi*" and pointed out the window. I followed the line of his arm but saw nothing apart from dense foliage.

At last, we emerged into dappled sunlight, this time at a crossroads. A single lane bridge over a river led in one direction, while another seemed to be a driveway up to a farmhouse on a hill. The third wound past a small shrine, a family monument perhaps, elevated by five or six stone steps. Hanada-san made a point of checking each road carefully, though we had seen no other drivers for miles, then turned left, passing the shrine. More orchards and pine groves laid out in deliberate, linear rows. Finally, we drove over a bridge spanning the same river I had seen at the crossroads, this time further upstream. I felt some relief to see telephone poles marching alongside us, paralleling the waterway, a familiar sign of civilization. Vines wound themselves up the poles then cascaded in waterfalls of purple blooms. The neighboring mountains, thick with untamed wilderness, seemed a place where ancient spirits must reside.

I knew we had reached Michikusa House before Hanada-san even slowed the truck. The tidy farmhouse, with its wraparound veranda and well-tended ornamental trees, felt as familiar as if I had visited it with my mother. Various outbuildings, including the one that sheltered the studio and kiln, surrounded it like a gaggle of hens. And there, behind the low stone wall separating the house from the road, was the most vibrantly crimson Japanese maple I had ever seen.

The road bypassed the house, crossed the stream one last time, then dead-ended at a corrugated metal garage that had once been vibrantly blue but had since faded almost entirely to rust. Inside I spied another flat-bed truck and various bits of farming equipment. We parked in the open lot and Hanada-san collected my suitcase. Rather than roll it along on its wheels, he hefted it toward the house.

When I entered the Hanadas' home for the first time, I slipped off my shoes, turned them around, and left them there in the *genkan*, the recessed entryway found in most Japanese homes. It was one of the many polite customs my mother had me rehearse in advance of my stay. Then, in my stocking feet, I stepped up into the hallway onto polished, wide wooden boards. Hanada-san located pairs of house slippers, one set for me and one for himself. Shoko arrived a moment later, drying her hands on her linen apron.

"*Ojamashimasu,*" I said, meaning "Sorry for the intrusion," meant as a sign of respect when entering another person's home, and handed her the gift box. In Japan, it's typical not only to give hostess gifts, but also souvenirs, called *omiyage,* after traveling somewhere else. Gifts of fruit and sweets are especially common. In my case, it didn't seem practical—or even legal—to bring food from home, so I had purchased a set of tea snacks, elegantly wrapped, from a Tokyo department store.

Shoko accepted the gift, bowing slightly, and greeted me in return. "*Hai, douzo, douzo.* Welcome, welcome. Come in. How was your journey?" she asked in English. I felt immensely grateful for her fluency, for the fact she still chatted over the phone with my mother and, presumably, other American friends often enough to have mastered the language. As for me, from the moment I landed in Tokyo it had been such a struggle to communicate that the sound of English words met me like a flood of relief.

It's difficult to convey just how unsettling it is to be surrounded by people you can't speak to or understand. Hotel clerks, train station patrols, cashiers…the language gap between myself and essential workers and other various points of contact had proved dangerously wide. More than once, and nearly in tears—I'm ashamed to admit—I had resorted to miming.

"Not bad," I said, smiling. "Your house is so beautiful," which was true, an elegant wooden structure that must have been at least partially renovated in recent years, given the modern bathroom I spied down the hall, the buffed, light-colored floors, the contemporary light fixtures, like lanterns, made of thin reeds and washi paper.

"Ah, yes. My husband's family home," Shoko explained, though Hanada-san had since disappeared with my suitcase. "Over one hundred and twenty years old! The house, not my husband," she teased. "Though you might not know it from looking at him."

I managed a small, hesitant smile.

"You will want to freshen up. Come, I'll show you to your room."

Shoko led me past rooms hidden behind sliding doors, and others, visible from the hallway, with woven *tatami* mats laid out over the floors. In one room, I spied a butsudan, a small altar used to pray to the Buddha and to family ancestors.

My room was upstairs and had also been given the *tatami* treatment. It contained only a low table and a cushion to sit upon. No bed, but I had expected as much. Doubtless I would find a *futon* and blankets hidden away in a closet, along with my suitcase. Shoko pointed out various features, showed me how to click on the overhead light, how to force the window open should I want a breeze. I thanked her, and she told me to meet them downstairs after I had settled in.

"Do you have a phone I could borrow, to call my parents? I didn't bother bringing one," I explained. "I didn't know whether an American phone would work here."

"There is a landline downstairs, on the table beside the genkan."

I thanked her and Shoko slid the door closed as she made her exit. I changed into fresh clothes and hung the scant items I'd packed in the closet, hidden behind yet another sliding door. With nothing much else to do to "settle in" I returned to the foyer to place my call. I dialed the extension, then my mother's mobile number. Unsurprisingly, she didn't answer. The thirteen-hour time difference meant it was something like three-thirty in the morning her time, but I had promised to leave a message. In it I explained I had made it to Michikusa House safely and would call again soon, keeping it to under a minute to avoid a pricey international call on the Hanada's phone bill. I repeated the gesture, this time leaving a quick message for Liam, then I wandered into the adjacent sitting room. I found Shoko and her husband kneeling at a low table in the main living quarters where meals were shared, where they watched the news, and entertained guests. I was not, however, the only guest. Another young man, about my age, knelt alongside them.

"Ah, Win-chan," Shoko said, inviting me in. "You found the phone?"

"I did, thanks. I left a message."

"This is Nakashima Jun," she said. Then to her guest, she said something in Japanese. I caught nothing apart from my own name: Win-chan, a name once exchanged only between Shoko and my mother, in reference to me, which later became Win-chime—as in 'wind chime'—a pet name my mother employed to this day.

"*Konnichiwa,*" I said.

"*Konnichiwa,*" he repeated, with a small bow.

"*Watashi wa Winona desu. Yoroshiku onegaishimasu.*"

"Nice to meet you, too," Mr. Nakashima said in near-perfect English.

"Oh! Hi," I spluttered. I had not expected other guests, nor anyone apart from Shoko, to speak English.

"Hi," he said, smiling. Genuinely, warmly, as if welcoming me to the table, but it seemed a bit cheeky, too, one corner of his mouth lifted slighter higher than the other. He wore black jeans and a white sweatshirt pushed up to his elbows, but that's all the detail I could absorb before Shoko beckoned me to sit. I chose the only seat available, across from Jun. I tried not to stare but also to not look vacant as I concocted something to say.

Is he a neighbor, I wondered? Shoko never had children otherwise I might have expected Jun to be a friend of their son, a love interest of their daughter...or vice versa.

"Nakashima-san is also doing a residency with us," Shoko explained, answering my unasked question. She passed me a small ceramic plate—one of her own, by the looks of it, uniformly shaped with a light-colored glaze, much more practical than my mother's style. Upon it she had placed an assortment of snacks, homemade mochi coated with toasted soybean flour, wedges of fresh fruit, and a few of the sweets from the *omiyage* assortment.

"Oh, thank you," I said, taking the plate. "*Arigato.*" Again, Jun smiled that cockeyed grin of his, amused by my weak attempts at speaking Japanese. "So, what sort of residency is it?" I asked, tossing the ball back at him.

"I am staying above the studio, in a separate place, so I won't be in your way," he said, perhaps as a joke, though I couldn't quite tell. Either way, he hadn't answered my question.

"So, you're a ceramics apprentice?" I reasoned.

"Sorry. I meant to say, I sleep there, but work more with farming and in the kitchen, doing the cooking. Not so good with ceramics." He grinned again, this time more self-deprecating. He had a nice face, narrow with prominent cheekbones and kind, discerning eyes. He seemed to be evaluating me, working out the type of person I was. In the face of such open scrutiny, I stared back, a challenge. He broke into a wide grin, a truce offering, then sipped his tea. Had Shoko or Hideyuki noticed this exchange?

"Win-chan is here to do a bit of everything, I think," Shoko said, as if nothing had just transpired between her guests. "A bit of farming with my husband. With me, a bit of pottery. Maybe the two of you can cook together sometime."

Jun did a little bow, almost imperceptible. "I would like that very much," he said.

*   *   *

I'm sitting on the sofa, reading articles about luring cats from closets when my phone vibrates. I answer it. "Hey, Mom."

"Winona? Are you there? I can hardly hear you," my mother says loudly, spanning county lines.

"I'm here, Mom."

"Is your phone dying? Do you need a new one?"

"It's fine. Probably just bad reception." I gaze out the wide panel of leaded glass windows overlooking the porch and the cemetery beyond. The clouds have turned dark, billowing like smoke from a steam engine. Maybe they'll roll past before I leave for work, my evening shift at the medical library. As I try to recall where I left my umbrella, my mother says, "I hear you and Liam had a fight last weekend."

No preamble then. "Not really," I say, lightly, dismissively, hoping to dodge this particular discussion, though I sense it's unavoidable. Four days have passed since Liam suggested moving in together. I have yet to make a decision. I should have known my mother would get involved. Liam talks to her nearly as much as he talks to me. I think they enjoy the overlap between their respective disciplines, between art and engineering, the structure and creativity of a thing. That, and I know Liam thinks of her as a second mother. For three years in high school, after his dad died—very suddenly, of pancreatic cancer—Liam spent more time at my house than he did at his own. He's been close with my mother ever since.

"I know you don't want my opinion, but I think it would be good for you," she says.

"You mean it would be good for the family bank account?" I mutter.

My parents were decidedly successful, financially speaking. Apart from their academic careers, they both published books in their respective fields, traveled broadly both for work and pleasure, served as a political consultant, in my father's case, and, in my mother's, sold art in the range of four to five figures for over two decades. I know they can afford my studio apartment. Still, I feel guilty about it, am socially conditioned to feel guilty for not making my own way in the world, like Liam managed to do. Especially at my age, edging on thirty.

"Oh, for god's sake, Winona." She exhales, then gathers herself for round two. "You two are…you're so great together. He's always, always been such a good influence on you. He's such a hard worker, put himself through school all on his own—do you even remember…? Oh, never mind. Even now, he's willing to drive that awful distance, that awful commute for the sake of—"

"His drive time isn't what's on my mind," I say, straining, tightening. Why do conversations with my mother always put me on edge?

From the closet, I hear a faint rustling. Lately, Claymore— Clay, his name is Clay—has ventured from the attic crawl space and has taken to sleeping in my coat closet on the pile of paper bags I use for recycling. The sound of another being close at hand calms me a little, though he's not the only one who lives here. I have, dare I say, an impressive succulent collection and a range of living herbs gracing each windowsill. The potted palms, which decorated my porch all summer, now sit in clusters around the living room keeping one another, and me, company. I grab the bit of string I've been using to encourage Clay to play, wiggling it through the gap in the closet door. I hear the cat swat a couple times, slapping the sturdy brown paper, and smile to myself.

"Well, it's your decision," says my mother, as if expecting me to make another poor one. "The reason I called, though, is I wanted to invite you both to the Faculty Art Show this weekend. If you feel like joining us, that is. It starts at seven."

Ah yes, the annual shindig I've attended nearly every year since childhood, at the opening of the academic year. Though never before has my mother waited so long to mention it. Nothing like holding out till the last minute. Possibly she had been waiting on me to inquire. More likely, she expected I wouldn't want to go. I skipped out on the previous few years' events, after all. Should this year be any different?

"Wouldn't miss it," I say, surprising us both.

"Alright then. I'll reserve two more tickets. Oh, and please wear something nice, will you? Something other than jeans."

"I did that once, Mom, like five years ago."

"Seven o'clock," she chimes. "Don't be late. No barging in during the Dean's speech."

"Don't worry, I'll be coming with Liam," I remind her. The guy is habitually punctual, bordering on neurotically conscientious.

As we exchange our goodbyes, I hear rain start tapping on the glass, trying to get in. Outside, the evening sky takes on another layer of darkness. Wonderful. Looks like I'll be trekking across campus in a downpour. With fewer than thirty minutes until my shift, I change into something a bit more workaday than torn jeans and a sleep shirt with no bra and go searching for my umbrella. I find, instead, the one belonging to Liam, or rather to his workplace, a sturdy, heavyweight model that won't turn inside out even if you try. Engineers, I tell you what. On my way out the door I portion out a serving of cat food for Clay, knowing both it and he will have disappeared by the time I return.

As the cathedral clock on campus tolls seven, I run the last few yards to the library's front steps, landing gracelessly in an ankle-deep puddle. Water seeps into my boots and I consider the hours ahead of me, facing them with sodden socks. Luckily, I find Erin, my late-night coworker, with her space heater running at full capacity underneath the reception desk. Despite her fiery, confrontational demeanor, she chills easily and turns even crabbier for it. Hence the heater. Erin is just about the tiniest, skinniest girl I have ever met, far beyond what I ever was but in her case, it must be genetic, or possibly a thyroid condition. The girl lives on namkeen snack packs and coffee concoctions that are more whipped cream than caffeine. Her hair is an indecisive strawberry blonde with manic curls that turn to frizz whenever it's humid. Apart from Liam, she's about the closest thing I have to a friend.

"Oh my god, this weather. Ugh!" she groans, pulling her hood up over her head to hide the explosion of curls. She peers out at me like an animal from its den. "You're late."

"Two minutes," I say, shaking off the umbrella and taking my seat at the desk beside her. The library's mostly empty, just a couple stragglers with their laptops occupying workstations. The weather is keeping people indoors. The giant glass panel walls face the darkening quad, creating the illusion of being stuck inside the eye of a black storm. I kick off my boots and shove my feet in front of Erin's heater. Rain, snow, sun, or hail, Erin's wearing the same thing she always does: black leggings under denim shorts, Converse sneakers, and a sweater of some colorful variant under her zip-up hoodie.

"You always expect me to cover for your scrawny ass."

"Well, I'm here now. Anything good?" I ask, spying the headlines on her laptop as they scroll up and up in a never-ending thread of breaking news.

"Warehouse explosion, hurricanes hitting both coasts...oh, look, cancer-causing pesticides."

"So...same old."

"I should be the one looking depressed, not you."

"What?"

"Girl, you look like hell and not just 'cause you're soaked. God, don't tell me. It's Liam, amirite?"

"He wants to move in together," I confess, pulling my own laptop from my bag. Apart from handing over reserved materials, directing people to study rooms or restrooms, or sorting out the printer when it jams, not many medical students require our help—not this late at night, not until exam season—so we bring our own work to do. Or, in Erin's case, dispiriting headlines to scan.

"You sound thrilled. What gives?"

"It's a studio. There's not a lot of room for, you know, guests...or roommates."

"So, you're saying he'll want to move into another place, something bigger?"

"Newer too, probably," I concur, realizing as I say it that that outcome is most likely what he would expect. I would have to give up my porch and my view of the cemetery gardens to accommodate his living room set, his workstation, and his king-sized bed. The thing is, though, I like my quiet, dead-end street, the graceful trees overhanging the partition separating the living from the dead. I like my creaky wood floors and the weathered glass windows that let in an abundance of daylight.

"You make it sound like it's entirely his decision," Erin points out. "Want one?" She pulls a namkeen packet from behind her laptop.

"No thanks," I say.

"Good, 'cause I only have one left and I didn't really wanna share." She tears it open and, using a pair of disposable chopsticks, extracts the curry-flavored crisps one by one.

"It's not so much about moving in together," I counter. "I just...I don't know if I actually want to stick this out. The degree, I mean."

"Seriously? How come?" she asks, mouth half full.

Now that I've brought it up, I'm not sure I want to get into it. I've already worn myself out trying to explain my reasoning to Liam. I don't have the energy to review both sides, not in this context, up against someone notorious for her fixed opinions and generally "having it all figured out."

"I mean, I get it," Erin says, unexpectedly. "College isn't for everyone. I should know. I'm a psych major. It's my job—my future job—to help people sort out their terrible decisions and badly-informed life choices."

"And you think pursuing a degree would be the wrong choice for me?"

She shrugs. "Not necessarily." She consumes a few more crisps, dusting our shared workstation with orange powder. She sweeps it away with her sleeve. "You just seem super unhappy all the time. Like, you might wanna reevaluate."

Her unimpeded presumption makes me balk and I feel compelled to retaliate, though whether it's because she's entirely off-base or because she's struck dead-center, I can't say, so I say nothing.

"I mean, why not do something that makes you happy for a change?" she continues, as if the advice were unconventional. Disruptive, even. "That's what I'd do. If my boyfriend—god forbid I ever have one—if he made me miserable and pressured me into doing any-effing-thing, I swear I would dump his ass," Erin says. I look up fully from my screen. "Just saying," she shrugs.

"Liam hasn't pressured me into anything," I argue, automatically. "Besides, you've never even met him."

"Uh, yeah, and I don't want to. Based on what you've said he sounds like a total buffoon. No offense."

"What's that supposed to mean?" I demand. Who does she think she is? As if adding "no offense" gives her the right to say whatever she pleases.

"It means he's got, like, zilch personality and acts like he knows what's best for you."

I can feel my neck and face heating up.

"Lemme guess, you told him you're thinking about dropping out and he tried to talk you out of it."

"Wouldn't anybody?"

"Uh…no? Jesus, Win. What the hell? Do you think you actually have no say in this? He should listen to your side and be supportive of whatever it is that's right for you."

"What about playing devil's advocate?" I try, but Erin ignores me. Instead, her attention returns to the snack pack. Realizing it's empty, Erin starts chewing the cord of her hoodie. Her eyes glow a distorted neon blue, reflecting light off the screen. Without looking, she tosses the crumpled bag in the direction of the wastepaper basket. When she misses by a yard, I slide my feet back inside my wet boots and finish the job for her. "See? You're too much of a pushover," she says, as if she's just made an excellent point. "You gotta stand up to people. Stand up for what you want."

I turn away from her, furious, both with her and with myself. "If you're suggesting I break up with Liam, that's…that's not even what I was talking about. We've been together basically forever." On and off since high school, true, but mostly on. He stood by me when others would have fled. On the other hand, Erin, has no idea what I endured, what he and I suffered through *together*. I've never told her, never told anyone. Well, no one, except—

"He's the only guy you've ever dated, right?" she asks suddenly.

"Uh…not exactly."

The first time I went off to college, before I dropped out, I masked my fears—of loneliness and mediocrity and all-out uncertainty—with the numbing effects of bulimia and the highs of impulsivity. Liam and I were on a break then. I was feeling rejected and needed to prove I was lovable. There were plenty of one-night stands and longer-term hookups, guys and girls I'd meet in class or at parties, though nobody lasted more than a semester.

Erin gives me a sidelong glance, then laughs. "Hey, no judgment here. You do you, girl. I'll just say one last thing, then I'll shut up."

"Okay," I say, and feel my shoulders tense, as if readying for another blow.

"If you can't have fun, then at least go with your instinct, you know? And I don't mean, like, tuning into your overthinking brain or your emotional heart. I mean listen to your evolutionarily-tested gut. Most people have forgotten how, in my opinion, but I think it's the best guide we got." Erin pulls her hoodie away from her face, her hair mushrooming from her head like a toxic cloud. Then she plugs in her earbuds and says no more. Whatever Erin's faults, however dogmatic her beliefs, her advice strikes me as critical, but also genuine, coming from a sincerely caring place.

A student in perfectly round glasses and, strangely, a lab coat approaches the desk and Erin rises to help him find a specific journal article amid the dozens of new publications we have acquired and thousands we've archived. By the time she returns, I've made up my mind. The only question that remains is: How will I break the news to Liam?

CHAPTER 3

It's still raining when our shift ends so Erin offers to drive me home. She lives even closer to campus than I do but refuses to walk anywhere unless absolutely necessary—possibly her lean-ness can be attributed to muscle atrophy. As she pulls the car up alongside the cemetery wall, I wonder if she will comment on my choice of accommodation, but apart from the cones of orange light offered by streetlamps it's too dark to see much and we're both equally anxious to end the night. She has two seasons of some cooking anime to binge-watch, and I have to finish that godforsaken essay. I poke the nose of my umbrella out ahead of me, through the car door and into the rain. I wave my thanks and dart up the rickety, slick staircase. After fumbling with wet keys, nearly dropping them through the grate, I finally tumble through the door, all but melting in a puddle on the kitchen tile. From the adjacent room, two blue-green eyes peer out at me from complete darkness. I scream, dropping the umbrella. The eyes vanish and, as I fumble for the light switch, I hear little feet skittering across the floor.

"Jesus, Clay. You nearly gave me a heart attack," I say in the direction of the closet, though I might have scared the poor little guy back a whole week, back into the attic crawl space. I hang up my coat and umbrella, shaking his treat bag, but to no avail. He probably hasn't made the association yet: shaky sound equals crunchy snack. "Sorry, honey," I say, giving up and turning on the kettle. This will be a long night.

Once I've changed clothes and brewed a cup of earl grey, mellowed by milk and lavender honey, I set up my laptop on the little table beside the darkened window and open the unfinished essay. Five blank pages stare back at me. I rub my forehead with the heels of my hands, as if massaging an idea to the surface. The fact I've already mentally checked out of the entire program overrules any attempts at productivity.

I'll tell them this weekend, I decide, *at the Faculty Art Show.* Then I'll have all three of them—both my parents and Liam—altogether in one place. Just a matter of ripping off the bandage.

And then what? Live with Liam at his place? Find a job? Hell, go back to Japan?

I minimize the empty document, open my browser, and type *"Shoko Hanada Michikusa House"* in the search bar. The first link takes me to the farm-stay website, a sleek but practical model, much like the house, the pottery, and the woman who manages both. The text is entirely in Japanese, a combination of three alphabets of which I can pick out and name only about four individual characters. Shoko's ethos, however, is easier to understand. Simply by admiring the images, the color palette, even the site's layout, Shoko's personal style is displayed as the embodiment of elegance in everyday life. Her core belief is that commonplace objects, like her ceramics, should not only be practical and useful but also beautiful.

I learned so much from Shoko, like how to tend a garden so its bounty fed you year-round, how to store and ferment soybeans to make miso and soy sauce, and how to grill skewered eels to perfect crispness. But my first lessons began not in the garden or even in the kitchen, but in the pottery studio. Days at Michikusa House began early, at sunup. Breakfast was at six and was finished and cleared away in time for the daily NHK *rajio taisou*, or radio calisthenics broadcast, a sort of stretching warm-up performed to music. Then it was off to the garden, studio, or garage, depending on the property's needs that day. When I arrived in late autumn, the farm work was winding down and Shoko spent most days behind her pottery wheel.

My first morning at Michikusa House, I overslept. I found a hot breakfast of fluffy steamed rice, grilled fish, and miso soup waiting for me under a tea towel at the table. I ate quickly, then bundled myself into my coat and boots and hurried outside to find the others and apologize for my tardiness. I noticed lights on across the way, so I crunched along the gravel path connecting home to studio.

"*Ohayou gozaimasu*," I said, sliding open the wooden door and letting myself in.

"*Ohayou*," Shoko called back. "Come in. Over here!" She waved at me from behind several rows of shelves, stacked high with unfired pottery. I found her elbow-deep in a vat of unkneaded clay in the back of the studio. "Want to help?"

"Sure," I said, and rolled up my sleeves, diving my hands into the cold, damp mass. The studio, like the wet clay, was freezing. Most Japanese homes, even modern ones, are not heated throughout. Her studio, external from the house, was no exception.

"You know the chrysanthemum method?" Shoko asked.

"I'm not the best at it, but my mother showed me."

"I thought she might. Her clay, she could make so smooth, like butter. No air pockets at all."

"I'm nowhere near that gifted," I warned Shoko, but she waved it off.

"Not to worry. This is practice. Just for fun," she assured me. We each grabbed a large lump of clay, set ourselves at the table, and began kneading the clay by hand, not like you would a bread dough, but by lifting, pivoting, and wedging the sides with the heel of your hands, quickly, over and over, creating the look of chrysanthemum petals. "See? Not so bad. Looks good! You could have been a potter too!"

"I don't know about that," I laughed. "I'm not talented like you, or my mother. I could never match her, or even come close."

"She has her own way, you have yours. No need to compare. No two artists are alike, no matter how hard they try. Even master and apprentice. I should know," she winked, referring to the age-old tradition of Japanese craftsmanship, passed down from teacher to student through oral tradition and demonstration alone, through the generations. Traditionally in Japan, few apprentices were encouraged to deviate from the tried-and-true methods of their craft to find their own interpretation. It was a souvenir criticism my mother brought back from her study abroad experiment. Personally, though, I liked the idea of having the solid foundation of generations of masters behind me, supporting and guiding my work. Then again, I wasn't an artist. I wasn't much of anything, really.

"Can I ask you a question? About ceramics," I clarified, not wanting to seem overly prying.

"Yes, please ask anything you want," Shoko said, her hands working rhythmically to smooth the clay.

"You and my mother, you both studied together but developed totally different styles."

"And you want to know how that could be?"

"Your work is so, I don't know, lovely and delicate. Hers is so demanding. It's big and loud and in your face. You know what I mean?"

"Yes. I know. We studied at American university together, she then came here to Japan. Your mother, she studied for some time in my hometown. She told you this?"

"It's not too far from here, right?" I said, implying the distance between Michikusa House—her husband's family home—and her own.

"Yes. Not so far. My town is in another prefecture. Right next door," she smiled, then stopped to check my handiwork. "That looks good. Grab a bat," she said, and pointed to the stack of round pallets used to support the clay on the potter's wheel. I followed her lead, setting myself up at the second wheel beside hers. As we started them spinning, I watched Shoko guide the clay, like leading a partner to the center of the dance floor, a familiar step she'd performed countless times. I struggled with mine, but eventually got it to where it needed to be in order to work it.

"Why didn't her pottery end up looking like yours, then, like the pottery your family makes?" I asked, but actually what I wanted to know was why my mother's work was featured in galleries worldwide, both public and private, and sold for thousands, while Shoko's work asked only a modest sum and graced only dinner tables.

"I wondered the same thing at one time," Shoko admitted. "Eventually, I think I learned what made Juliet," she said, pronouncing my mother's name slowly, each syllable deliberate, "do things the way she does. In her heart, Juliet is a sculpture artist who happens to love clay as a medium. Her work has an...uneasy sort of beauty. It does not ask for attention, it demands it."

Yes, I thought. It's exactly like her in that way, demanding attention. My mother's artwork, while strikingly freeform thanks to her hand-built technique, is almost completely non-functional. Her bowls might have holes, her vases none at all. The surfaces erode, like chalky windswept cliffs, integrating rounded shapes with economic lines, using minimal detail and color. Her art has been called "hauntingly, painfully lovely", "daring, unconventional, almost twisted," and "the closest thing we'll ever see to perfection." Each line of praise, however, could just as easily be describing the artist, herself. People adore my mother. Critics and collectors, of course, but also colleagues, friends, neighbors, baristas, and cashier clerks, for chrissake. She's lauded by, worshiped by her students, and not just for her artistic prowess. They love her for her clever wit, her intolerance of mediocrity, even for her stunningly plain features—minus that amber-red hair of hers, naturally lustrous and perfectly straight. She's admired in our small community as the artist who never abandoned her Midwest roots for the likes of New York or London.

"As for me," Shoko continued, interrupting my thoughts, "I am content to make pretty things for everyone to use every day, cups to hold favorite drinks, or plates to serve special food for celebrations. That is who I am," she said, adding a single, definitive nod, almost a bow. As I looked up at her, though, my attempt at a bowl collapsed. "Ah! There it goes," she laughed. "No problem. You can always try again. As many times as you need, to find the right shape. There is no shame in making mistakes or starting over." She laid a delicate, slip-covered hand on mine, smiling. Then she returned it to her own perfectly formed creation, pressing into the clay, deforming it beyond repair. "There. Now we can both start over together."

We returned to the house around midday to find Hanada-san under the *kotatsu*, enjoying a cup of *hōjicha*, a type of green tea that's harvested in autumn and winter then roasted in a porcelain pot, giving it a warm smoky flavor reminiscent of fires in a hearth. Jun, by the sound of it, was in the kitchen.

"Maybe you could help Nakashima-san," Shoko suggested lightly, nudging me in that direction before taking a seat beside her husband.

It seemed I had no choice. In slippered feet, I shuffled through, parting the noren curtain and stepping down into the kitchen. Jun stood over a simmering soup pot, steam billowing past his face.

"Hey," I said.

"Win-chan, right?" he said, not looking at me but scrutinizing his concoction.

"Shoko thought you might need help."

"You can be my taste tester if you want." He grabbed a clean spoon and ladled out a small serving for me to try. I blew on it, inhaled its rich fragrance, then sipped. "It's delicious!" I said. "What is it?"

"Instead of a traditional *dashi* broth, I used chicken stock," he explained, indicating what appeared to be an almost intact, albeit featherless, bird in the soup bath. "Plus, plenty of *miso* and *shoyu*." This time, he removed the lid and gauze from a giant earthenware jar sitting nearby on the floor, revealing a bubbling brown mass. "This is the house *miso*," he said. "Soya beans, wheat, salt, water, and *koji* bacteria. They live together in this jar for many months. Then it gets pressed and fermented again. The liquid on top is *shoyu*, soy sauce."

The bubbling goo looked far from appetizing to someone used to soy sauce in neat little bottles. It smelled salty, almost briny. Again, a clean spoon appeared, and Jun scooped out a pea-sized portion of the *miso* paste for me to sample. Salty, yes, but deeply flavorful, surprisingly rich, smooth, and delicious. I stood awkwardly beside Jun, who seemed so at home in this place. What a gigantic world that must be, inside a kitchen. Knowing so many strange ingredients, how to combine them, adding heat and seasonings and time to get a perfectly delicious blend.

"I wish I knew how to do that, just whip things together and have it taste good," I admitted.

"It's easier than people think," he told me. "Most of the time, in Japanese cooking, you use the same base ingredients: shoyu, mirin, sake, dashi, miso." He counted them off on his fingers, one by one. "Then you combine them in different ways with fish or vegetables, then serve with rice. Very simple. Always fresh," he explained, and in perfect English.

The months' old miso didn't appear particularly "fresh", but I let that one slide. I understood the concept, the point he was trying to make.

"We also eat fermented pickles, *tsukemono*," he added. "When summer vegetables break down for some time it increases their flavor and makes them last year-round. So today, we will put a few inside onigiri. Can you make onigiri?"

"Rice balls?"

"Very easy, like this," he said, stepping around me to reach the rice cooker. He wet his hands, then scooped out a portion of freshly steamed rice. Using both palms, he quickly, but delicately formed a fat triangle around the pre-diced pickles, then set the finished onigiri on one of Shoko's plates. "See? You try."

I took up his place and scooped out a portion of rice.

"A bit less," he said.

"Like this?"

"*Hai.*"

"Who taught you? To cook, I mean." The glutinous rice was stickier and harder to work than he had made it appear.

"*Okasan*," he said. "My mother."

"My mom lived here for a year. Two years, actually. The first time was in college, then later she did a sabbatical with Shoko, but she always said she never liked rice. Isn't that weird? How can someone not like rice?" I finished my first malformed onigiri and set it beside Jun's. "She's a decent cook, but I never bothered to learn any of her recipes."

"My mother is an excellent cook. She grew her skills at the school in our district."

"She took classes?"

"No," he laughed, returning to the soup, taste-testing for flavor, adding a few pinches of salt and other seasonings I couldn't identify by sight alone—probably not even by smell, if given the chance. "She makes *kyushoku*—school lunch—for primary school students. Not the nutritionist who plans out every meal, but one of many cooks in the kitchen."

"I'm pretty sure that's not a job anyone has in America."

"In America, students bring their own lunch?" he asked.

"Some do, but they also have lunches for sale, like in a cafeteria. But no one really 'prepares' them. Not the way your mom does, anyway."

"I forgot, Western students don't eat in their classroom, or serve lunch to one another."

"Nope. We have big, separate rooms just for eating in," I said, thinking, as I said it, how excessive that made us sound.

"I always liked *kyushoku*, especially when I got to be on the team that served the meal, wearing an apron and everything, but some of my classmates cried when they had to eat food they didn't like, especially milk. We all hated the milk, the kind that came in boxes."

"We had those, too," I laughed.

"It was like, some government requirement or something, that we had to have milk at lunch."

"Aren't most Japanese people lactose intolerant?"

He nodded. "Stupid, right? I think the rule might be from the post-war era."

"Talk about outdated."

"But overall, *kyushoku* was a good program, I think. It taught us about nutrition and manners and responsibility, that kind of thing."

"I'm sure there were plenty of American students who felt like crying after eating one of our school lunches," I agreed, only half joking. "Uh, how many of these do we need, you think?" I placed another rice ball on one of Shoko's lovely plates, my hands dotted with sticky grains.

"A few more, maybe three?...I thought Americans were rich, I mean, always eating rich food." He said it with such seriousness that I couldn't even rally a smile.

"Nope. For some kids, those lunches are all they eat in a day. Homelessness is a huge problem. We grow and import, like, three times as much food as we can eat—some crazy amount like that—but there are still people who go hungry. It's pretty messed up, the whole situation."

I decided not to delve into how racism, colonialism, and abuses of power affected America's food system to this day, or how a girl like me had, for years, given no value to the thing keeping her alive. Preferring to invoke drama and risk for no other reason than not wanting to seem ordinary or ugly. I was still trying to disentangle myself from my own perceived hardship when my mother suggested I go abroad. Stay with Shoko and Hideyuki, she said, like the good old days. Meaning, presumably, when the wealthy fled to the countryside to recover or escape from illness. No computer, no Wi-Fi, no mirrors. Only rest, farm-fresh food, and mountain air. My mother said, it would do me good to stop fixating on minutiae and "live in the real world for a few minutes." I could have interpreted her comment as flippant or, worse, cruel. Except for the fact I knew, deep down, she was right. I needed to quit obsessing over myself—my appearance—for a change. Besides, sitting alone in my room gave my mind too many opportunities to hijack my attention. Doing something practical, something hands-on, even if it was just gardening or kneading clay, would ground me in the present.

Jun stopped stirring the pot but didn't reply. *Great, I've already scared away the only other person my age within a hundred miles who speaks English*, I thought. "Sorry, didn't mean to be such a downer. We can talk about something else."

"A downer?"

"I only meant, we don't have to talk about sad things like that," I said.

"It's easy to feel sad when there are so many big problems," Jun agreed. "When you are just one person."

"How do you deal with it?" I asked, wondering whether he might have an answer to a question I had often struggled to answer, myself.

With the soup ladle he gestured around the kitchen. "Cooking."

"That's all?"

"With food, I can honor people's hard work, honor everything that grows what I eat. It's one thing I can do every day." The attitude I had taken for cheekiness the day before faded, replaced by a subtle confidence that spoke of a man prone to deep introspection.

"That's...a really good point," I said, meaning it. "The way you put it, it sounds almost religious." I laid down another pillow of rice.

"Yes, I think so. Cooking connects us to everything." His hands stilled and he looked to the ceiling, as if redirecting his energy to find the exact words he wanted to say. "If not for sun and rain and insects and many hard-working people, so many things working together in just the right way, we wouldn't have ingredients to make a delicious soup like this one to warm us on a cold day." The cockeyed grin returned, but I found myself drawn in. I couldn't help but smile back briefly, hurriedly, before looking away.

"Is that why you're here?" I asked. "To learn about food production, start to finish?"

"Part of the reason. Another small part is, I'm staying here at Michikusa House to learn about cooking with the most delicious ingredients I can find, honoring each one so that one day I can be the best *kaiseki* chef in Kyushu."

"Really? That's the traditional multi-course meal in Japan, right?" One of my mother's fondest memories from her sabbatical took place not in the studio, but in just such a restaurant. From what little I knew, *kaiseki* cuisine used seasonal ingredients, each prepared specially by the chef to showcase its best features, color, flavor, texture, and the like. The ingredients, cooking methods, and presentation are not repeated in any course of the meal. It's an intricate display that tests the skills of the chef on every level.

"You don't believe me?" he asked, one eyebrow raised, but he was grinning.

"Sounds tough, is all." I said it lightly, joking, but he turned away.

"I think it's done," he said, a shock of coldness in his voice. Had I offended him? Silently, he ladled out four bowls of the fragrant, steaming broth, laced with strands of seaweed and chunks of white chicken meat.

"I think I'm done, too," I said, placing the last misshapen onigiri on the plate. None were exactly the same size, which made me feel oddly embarrassed. "You'll have to tell me more about Japanese schools sometime," I said, going for placating.

He arranged a tray: soup, rice balls, pickles, and other home-made condiments. "Not much to tell. I was a very bad student."

"I don't believe you. Your English is phenomenal," I said.

"I speak okay, but I can't read English. I tested very badly."

"Yeah, but your speech isn't academic, either. It's natural and conversational."

"My first job was at a *gyudon* restaurant, across the street from a major train depot. It was close to a popular shrine also, so foreigners would come in to eat or ask for directions."

"You learned fluent English from working in a restaurant?" I asked with unveiled skepticism.

"It's a long story," he said, then whisked the tray through the curtain.

CHAPTER 4

"You've been awfully quiet," Liam says, staring straight ahead, hands at ten and two on the steering wheel. The dipping sun backlights stretches of black locust and white ash lining both sides of Route 2, setting the last of the seasonal color display ablaze. Light and color, both, will disappear soon.

I wriggle in my seat. The green dress hugs my waist uncomfortably, too tightly, a relic from a body sacrificed to the past. A past when there were dresses to fit into. I should've worn the other one, the black shapeless knee-length I bought to hide inside during my worst recovery months, when my tummy ballooned and my returning weight arrived ill-distributed, in all the wrong places.

Liam, on the other hand, looks polished, like that wool suit jacket was tailored to fit him. His posture, always erect, does its form justice. I, however, will always remember Liam the way he was in middle school, a head above the rest. Back then, he let his dark, curly hair grow wild as a riverside thicket. Both his wire-rimmed glasses and baseball jackets were oversized—hand-me-downs from his brother, Mike—both much too big for his face and frame. He grew so tall so fast his jeans couldn't keep up, the white cotton ribbing of calf-high socks permanently exposed around the ankle.

"Do you think we would've ended up together? If not for alphabetical seating in sixth grade, I mean," I ask, and not for the first time. "Heeley, Hoxley…"

"You think maybe I should've sidled up to Fiona Justice, instead?"

"No, I meant Uriah Grenson—Grenshaw? He might've been more my type."

"Uriah Grant, you mean? So, you're into effeminate homosexual men now, is that it?"

I feign a shrug.

"Win, we've been together—we've been friends," he corrects himself, "longer than we haven't been. Come on. That has nothing to do with the alphabet."

"But why me? Why not Fiona Justice?"

"She chewed her cuticles."

"Oh. Well then."

"Something's going on in there," he says, reaching over to smooth a strand of hair away from my face.

"I just wonder 'why me?' sometimes, is all." What I wonder is, what was left to love after the artificial guise of misfortune, the flawless white skin stretched over bone, was stripped away?

We leave the highway, turning south toward our old stomping grounds, the town where we grew up, toward the college where my parents still teach, where we'll soon laud my mother's brilliant artwork.

"Okay, how's this for a reason: You were the only girl in Science Olympiad in seventh grade."

"I only joined because you talked me into it," I argue.

"And why do you think that was?"

"My charming wit?"

"Because we were lab partners, which meant I got to know you. You were sweet and generous and very cute."

"Were?"

"Are."

"Don't you mean quiet and introverted?"

"That too. Where did that girl go, I wonder?" he says, sliding a hand along the emerald silk covering my thigh. I cross my legs.

"She left after you dumped her senior year." *When you weren't there to act as a crutch anymore,* I think.

We're quiet for a few minutes, lost inside old memories. Lights from the campus draw us in. The sun, by now, has fully set.

We've gone over this so many times, what happened to us back then. It's funny how small events bump people onto a track they didn't anticipate, the lengths they'll go to not to feel lonely and unwanted. We worked it out in the end, though. The storm blew us to where we are now. I'm healthy, back in school, we're together. Isn't that enough? Why doesn't it feel like enough?

Liam asks, "Have you thought any more about…?"

"…About what?"

"Moving in together," he says.

"I have. I am…thinking about it."

We circle the familiar quad, pull into the lot, circle to find parking. Our headlights illuminate smartly dressed students and professors heading toward the gallery where the Faculty Art Show is about to begin. The tall gallery windows cast orange rectangles of light across manicured gardens. Inside, among dozens of well-dressed attendees, I spy the elegant frame of my mother, her back to us. My father, looking comparatively stocky but equally smart, stands beside her. It'll be hard enough facing this evening, my parents' friends and their sidelong glances—people who knew me before and during my worst years—without a deep dive into my past as a warm-up act.

"If we're going to do this, Win, we need to—"

"Yeah, there's a lot to figure out," I say.

"The lease, the cat."

"Right. I know. That's why I'm taking my time, not jumping into anything."

Liam leans his head back against the headrest, rubbing his face with his hands. "That's not like you."

I let him have that one. We sit in silence. The numbers on the digital display tick by.

"What is it?" he prompts.

How long had I ached for Liam's company, his companionship, his commitment and love? Now that I have it, a hundred percent, why even consider rocking the boat? *Yet here*

I am, ready to toss myself overboard without a life preserver.
"Nothing. Come on. Let's go inside. I see my mom." I lean
over and kiss his cheek. "She'll blame me if we're late."

The annual Faculty Art Show is a semi-formal event, but
everyone comes dressed in full regalia. My emerald silk dress
slinks across the floor, trailing a step behind me as Liam and
I approach my parents. I sense, or maybe just imagine, peoples' eyes following me, scrutinizing. Judging. Friends of my
parents, old professors whose names I can't remember, who
once voiced "concern," either to my mother or directly to
me, regarding my weight, my habits, my attitude, my falling
GPA, sleeping in class, failing to show up at all. I don't want
to talk to them, answer probing questions, or invent excuses.

The last time I attended was five years ago, right before I
dropped out of school, this school as a matter of fact. I wore
skinny jeans, a heavy leather coat, and combat boots—just
about the only clothes that still fit. I weighed almost thirty pounds less than I do now, not even close to reaching
triple-digits. No doubt my mother's given excuses for my
absence in the years since—Winona's not been feeling her
best, she's taking some time off; she's in Japan, staying with
a family friend; yes, you remember Shoko Hanada, the ceramicist; oh, Win? She just took up a new program over on
the East Side, it demands so much of her time, she couldn't
possibly make it this year.

In the background, the school conservatory's string quar-
tet plays a lesser-known Bach piece I've heard once or twice
but can't name; a predictable choice. Pleasant and upbeat,
no dissonance whatsoever. Wish I could say as much for the

atmosphere. Or maybe I'm only imagining it. Even if it is all in my head, why agree to come this year? What on earth was I thinking?

"Oh, thank goodness," my mother says, hugging me. "You made it." *On time* being the unsaid implication. "How are you feeling, honey? You look flushed." She holds me at arm's length. We examine each other. This evening, my mother's chosen a silk-satin dress with a bold iris motif: violet, sage, turquoise, and copper against a dark navy background. The flowing balloon sleeves balance the otherwise figure-skimming fit. On her, it looks like art.

"I'm fine," I say. "Chilly outside, is all," though it's nowhere near cold enough yet, not even late in September, for burning-cold skin and reddened cheeks.

"Liam, you're looking wonderful, as always." They exchange greetings and hugs before my mother turns back to me. "I always loved that dress on you," she says. "Glad it still fits after all this time, all the trouble we went through having it made."

"Thanks," I mutter, but she doesn't hear me. Although, frankly, I don't think she hears herself half the time. "Hi, Dad."

"Win, glad you two came this year. Love that dress."

"Thanks," I manage. I had thought so too, until we arrived. These days, I just look...normal. Average. Though "normal" for a girl who once deliberately went out of her way to appear anything but means I now stand out like a giant purple-green bruise to anyone who knew me "before", for exactly that reason. It's a stark contrast. Students hired as wait staff whisk trays back and forth. I accept the closest alcoholic beverage on offer and finish it in one swift swallow.

"Delightful," my mother says, a mild but deliberate scolding.

Meanwhile, the Dean of the Art Department, Dr. Anita Chowdhury, steps onto the stage in a stunning gold and magenta saree. She's worn a different one to each of these events. Despite my reservations about the Dean, herself, I can't help but admire the vibrant, abstract print and the dashing amulet hanging from her neck. All but the spotlights dim, leaving only the Dean and the art, paintings and photographs and sculptures positioned expertly throughout the room, in full illumination. The mic echoes on and she begins her opening remarks, welcoming guests, thanking patrons, and championing artists. She carries on for some time, so I quietly disengage myself from Liam and my parents and wander in the direction of the restroom. Thankfully, I find it empty. I need a moment to steady myself. I lean over the sink, bracing my weight against the cool countertop. All that in the car, my mother's flippant remarks, the fact I plan to break the news this very evening about my decision to—

The door bursts open and a woman hurries into a stall. I hear her fiddling with the toilet paper, a zipper, and figure that's my cue. I exit, but don't return to my family. Instead, I wander outside, onto the garden patio where a few guests are chatting and sipping drinks under heat lamps. It's chilly and the breeze raises goosebumps on my bare arms. In years past, I wouldn't have been able to stand ten minutes outside, even in mild weather, not without a coat, since my own body carried none of its own insulation. *The things we take for granted*, I think, *the ability to enjoy a breeze on a cool night.*

"Winona, there you are. You missed the speech," my dad says from the doorway. "Let's take a look around. I've been eyeing Professor Whang's portrait collection." With his arm extended, Dad draws me back inside.

Together, we circumnavigate the room as I actively avoid making eye contact. I see no sign of Liam. My mother, on the other hand, stands out in any crowd, a beacon to which others are naturally drawn, like the proverbial moths to the flame. She's in her element, and the two of us—Dad and I— we've learned to let her bask in it.

"Your mother mentioned Liam's idea," Dad says. We're standing side by side, admiring one of Professor Whang's unconventional portraits. Whang's work, I read from the little plaque posted alongside the collection, *relies heavily on traditional Chinese calligraphy techniques. She combines incense ash collected from temples into her ink to create intense black-and-white portraits that aim to capture human suffering.*

"Why does art always have to be about suffering?" I wonder aloud, ignoring Dad's comment. I can't talk about Liam's idea, about he and I potentially moving in together, without mentioning what I've decided to do about it. "This is depressing. Let's go over there."

I'm drawn to the work of an Argentinian textile artist, the newest faculty member, who has created murals made entirely of felted wool dyed wildly pigmented colors. The way they're laid out, the figures and symbols nested neatly within a circle, reminds me of the sand mandalas created by Tibetan monks.

"Have you thought about it?" Dad presses. "Just so you know, your mother and I are on board, whatever you decide. If you think you want to keep the place to yourself, to focus on school—"

"Thanks, Dad. I'm...still thinking about it," I lie.

He nods approvingly. "No point rushing into a big decision."

After we complete our circuit, I go in search of Liam. I find him on the same patio I vacated, overlooking the gardens and water features. He's talking with—laughing with—a young woman I vaguely recognize, though her indigo headscarf and decadent gold-and-turquoise jewelry fail to offer additional clues. She's about our age; too young to be one of the professors. Probably a teaching assistant or graduate student.

"Liam, I was looking for you," I say, cutting in, the second flush of the evening rising to my cheeks. He holds out a hand, reaching for mine, and pulls me in.

"Win, you remember Fiona, right? Fiona Justice," he says. As in cuticle-eater Fiona Justice? When she offers a hand for me to shake, I slyly check her nails. They're beautifully manicured, painted an ivory color that matches the accents on her headscarf. Did we conjure her, I wonder?

"Do you work at the college?" I manage.

"I'm doing my thesis with Professor Mathenge. We're both interested in traditional Kenyan dress. For me, it's all about jewelry-making and beadwork."

"That sounds interesting," I admit mildly, albeit unwillingly. "It's great you found such a…niche focus."

"Well, it was either that or dance," Fiona says, lifting her lithe arms gracefully, her fingers snapping like castanets.

"You dance?" Liam asks.

"Thirteen years, can you believe it?" she laughs, as if even she can't fathom so great a passage of time.

"You must've started, what, back in middle school?" Liam calculates. "I had no idea."

And why would you? I want to ask, but don't.

"I didn't advertise." Fiona actually winks.

Are they flirting right in front of me?

"Really, though, I feel like it's important to become an expert in one particular niche, as you put it," she says, and her amber eyes flash in my direction for a split second. "If nothing else, it's a way to honor my heritage." She smiles at Liam then, who nods as if she's said something profound. I roll my eyes towards the door, the exit, hoping for an escape. "So, are you two…?" she lets the question hang.

"Still dating," I say.

"Really? Not engaged yet?"

"Not yet," Liam admits. I expect him to take my hand again, but he doesn't. I want to walk away, right now, but I don't trust him to follow me.

*   *   *

There's a tradition for the families of the presenting faculty to go out to dinner together after the show, to the only sit-down restaurant in our tiny college town. The little Italian place, *Catania*, serves Sicilian-inspired dishes that appeal to almost everyone. This year, however, there's been a change in venue: a new Japanese restaurant, whose name I can't remember, sits half a block from *Catania*. In clusters, we walk there from the gallery, our path lit by antique-looking streetlamps that line the quad and each of the major roads through town.

Now that Liam and I are alone again, I ask, "So, you going to tell me what the heck that was about?"

"Hm?"

"Oh, come on. What was that, with Fiona? Don't pretend I wasn't standing right there."

"She's an old classmate. You know her as well as I do."

"Maybe, but I wasn't the one batting my eyelashes."

"God, Win. Why do you have to turn everything into a fight?"

"Because my boyfriend is flirting with other women right in front of me!" I whisper angrily, not wanting the couples ahead or behind to hear.

"Don't you think if I were interested in pursuing her, I'd do it behind your back?" he asks, and I flinch. He softens at once, as if he's slapped me, eager to apologize, take it back. "I'm sorry, I didn't mean that. You know I wouldn't do that."

I can't even muster a reply.

"Win, you know I'm not like that, right?"

"Yeah, I know," I say, but without much conviction, and we walk the rest of the way in silence.

Even before friends and complete strangers alike started commenting on my choice of entree, I hated this part of the annual event most of all. My feet are tired from the hours I just spent standing in heels, and thanks to the late hour I'm starving and irritable. Nor does the constant chattering of people congratulating one another help my mood.

Liam and I are seated at a neat wooden table along with my parents and another couple. Professor Salk and his wife, Roberta, neither of whom I know well, seem nice enough and older than most of the other diners. Luckily, Fiona Justice is nowhere to be seen. Professor Salk is trying to engage my father in a discussion about political reforms in Eastern Europe, but the poor man is so hard of hearing that Dad's practically shouting. Liam, on the other hand, is quietly chatting with my mother about god knows what, so I'm left with Roberta.

"Do you like Japanese food?" I ask her, just to be conversational.

She scans the menu through a pair of reading glasses hung on a chain around her neck. "Seems a bit of an odd choice, don't you think? What on earth is this natto I'm seeing under the appetizers column?" She takes a moment to wipe her glasses. "I can't read a word of this."

"In terms of acquired tastes, that one's pretty advanced," I warn her. "I'd pass if I were you."

"Ah, you've tried it, then?"

"Once. I lived in Japan for a year."

"Did you now? Ed and I went to China a few years back," she informs me, but I decide not to point out that the two countries probably aren't all that similar. "Such a lovely place, the Far East. Did you enjoy it?"

"I did. I miss it a lot, actually. The woman I stayed with is a friend of my mother's. She has a farmhouse in the countryside."

"Sounds lovely."

"We worked in the garden, made pottery…"

"Oh, how nice for you."

"Japan is where I learned to cook, actually. I feel like I know more about Japanese cuisine than…American… food."

"Well, I'll rely on you, then, to help me choose," she smiles, and leans over with her menu.

"Do you like seafood?" I try.

"Not especially. All those little bones," she says, with a look bordering on disgust.

"How about *nabemono*," I suggest, pointing to the line on the menu. "That's one of my favorites for chilly nights."

"It has gotten rather cold lately, hasn't it? A hot pot, it says. Hm…"

"It's nice, like soup almost. Hot broth with fresh ingredients, simmered and served in a clay pot."

"I see. Very well then," she says, folding the menu decisively.

I recall the first time I made *nabe*. It was the first dish I learned to make from scratch, if you want to call it that, since *nabemono* are really easy to throw together. I had asked Jun Nakashima what he thought the easiest Japanese dish to make was, and whether he could teach me.

We had been snowed in for the first time that season, though the accumulation amounted to little more than drifts around the old farmhouse and white mounds blanketing the garden beds. The four of us, Shoko, Hideyuki, Jun, and I had spent that afternoon huddled under the domed warmth of the *kotatsu*, reading and chatting, watching the news and playing card games, leaving that small, cozy shelter only to refresh the teapot.

"The easiest Japanese dish to make?" Jun wondered aloud. "*Nabemono*, I think. The perfect winter comfort food."

"And you can teach me?"

"I can teach you," he assured me with that cockeyed grin I had already come to love. The grin that meant he was hiding, or was about to reveal, a precious secret.

Wrapped in a heavy sweater and two layers of socks, I followed Jun into the kitchen where he began collecting ingredients: a block of tofu, root vegetables—carrot, daikon, yams—winter greens, three kinds of mushrooms, a hunk of marbled beef, and udon noodles. Then he pulled out a large earthenware pot and the portable gas stove.

"We'll use this," he indicated the stove, "to cook everything, right at the table."

"Oh, okay."

"But first, we prepare the ingredients. You cut the vegetables. I'll slice the beef. Bite-sized pieces," he instructed.

By that time, two months into my stay at Michikusa House, I could handle that much, at least. I went to work on my ingredients while Jun, meanwhile, shaved the beef down to tissue-thin strips.

Jun passed me a large ceramic plate. "You have to arrange the food to maximize its presentation. It makes food appear more delicious, but it tastes better too."

I looked over at him, questioning his sincerity, making sure he wasn't messing with me. "Really?"

"Yes," he swore. "When ingredients are plated in an attractive way, we take time to appreciate them individually, we eat more slowly, and enjoy the flavors and textures more completely, which also boosts digestion."

"Alright," I said, feigning distrust. "I believe you, but I can't believe you've never said that to me before, *Senpai*," I said, teasing him, but also genuinely surprised.

"What is this, an after-school club? How do you know that word?"

"I only meant we've been cooking together for a while now."

"There are many secrets to cooking you don't know yet, Win-chan. Before you can learn a new lesson, you have to advance to the next level," he said, joking, I think, though sometimes it was hard to tell with Jun since he took cooking, above all, so seriously.

"What level am I at now?" I prodded. "Gotta be two or three, right?"

"You started with zero, no skill whatsoever. Now you're maybe at level two, I think," he said, and we both laughed.

"I was pretty useless at the start. Remember those onigiri?"

"Too big, too small, too packed together."

"I'm surprised you let me in the kitchen after that."

"Shoko-chan made me," he said, thumbing over his shoulder toward the dining room, where we could hear the sound of the television, the evening weather report.

"Hey, don't be mean. Somebody had to teach me. That's partly why I'm here, right? To learn."

"Lots to learn," he agreed.

After a beat, I asked, "Did they tell you why I'm here?" trying not to sound overly curious. No doubt my mother had told Shoko the basics, if for no other reason than to ensure I ate every meal served to me without immediately emptying it into the toilet. Had Shoko passed any of that information on to her husband or Jun?

"They told me an American girl would be staying here. That's all."

"Why are you staying here, of all places? A full year, right?"

"*Hai*, one year," he confirmed, then went silent, but I sensed there was more to come. Finally, after whisking together two dipping sauces, Jun admitted he came here after dropping out of culinary school, a prestigious institute in Sydney, Australia. "So, I am here to start over."

I desperately wanted to ask why he had dropped out but didn't want to pry. We weren't close enough for that. Nor did I want to explain my reasons for terminating my first attempt at higher education, for staying at Michikusa House. Not yet. But I could, at least, reciprocate.

"I dropped out of school, too, actually," I admitted. Jun looked up. "Not culinary school," I clarified. "Just a small, liberal arts college. I guess I'm here to start over, too." Jun paid me the same respect, reigning in whatever curiosity might tempt him to ask "why?" I didn't offer more, keeping us on equal footing, so to speak.

Jun looked at me differently then. I remember it vividly, that singular moment. Since that first day we met, Jun had struck me as openly curious and inquisitive, unlike most Japanese people who are generally habitually polite and respectful of other people's privacy and personal affairs to the point of seeming a bit withdrawn or overly formal or, to American sensibilities, even unfriendly. That's why, when Jun looked at me just then, I felt very—he wasn't scrutinizing or judging—but I felt seen, like he was taking me in for the first time. Like I wasn't merely a shadow passing through the room, but a person with unusually attractive features worth admiring more closely, politeness be damned. The intensity of those eyes startled me, and I turned back to my little task, haphazardly putting the finishing touches on my plate of arranged vegetables. He did the same, but a bit too quickly. He bumped into an open drawer and knocked both his precious kitchen knife and the sauces he'd just prepared to the floor. I jumped as the knife spun out. I could feel my heart pounding, but whether it arose from the clatter or his intense gaze, I couldn't have said.

"*Sumimasen!*" Jun apologized, ducking to wipe the mess and retrieve his knife.

"It's fine," I assured him, a bit breathless, looking down as if from a height. The thinness of his t-shirt revealed the curved arc of his spine. He moved so gracefully, I thought—oddly—hunched there on the floor, strong hands working rapidly to clean every surface. I wondered if I should help, and in my mind, I pictured us kneeling, our hands brushing around one another, our heads almost touching, sweeping up every last drop of the spill. Instead, I blinked the image aside and hurried, bearing my plate, out of his way.

"Everything okay?" Shoko asked, as I laid the plate on the table. "Ah, how beautiful. Well done," she said. "Your skills are improving."

"You think so?"

"Mm," she nodded, then said something to her husband in Japanese, who also nodded.

I joined them under the *kotatsu*, feeling a bit lightheaded.

"You okay?" she asked for the second time.

"Jun dropped the sauces. I don't think the dishes broke. Just a spill."

Shoko craned her neck to peer under the noren curtain separating us from the kitchen. "Nakashima-san?" she called out to him. "*Daijōbu ka?*"

Jun appeared then, looking both rigid and flustered. In one hand he carried the portable stove, his plate of shaved beef in the other. He made several trips, bringing out various dishes and utensils, the clay pot containing the rich *dashi* broth, but never once did he look at me. Throughout dinner that night, as we simmered and stirred, helping ourselves to the array of ingredients, Jun said very little. Usually so amusing and conversational at meals, Jun for once seemed lost in thought. Or in memories, perhaps best forgotten. If his reasons for starting over were as troubling as mine, I could understand why he'd prefer to keep them buried under layers of civility and the passage of time. Whatever his reasons, however, I felt sure Jun Nakashima was hiding something.

CHAPTER 5

"How does it compare?" Roberta Salk asks, leaning in. In the end, we had ordered the same dish. I couldn't resist.

"Similar," I lie.

The *nabe* is fine, edible, but tastes decidedly homogenous. Nothing like Jun's exquisite cooking, no surprising layers or nuance. His dishes always tasted rich and wholesome. Like coming home, but with an unexpected twist: a bit of crunch, a little zest. With Jun's cooking, you could sense the terroir, where the ingredients came from. They melded together, reminiscent of the season, of a special place in time.

These ingredients, I can tell, did not come from a wholesome food community, but from a wholesaler. The vegetables represent a spectrum of color, but not taste. These carrots, this cabbage, probably came from Mexico, grown out of season and harvested before fully ripe. By the time they reached my clay pot, they would've traveled thousands of miles, withstood days if not weeks of heavy handling. Not all restaurants function this way, but most do. To source ingredients locally, from nearby farms, presupposes a chef who can adjust the menu according to the seasons to accommodate the natural growing and harvesting schedule of different plants. This also assumes the chef has some knowledge of regional cuisine, the types of grains, vegetables, fruits, nuts, legumes, herbs, and edible fungi that grow well in the surrounding soil and climate, and how to prepare and combine each to best effect. Jun, I'm certain, would have sent this dish back to the kitchen.

I slurp a few chewy noodles, then push the bowl away. I don't have much appetite, anyway. The talk I've planned to have with my parents and Liam—I rehearsed a speech but have already forgotten every point I wanted to make. *What am I doing? Can I trust myself to make the right decision after so many regrettable ones?* As my mind whirs, second guessing, I picture Erin, hear her telling me to do something that makes me happy for a change.

"You haven't eaten much," my mother comments. "Do you want something else?"

"No. I'm fine." My frayed nerves finally push me over the edge. "Actually, there's something I've been wanting to talk to you all about." Everyone at the table, including Professor and Mrs. Salk, looks up from their plates. "Uh, the thing is…" My palms feel clammy. I press them between my knees. "We talked about moving in together," I say to Liam, "but the thing is, I don't want to finish this program. This degree, it's not what I thought it would be. It's…I'm not going to finish." Period.

"Excuse me?" my mother says, her hand gripping the edge of the table, as if to steady herself or possibly tamp down her rising blood pressure.

"What are you saying?" my father asks.

Liam glares at me. "You're dropping out?"

"For heaven's sake, Winona. What on earth do you plan to do if you're not in school?" my mother asks.

"I'm not…entirely sure yet. I just know I don't want to waste any more time and money on a program that doesn't interest me and that doesn't align with my beliefs."

"For chrissake, you're not studying world religions," my father grumbles. "It's a nutrition course, what's there to believe in?"

"You'd be surprised," I mutter, knowing that even if I explained, they wouldn't understand or, I think, especially care.

Liam scoffs. "God, if I'd thought you were serious—"

"You knew about this?" my mother demands.

"Juliet, leave him alone," my father cuts in. "It's certainly not his fault."

Despite the pointed accusation, I agree. "That's right. It's my decision. Leave Liam out of it."

"Leave me out? Do you even hear yourself, Winona? What are you planning to do? Where are you going to live? I think this very much concerns me." Liam struggles to remain seated.

"Goodness," Roberta Salk mutters, then turning to her husband, adds, "I think we should go, Ed." The Professor nods and rises.

"I meant, the decision isn't up to you, Liam," I continue. By now our raised voices have turned heads. Dean Chowdhury, who's been making the rounds, steps over to our table.

"Everything alright over here?" she asks, her voice cool and level. Years of managing highly emotional artists—faculty and students alike—has trained her steady composure.

"Yes, we're fine," says my mother. "We've just had a bit of a shock."

"Oh, please. Don't be so dramatic," I scoff.

Dad says, "Winona, don't speak to your mother like that."

"Can I help?" Dean Chowdhury asks, aiming, no doubt, for a quick resolution.

My mother presses her fingers to her lips, as if to stifle a scream. When she speaks, she fails to exude the same calm as the Dean. "Winona just informed us that she wants to drop out of school. Again."

Roberta Salk stands, offers her chair to Dean Chowdhury, then lays a hand on my shoulder. "Good luck," she whispers, then totters away to retrieve her coat.

The Dean sits. I recall the day I got called into her office to discuss my failing grades and various reports of falling asleep in class. At the time, I still hadn't declared a major but knew the Dean of the Art Department thanks to my mother's position and, of course, these annual events. She'd sat me down across from her, me with my arms folded, glaring, hating everyone, anyone who got "involved". What business was it of hers what I did with my life, academic or otherwise? After twenty minutes or so of questioning, interrogating me, she phoned my mother's office. My mother came in. The three of us talked. And talked. By the end of it, after what felt like hours, Dean Chowdhury had convinced my mother to pull me out of school and enroll me in a recovery program. Thus began my extended medical leave and what would become the worst years of my life.

Immediate entry into pharmacotherapy, the experts said, was the solution. I have chemical imbalances, they said, too much of one, not enough of another. They make pills for that. Pills that, in one case, indulged depression and, in another, shot my skull so full of exit wounds I couldn't brush my hair without wailing. The third pill flooded the room of my body with water, suspended, anesthetized. I'd already spent years being numbed out. I didn't need pills to help me achieve that. So much for psychiatry.

Once I'd committed to finding wellness, I refused to suppress the problem without addressing the underlying issue, the pervasive fears: of abandonment, of loneliness, of imperfection and mediocrity, of the future and its uncertainty, and of a self too cowardly to face any of those possibilities. Talk therapy fared marginally better but was hindered by the fact that they—the therapists—were so overburdened with patients they were unable to schedule regular appointments and often canceled at the last minute. After struggling to reschedule over the phone, one secretary helpfully informed me that finding a doctor in-network is especially difficult for patients like me because "Nobody wants to touch eating disorders."

Over the course of two years, I saw more than a dozen health experts, few of whom had any experience treating my specific form of craziness. Mainly, I muddled through on my own—at least it felt that way—reading as much as I could on the subject and its more tangential aspects. All that, to say nothing of the fact I was literally forced to eat for the first time in years, was scrutinized at every meal while my stomach, my whole body ballooned, screaming in agony with the unfamiliar sequence of processing food into waste. I had to shower and shit with the bathroom door ajar. I hated it, hated myself, hated my life. That's what I associate talks with Dean Chowdhury with. She was literally the last person in the world I wanted to intervene.

"I heard you enrolled in a nutrition program. Sounds like a good match," the Dean says to me, without any irony I can detect. "We were missing you at these events for a while."

I decide not to mention that most of that long, long while I was not enrolled in anything. "Turns out it wasn't what I hoped it would be," I say, hoping I don't have to explain.

"That's a shame," the Dean says. "I'm sorry to hear that."

I'm not especially interested in platitudes, and I don't need to defend myself to her, not this time.

"It took years, so much convincing to get her re-enrolled," my mother explains.

The Dean nods, listening. "But don't you think Winona probably knows what's best for her?"

Her acknowledgment stuns both of us to silence. She took the exact opposite stance all those years ago, convincing my mother to step in and act on my behalf.

"You know, my son never got a degree," Dean Chowdhury admits. "He dropped out of technical school while also working for a distribution company part-time. He kept on with that and now he's a manager. His job ensures products are shipped in the fastest and most efficient way. It's an important service these days; he's earning six figures. It wouldn't be everyone's dream job, not even the most fulfilling, maybe, but it serves a purpose and gives him freedom to do other things he enjoys."

"Well, thank you for that, Anita. I'm sure there's plenty to talk about," my mother says in such an overtly dismissive manner I'm a little stunned. Dean Chowdhury, however, doesn't seem to take offense. She smiles, making her exit. My mother says to me and Liam, "Why don't the two of you stop by our place on the way out. We can talk more there."

"I've made up my mind," I say, rejecting the idea of dragging this out any further. "I'll finish this term while I work out a plan going forward, but once this semester's over, I'm done."

"There's a lot to think on. How 'bout we sleep on it?" Dad suggests reasonably, though I can tell both my mother and Liam have plenty else they would like to say, right now.

After a silent car ride, Liam and I return to my apartment. I can tell he's ready to duke it out. He throws his jacket onto the bed and paces the room. I, on the other hand, feel calmer than I have in weeks. For once, I feel like I'm moving in the right direction, rather than a direction someone else has chosen for me. I have no idea where this path might lead, but it's exciting to consider the possibilities.

"I should've known you'd do something like this," Liam says at last.

From the kitchen, I say, "What, make a decision on my own, you mean?" I set the kettle to boil, checking to see whether Clay finished his dinner. He's polished his bowl, but I see no sign of him otherwise and I wonder if he, too, can sense the tension in the room.

"Why didn't you talk to me first, instead of making me look like an idiot in front of your parents?"

"The way I remember it, I did try, and you dismissed everything I had to say. For another thing—and let me say this loud and clear—this is not your decision." Liam appears in the kitchen doorway. I work to occupy my hands, going from cupboard to counter, readying a mug, choosing a teabag. "For once, I'm making up my own mind about my future. I'm not following you around; I'm not letting my parents' jobs influence where I go; I'm not letting my mother ship me overseas. I'm listening to my gut and it's telling me this is not the right path for me. I'm not happy in this program, or at this school, and—"

"So where are you planning on living? Do you expect your parents to keep forking over the rent for this apartment, or are you just going to crash at my place?"

My entire body tightens, as if absorbing the blow. I shake my head, shaking it off, and let out a held breath. "Thank you for that, Liam. How kind of you to consider of my wellbeing."

"Oh, stop acting like a child."

"You can't try to make my decisions for me one minute then tell me to grow up the next. And for your information, I'm not coming to live with you."

He shoves his hands in his pants pockets, nodding condescendingly.

"Actually, you're right about one thing: I'm not going to leave this apartment," I inform him, only realizing that truth the moment I say it. "I like it here. I like the location. I just don't like what I'm doing with my life. I'll get a proper job and pay for it myself."

"Fine. Good luck with that," Liam scoffs, then disappears around the corner, locking himself in the bathroom. I hear the shower running. It stays on for nearly an hour. I change out of the green dress and into leggings and one of Liam's old t-shirts, then plop myself at the table behind my laptop with my mug of tea. When he emerges, wearing only boxer briefs, Liam gets into bed without saying a word to me. With his head already on the pillow, facing away from me, he says, "You coming to bed? It's after midnight."

"I think I'll stay up a while yet," I say, my voice deliberately cool and unaffected. When Liam doesn't reply, doesn't argue, I plug in my headphones and watch a couple mindless videos until his breathing evens out and I'm certain he's asleep. Then I pull up a search bar. I consider looking up Fiona Justice but decide she's not worth my time and effort. If I'm lucky, I'll never hear her name again. Instead, I type: Jun Nakashima, Kumamoto. Briefly, I consider other signifiers I could attach— the words chef, farm, and kaiseki come to mind—but I decide to begin broadly and narrow my search from there. It's a process I've repeated many times, though not since living in this apartment, and never with Liam in the room. I blink up at him, making sure he's still fast asleep, then begin scanning the results, those automatically translated into English.

The work of a scientist by the name Okabe Nakashima at Kumamoto University claims most of the top headlines, but it's unlikely the two are related. Nakashima is a common enough surname. Other results include links to a famous American woodworker and another, an inventor, with several patents registered under his name. When I search the name in relation to farming, I get results springing up across the United States, family histories and farms that ended with Japanese internment. Would Jun have started a cooking channel? Or maybe he's retweeting funny one-liners. I try typing Jun's name into major social media websites—first in English, then using the same Japanese characters I used to address the letters I mailed to his parents' house. Neither search proves fruitful given how few people use their real names on those sites, preferring a catchy nickname or phrase. Nor, it seems, can I track down the old Facebook account that belonged to my friend. Either it's been deleted or privatized.

At last, on a whim, I try a popular photo-sharing website. Like anyone, Jun occasionally took pictures of his culinary creations, of interesting features in a landscape, things he wanted to remember. Whether he uploaded them here or elsewhere, and under his own name, is another matter. Once again, the Kumamoto scientist, Dr. Okabe Nakashima, appears, or at least someone advertising his lab and their research. There are plenty of J— Nakashima combinations, but careful perusal reveals none to be the Jun I'm looking for. But there is one other. Someone publishing under the name @j.nakashima.j, a real photographer by the looks of it, and a talented one at that. Not that I'm any great judge, only to say that when I look at the photos on this J— Nakashima's page, I *feel* something. Like listening to soothing music, this set of images evokes a profound sense of calm. Of traveling through the world without haste, taking great care to capture the beauty of everyday scenes.

Mainly, @j.nakashima.j has posted photos of water. Water reflecting the silhouettes of trees. Water blanketing a rice paddy. Water embracing freshly fallen cherry blossom petals, like candy-pink sprinkles. Water rushing under a wooden bridge. Ducks floating on a pond. A riverbank dappled by raindrops. The unmistakable white-and-orange of a koi fish in a dark pool. I scroll down. The photos of water are interspersed with shots of what must be the Japanese countryside, though only rarely do any features give clues as to location. Only a person familiar with the topography, the finer points of Japanese culture, the types of grasses and flowers native to Japan, would recognize these photos as being of Japanese origin. No towering castles or torii gates, no images of sushi or kanji characters or bonsai. No people, even. Not even from a distance.

Were these photos taken by a woman? They seem so...sensitive. Delicate, almost. Or could this be Jun?

My Jun?

My heart beats faster as I scroll further down the list, looking for clues, for images potentially taken during our shared time at Michikusa House. Could that stream be the same one that ran alongside the farmstead? Are those patches of moss clinging to the same road that dead-ended at the farm? The fronds of grass set ablaze by late afternoon sunlight, are they waving the viewer toward Shoko's studio and kiln? It's impossible to say, not least of all because the owner of the account failed to include any subtext or hashtags alongside their images. I scroll back to the top, thinking maybe they listed contact info. Surely any artist would want to connect with potential collaborators—though the fact they haven't used hashtags doesn't bode well for this theory. Sure enough, there's no email address or link to the artist's personal website. The private messaging avenue has been disabled as well. Why even keep the account public, I wonder, when only the commenting feature on individual photos remains active?

I curse silently, wondering what I should do, if anything. Admittedly, I hadn't been holding out hope of actually finding Jun this evening, if ever. Still, the disappointment stings like an oncoming headache.

Lazily, I scroll down one final time, thinking how like Jun it would be to withhold contact information. For two years, he has been impossible to track down. If this account does indeed belong to Jun Nakashima, the same Jun I befriended at Michikusa House, it would stand to reason he would keep himself hidden behind a barrier, just like this.

Liam shifts in bed, startling me back to the present, to the studio overlooking the darkened cemetery. He sits up in bed, then totters toward the bathroom, shutting the door behind him. He'll be back any minute. I clear my search history and close the laptop. Only then, with the room completely dark, apart from the sliver of light under the bathroom door, I spy emerald eyes glowing at me from underneath the bed. Clay, it seems, is becoming a little braver, a little more confident in himself. He may shy from Liam, but I can tell he's no longer terrified of me. Trying hard not to startle him, I slip quietly under the covers and close my eyes, pretending to be asleep. Predictably, Liam doesn't notice my change in position when he returns. He flops down beside me, landing heavily, instantly asleep.

As for me, I lie awake a while longer, wondering, of all things, when those images were posted. At Michikusa House, after all, we had no Wi-Fi—internet wasn't installed until after I left, presumably so Shoko could create a website and manage her business digitally. Meaning, if there was a gap in the upload history where no photos had been posted, around the time Jun and I were living together on the farm...

I resist the urge to spring out of bed, to check the dates the photos were uploaded, telling myself nothing could be done about it anyway, not tonight. It's been an awfully long day. Better just to rest on it. No doubt I'll have to do battle again come morning.

CHAPTER 6

Sleep fails to improve Liam's mood. He's grouchy and more prickly than my mini windowsill saguaro, galumphing around the house. Ready to be back at his own place. Alone. I do my best to stay out of his way, but to no avail.

"I'm going for a walk," I announce, slipping on my coat and boots. "Try not to terrify the cat with all your stomping and huffing, alright?"

I shut the door behind me before he has a chance to call me back. I rattle down the fire escape and around the front of the house, diving along the shortcut between the neighbor's house and the cemetery. I'm fairly sure Liam won't come after me, but if he wanted to, he would know where to look. I cut over two more blocks, tracing the stone wall, eventually reaching the north entrance to the cemetery, its iron gates flung wide. I slip through. Groundskeepers work at intervals along the road, still raking leaves into piles. A bit further off, a funeral gathering blankets a patch of ground in black, though not the leather and denim varieties I used to prefer. Though that didn't stop my mother from telling me I looked like I was habitually in mourning. Perhaps I was, in a way, mourning the girl I used to be, the healthy, happy one that never drew questioning eyes or provoked concern.

Jun Nakashima asked me about it once, too, why I always wore black, though by that time, at Michikusa House, I did wear some colors. Earth tones, I guess, are what you'd call them: chalk and slate. My mother had insisted I not put my past on display whilst abroad, lest I embarrass my hosts. She had given me her credit card and told me to "buy farm clothes, things to wear in the studio, in any shade other than noir." The gray and navy items I chose did not amuse her. Against all odds, however, she didn't make me return them. Maybe she sensed I was suffering enough of a transformation as it was.

The day Jun asked me about it was the first time he and I had been sent out on an errand together. The first time I had left the property, as a matter of fact, since my arrival four months earlier. Hideyuki had come down with a fever and couldn't leave his futon, so Jun drove the little green keitora pickup while I rode shotgun, though the whole setup felt backward: me on the left, him on the right. We cruised along, paralleling the stream that hugged the little dead-end track. I looked out over last year's dry grasses, locked in January's icy hold.

"Do you always wear black?" Jun asked. "Is it out of respect, like a funeral?"

"I didn't think you were allowed to ask personal questions like that," I said, but Jun seemed unflinching and unembarrassed. He had experience with Westerners, having lived among the Australians of Sydney for a good chunk of time. Besides, by then he and I had logged hundreds of shared hours together, so the formalities were slowly disintegrating.

"I'll have you know," I said, pinching the collar of my sweater, barely showing under my zipped-up leather jacket, "I don't. Not always."

"Grey," he said, pronouncing it gurē. "Close enough."

"And these." I lifted one knee, revealing the hem of an argyle sock, an inch of tan and cream fabric showing through the gap between my black denim jeans and waterproof winter boots. "Maybe I should say the same to you: Why do you always wear white, or colors?"

"Alright," he said, lifting his hands off the steering wheel in mock surrender. "You win, Win-chan."

"I'll tell you, if you really want to know," I said, settling back in my seat. Jun raised an eyebrow. "Have you heard of that designer, Yohji Yamamoto?"

"You like Japanese fashion?"

"Don't you? God, you've got Rei Kawakubo, Issey Miyake… Anyway, he said something that struck me, like: black is mysterious but, above all, black says 'I don't bother you, you don't bother me.' I can't afford his clothes," I said, thinking that my mother, on the other hand— "but I do like his ethos. He makes clothing like armor. I always liked that."

"Armor?" Jun didn't know that word, and I didn't know the Japanese equivalent.

"Like, to protect you." I shrugged, and with a wry smile, said, "It's a vicious world out there."

Surprisingly, Jun agreed. "For a while, I felt that way too, like I always had to defend myself." It was probably the most personal thing Jun had revealed.

"But not anymore?" I prompted, willing him to say more. I was, admittedly, desperately curious about Jun, about his past.

"When I was in Australia, I had to stand up for myself. It was like a battleground at that school. The people were…very focused on the competition."

"That's why you left?" I asked.

"I left because I couldn't continue."

We were quiet for a while after that. I stared out the window, watching the perfectly flat white rectangles that would, come spring, become planted rice paddies. What did he mean, I wondered, "couldn't continue"?

Finally, Jun spoke again, both hands gripping the wheel. "You said you also dropped out of university. *Sou desu ka?*"

"Right. We're both here to start over," I said, repeating the line that had nearly sent Jun into a tailspin the evening he taught me to make *nabe,* the winter hot pot. This time, however, he didn't spin out or drive off the road into a ditch. Steadily, I continued, "In the broadest sense, I'm here to learn about food. Growing it, cooking it. I'm here…I had to come here to learn to appreciate eating again, because for a really long time I didn't."

I could feel the energy of Jun's intense focus from across the cab, listening hard so as not to misinterpret.

"For a long time," I continued, "I refused to eat, and if anyone made me—" I performed a weak mime of reversing the cycle. Jun was quick to interpret.

"Ah, yes. It's common here also."

"Really? Everyone always seems so, I don't know, naturally healthy and thin in Japan. Not artificially so."

"Many people are very healthy. We have high-quality food and clean water, people walk and cycle everywhere, but…"

"Western culture is invading?" I tried.

He nodded. "But also, the government can fine your employer if you are overweight. And many clothing brands are one-size-fits-all, so people do anything to conform."

I balked. "I didn't know that."

"People don't talk about it. Most people don't care either way. I only know because a student I went to junior high school with ended up in the hospital because she was starving herself."

"Most people don't end up there till it's almost too late," I acknowledged.

Jun was quick to ask, "Did you?" but then retracted. "*Sumimasen.* You don't have to answer that."

I did anyway. "No. I was lucky."

Again, he nods. "That's good."

"You wanna know what's crazy, though?"

"Okay."

"It started because I was lonely. At first, I thought being thin would make me more attractive, so I did it so I wouldn't lose the only friend I had. Funnily enough, I lost that friend anyway. After that, I did anything to get basically anyone to like me," I explained. "It didn't help though, being admired but not cared for."

"Are you still lonely?" Jun asked.

"I'm not sure," I admitted. "When I dropped out of school, I went on medical leave. I was in pain all the time which put a stop to doing pretty much everything. I didn't see anyone other than my parents and doctors, so that was a pretty lonely period."

What I did not tell Jun, however, what I deliberately withheld, was the extent to which Liam came back into my life at that point. How, for the first time since graduation, Liam wanted me back. Even though he was away at school in Pittsburgh he sat with me through my most excruciating days. When I didn't want to live out another minute, let alone wait for the pain to pass, he stayed on the phone with me for hours, talking about shared memories, about a funny television show his roommate was watching in the background, about nothing in particular. Sometimes he even drove home, for a weekend or just an afternoon—the drive only took two hours, but still, it made all the difference just to have him there.

Instead of telling Jun about Liam, the partner I had waiting for me back in America, I talked about my mother. I explained how she came up with the idea to send me to Japan, a place she thought might expedite, or at least support, my recovery. The idea, in part, was to get me away from American media and ideals and go someplace where people still had a rich food culture, where—now that I could eat normally without becoming viciously ill—I might start to enjoy food again…or maybe for the first time.

"Sounds like Japan might not be as golden as she thought," I said, finally.

"No place is perfect, but it's not so bad here, in the countryside," Jun said. "No *konbini* overflowing with anime porn mags."

We both laughed at that, clearing the air.

"I do like it here; *inaka*, right? The word for countryside? Uses the characters for 'rice paddy' and 'cottage,'" I said, tracing them out on the dashboard with a finger.

"Hai, sōdesu."

"I wish I knew more words. I never planned on coming to Japan, though, not until I was practically on the plane. I only had time to memorize a few phrases."

"I want to hear it," he grinned.

"God, don't put me on the spot."

"I could help teach, if you want."

"You've done plenty of teaching already. Thanks to you, your cooking, I've learned…so much. And I have an appetite for the first time in about a decade. Now you know why I couldn't even operate a rice cooker when I started."

"I'm glad you like my cooking," Jun said, then took a steadying breath, eyes trained on the road. "Now it's my turn to tell you why I left culinary school."

Honestly, I hadn't expected him to reciprocate. "If you don't want to," I protested weakly.

"I left," Jun began, "because I was also living under a shadow. By the time I got to Australia, I had been working in kitchens for many years, as you know."

"That place by the train depot?"

He nodded. "Sadly, many kitchens promote bad ways of thinking. It was because of kitchens that I started smoking. Smokers can take more breaks, longer breaks. The hours are bad, the work is hard, very fast-paced. Always on your feet, moving around in hot kitchens, around sharp objects and open flames. People can become very competitive, even becoming mean, wanting to ascend to a better position. Many workers start drinking to cope with the stress. I was already addicted by the time I went to culinary school. Being there only made it worse…more pressure to succeed." He let out a small, unhappy laugh. "The dependency I built up made me lose my mind. I felt like I was inside…ah, what is the word: *kiri*."

I thought hard, but nothing came to mind. Jun found the answer first.

"Fog or, uh, mist," he said.

"You were living inside a fog?"

Jun nodded. "I couldn't keep going. I crashed. I had to leave culinary school and go back to my hometown. For a while, I lived with an old girlfriend, then with friends, but they had many bad habits also. They never let me forget how badly I failed; they wanted to shame me. I had to give up on those friends and return to my family home to…uh…"

"To get clean?" I tried.

"*Hai.* After some time, I came here to start over, to learn about cooking and about food from the ground up."

"Literally," I said, then cursed myself for making such a flippant remark. Astonishingly, though, Jun agreed.

"Yes. Food starts its life in the ground. Soon we will begin that process by planting seeds."

Jun pulled the truck into the parking lot of the hardware

store, where we were meant to pick up supplies for exactly that task. After navigating into a spot, however, he didn't exit the car.

"Everything alright?" I asked.

He sighed. "I need to tell you something else."

"Sure," I said. "What is it?"

"When we first met, I thought you were just a regular artist, here to train with Shoko-chan."

"Well, for what it's worth, I thought the same thing about you. Remember? The first thing you told me was that you were living above the studio."

"What I mean is, I'm glad you're not. I'm glad that's not why you're here."

After a beat, I said, "It's funny...I feel like I'm the type: a white American tourist here to mess about with clay for a bit, not a recovering...whatever I am. Seriously," I insisted, before Jun could offer polite protest. "My parents could afford to send me here for an entire year; I can afford not to work because they both have stable jobs and savings; hell, I could afford to be wasteful with food and my education thanks to the stability that lifestyle provided. How ridiculous is that?" Inexplicably, I felt myself choking up. I bit my lower lip, refusing to shed a single tear in front of anyone, Jun least of all. "It's so pathetic it's funny."

"No person is pathetic," Jun said, his voice calm. "Everyone is doing the best they can to live in a world that is not always forgiving or kind."

I stared out my window, at the customers filtering in and out of the store. Snowflakes began to fall, dotting our windshield, sheltering us from view.

"I chopped my hair off before coming here," I sniffed, crossing my legs and leaning to one side, as if to ward off unwanted attention. "It was falling out anyway." I clamped my teeth down on the sleeve of my jacket to stop myself from saying any more. The leather felt dense and supple. I wondered if I could bite all the way through it, whether ruining something would make me feel better. Feel less. Then a hand reached out and touched my hair, short dark waves that ended above my shoulders. Jun rubbed the thinning ends between his fingertips. Those hands, always so assured in their task when gripping a knife or a spoon...

A thrilling chill darted up my spine, electrifying my entire body. Eyes damp, I took his hand, clasping it in mine as tightly as if he'd thrown me a life preserver. That little bit of compassion, the coiled charge of its possibility. I remember the warmth despite the calloused burn marks and healed wounds. We sat like that for a long while, our fingers interlaced.

I should have told him then, about Liam. I should have admitted I had a partner waiting for me back in America. The same guy, by all accounts, I was destined to be with. The one who had been both my best friend and my first love. The one I had all but ignored since my arrival in Tokyo, insisting every time he called that we had to keep our chats short. I invented half a dozen excuses: I was too busy to talk, the hour was unreasonable, the international call rate was astronomical, someone else was waiting to use the phone or was expecting a call. It was like I was hiding from him. Or, more simply, hiding his existence.

Why had I entrusted Jun Nakashima, someone I had known barely a full season, with my hidden past and then withheld this final, crucial detail? Maybe I expected Jun to withdraw that small bit of comfort if I confessed to anything more. Perhaps I didn't think I would survive if he did. But, even more likely, I already sensed my connection with Liam had begun to fracture. Unlike Jun, Liam had never known desperate hunger— for numbness, for belonging. Yes, he had suffered—the loss of his father, his mother's alcoholism—but he had never, for one moment, been alone. Once you've known the hollowness of unrelenting physical pain, of total isolation, you can never fully love those who have not.

*   *   *

By the time I've completed a full circuit through the cemetery, crunching my way over dried sycamore leaves the exact size and rubber-orange color of a basketball, I've received several texts from Liam. I find a bench overlooking a row of ivy-capped mausoleums and sit myself down to read them. Unsurprisingly, his messages grow more frantic and heated the longer he's gone without a response:

'Why did you leave like that?'

'Where are you?'

'Are you coming back or should I just go? Do you even want me here?'

'Are you kidding me right now?'

'Seriously, Win. This isn't funny anymore. Stop acting like a spoiled child and answer. Better yet, come home.'

'Fine. I'm leaving. Good luck with your terrible decisions.'

Well, I think with surprising clarity, that's that. I power off the phone without replying. No doubt I'll turn it back on this evening and find a dozen or so other missed messages and calls, but at the moment, I couldn't care less. For the first time in a long while I feel wild and free.

CHAPTER 7

On my belly, arms stretched over the side of the bed, I swish the neon orange mouse into the dark crevasse, then whip it out again, in and out. Finally, a furry monster explodes from the cave, diving after his prey, attacking so viciously that the flimsy wand is yanked from my grip. Clay carries his kill—wand and all—proudly across the room and drops it in his food bowl. He sits, staring up at me.

"What a good boy," I say, just as proudly. Over the past few days, I've not only lured him out from under the bed thanks to a colorful and textural array of cat toys, but I've also taught him to expect food after playtime. I portion out his dinner, then check the time. My library shift starts in half an hour. Erin already texted me saying her "effing space heater just crapped out" so I layer on another sweater and a pair of wool socks. I say goodbye to Clay, leaving him to his feast, then don the same leather coat I've worn since forever, plus knitted gloves and a hat. On the rickety old steps, I swirl the tartan wool scarf around and around until I can barely see over its heavy folds. The weather has finally turned bitter, abandoning the last of the dried autumn leaves to gray wind that stings the corners of my eyes. Resolute, I march toward campus.

It's well past sundown but students still hurry across the quad. No one, apart from the smokers, lingers outside tonight. I always see them—premed students, presumably—smoldering like coal stacks outside the medical library. The disconnect is mildly unsettling. I hurry past and into the building, drawing a gust of cold air in with me. I spy Erin huddled behind reception looking miserable, her forehead flat against her closed laptop.

"You alright?" I ask, genuinely concerned. I set my bag on the shelf under the desk and maneuver into my seat.

"Just run me over with a dump truck," she says. "I can't live like this."

"Chilly?" I ask. The glass cathedral that is this library does indeed feel inordinately frosty this evening, though I don't think they designed it for warmth, rather for its striking visual appeal.

Erin grunts.

"If you want to, you could take a break. Go sit in your car," I suggest. "Turn the heat on full blast." She sniffs, a sort of wet, sickly sound. I had hoped to get her opinion on last weekend's confrontation at the Faculty Art Show dinner, the run-in with Fiona Justice, the fight I had with Liam, and the fact I haven't heard from him since. I also need to give her a heads up that I won't be working here once the term ends. Seems like that'll have to wait, though. "You sure you're okay?"

"I've been here since one."

"Why?"

"I stupidly agreed to cover a shift. My ass cheeks are numb and I want to die." Whether the numbness is from the cold or the lengthy sit, she doesn't specify.

"Take a break, then," I say. "Really, I don't mind."

"You do kinda owe me," she agrees, though I honestly can't say for what. She slings her purse over her shoulder then loads her laptop into her backpack.

I decide not to ask whether she's coming back or not. Nothing I say will make any difference to the outcome. "Feel better," I say.

Her white Converse squeak across the polished floor. She disappears through the glass doors and around the side of the building.

I open my laptop. I should get some work done. I've promised myself not to flake out this term, even though it will be my last, but even the thought of reading one more journal article on the pathways involved in carbohydrate metabolism is enough to make my lids heavy. Instead, I'm pulled in the direction of the photo-sharing account I discovered, the one belonging to @j.nakashima.j. I've been meaning to go back and double-check the dates the images were posted. I navigate to the soft, soothing display. Taking a deep breath, I start to scroll, checking dates as I go. I have to click on the images one by one, but instantly recognize a pattern: one photo has been uploaded every day. It's possible the account owner used some kind of software, prepopulated with images, to schedule a daily post. Given the professional appearance of the account, the fact the photos are both color-corrected and given a white border to appear more cohesive as an entire set, it's probable that the artist would want to regulate and control the upload rate as well, rather than dumping them onto the page all at once. Meaning it's possible, regardless of when these photos were uploaded, an actual person would not have been maintaining the account in the background. Not entirely. It could have kept itself operational in the artist's absence, so to speak.

At last, I reach the bottom of the deck. The first photo was posted about four months after my return from Japan, less than two years ago. This fact gives me a sudden burst of irrational hope, a feeling I can't fully justify for at that moment I discover a student standing directly in front of me. How long has she been standing there?

"Uh, excuse me? Do you work here?" she asks, which seems an odd question given the fact I'm sitting at the library's information desk wearing an ID badge.

"Yes, can I help you?"

"I don't know where to find any of this." Exasperated, she slides a notebook page with a list of reference materials, copied out longhand, across the desk.

"Alright. Let's see…"

I switch over to the library database and jot down the location of each item on her list. I stow my laptop, so it's not stolen in my absence, then we go track down the materials she needs, a tidy stack of books and journal publications. By the time I return to reception there is, astonishingly, a small queue. It's another forty minutes before I've helped everyone in need of my services and can return to my little task.

Once again, I orient my laptop in front of me and pull up the photo-sharing site. Without an account of my own I can't comment or do much of anything, apart from look around. When the limitation proves to be something of an obstacle, I spend the next quarter hour setting up my own account, inventing a name—I settle on @Win__chime—and setting my preferences. I spend another half hour uploading photos from my phone, a combination of outdoor scenes, selfies, pictures of Clay and my apartment and my cacti collection, just so I don't have a completely blank page. The effect is nowhere near as lovely or cohesive as @j.nakashima.j's but it'll have to do. If nothing else, anyone looking at it—if the Jun Nakashima I know looks at it, he'll know it's mine.

Finally, I toggle back over to the @j.nakashima.j account. Whether the photographer checks this account or reads comments on their photos is difficult to say, but it's the only chance I've got to make contact. I made my own account, for heaven's sake. If not for this, then why? Alright, no turning back now.

I click on one of the few photos that feature food, a single-serving bowl of miso soup, and hover my cursor over the comment box. Before I type anything, however, I stop to consider: *The Jun Nakashima I know would have more food photos than this, wouldn't he?* The Jun I know would not have taken so many pictures of water and whatever else. Nor was he, based on what I can recall, the sort to amass enough photos to post one image every day for years on end. I feel my confidence drain and I close my laptop with a sigh, feeling, once again, disproportionately defeated. Deflated.

Just then, Erin appears at the library's entrance, her butt pressed against the glass door. For a minute I think she's trying to be funny, until I realize she's genuinely trying to open the door, pushing one that's meant to be pulled. I hurry across the foyer to help.

"Holy son of a motherless goat," she curses, breathless, her cheeks a startling flush of cranberry red. In her hands she holds two drinks from Upper Cup, the café and roastery on the edge of campus. The one without whipped cream she hands to me.

"I figured you weren't coming back," I admit, taking a sip. Amazingly, she got my order right: soy chai latte.

"Miss me?"

"Actually, I have some news."

Seemingly revived, Erin resumes her seat behind reception, facing me dead on. "Spill."

She's wearing a knit hat, one with wild tassels and a pompom on top, one I haven't seen her wear before. Her wild curls

explode below the hem. As I explain my decision to drop out
of school and the conversation with my parents and Liam that
resulted, she bats and tugs at the strings that hang from the ear
flaps with one hand, sipping at her drink with the other. She's
like a cat, I think, imagining the fun Clay would have with that
hat. By the time I've finished recounting my tale, she's slurping
the last remnants of her whipped concoction.

"Talk about a quick turnaround," she says.

I had expected her to say more, be more enthusiastic or offer
a merciful new angle. It was partly her idea, after all. She's the
one who agreed this program might not be the best fit and that
I should do something that made me happy for once. "Really?
That's all you got?"

"Dude, you kinda plowed over your whole life in literally a
week."

"Just because I only told you about a week ago doesn't mean I
haven't been thinking about it," I say, which is only half true. I had
only realized how unhappy I was two weekends ago, when I confronted Liam about it in the cemetery. I hate to admit she's kind
of right, though. Things have hurried along since then. I've already made an appointment with the student guidance counsel-
or, or whoever it is, to finalize the details academically speaking.

"Could be why Liam's pissed," she says. "If you want to keep
him around then you might wanna bring him along for the
ride. Otherwise…" When I don't reply, letting the implication
fall flat, she asks, "You do want him along for the ride, right? Or
has that changed now, too?"

"I do," I insist. "But he's not making it easy."

"Neither are you, by the sound of it."

This isn't helping. I'd expected to have at least one ally in
Erin. Why does everything have to be such a battle?

"So, what are you gonna do instead?" she asks.

I don't feel like giving her the satisfaction of an answer, but she needs to know my place at this desk will be vacant before long. "I'm going to try for the groundskeeping job I wanted from the beginning."

"On campus?"

"At the cemetery behind my house."

She waits a beat, as if it was meant as a joke. "Oh, wait, you're serious?"

"What's wrong with that?" I demand, probably more harshly than necessary, but I'm feeling heated. She's the one who's put me on the defensive, so here we are.

Erin raises her hands in mock surrender. "Nothing," she says. "When I suggested doing something that makes you happy my first thought wasn't 'spend more time in a cemetery,' but you do you."

"What did you have in mind?" I ask flatly, as if she had any say in the matter.

"Alright. Look, I'm backing off. Sorry. You're the one who brought it up."

Yes, I did. As usual, I think, wishing I hadn't, wishing I never said anything to anyone, ever.

It's nearly midnight by the time I get home, where I find Clay asleep on my bed, curled into a ball between the pillows. I smile as I unpack and undress, as quietly as I can. His ears twitch, attuned to all noises equally, irrespective of volume or frequency. He bolts the second I sit down on the bed, before I can even consider reaching out a hand. I'm anxious for the day he lets me pet him. Funny, I think, to have grown so fond of a cat everyone thought was a monster. Poor Clay. I curse Mike Hoxley, then forgive him and thank him for sending Clay to me, in a roundabout way. I wonder vaguely whether Liam's brother found happiness out there in the Texan outback, whether the greener pastures were worth the price. As I climb under the covers, I wonder, too, whether he's spoken with Liam since he left. If he has, Liam never mentioned it to me. Not that Liam and I are talking much either at present.

Erin's words, her warning, infect my mind all over again. If I don't bring Liam along for the ride, if I don't include him in my decision making, he might not stick around.

Why am I acting like this, like Liam's feelings and opinions don't matter to me anymore? Am I really that selfish, or am I standing up for myself? Honestly, I can't tell the difference. Is it entirely my fault, though? No one seems to understand how I feel. No one's even tried.

Besides, it's not like this is the only time the boat's rocked us lately. Liam and I have been navigating unfamiliar terrain ever since I returned from Japan. My time at Michikusa House changed me, dramatically, we both know it did. But Liam, while I was away…well, he stayed the same. Neither of us was used to the girl, the version of me who wasn't submissive, who didn't need him anymore. I had relied on him as my sole friend, confidant, social support, mentor, and love interest for so long that we hardly knew how to act around one another when I came home a—dare I say—more independent person. Suddenly, Liam couldn't make all the decisions for us: where we went, what we did, and when. I had developed my own set of interests and opinions, many of which differed from his. And for the first time in my adult life, I had started to care about people other than myself and Liam. I cared deeply about Shoko and Hideyuki Hanada, their farm and their livelihoods, and I cared about…no, I loved Jun Nakashima.

*   *   *

With only tepid warmth and a flicker of added daylight clawing through the heavy grey sky, spring reawakened the sleepy Japanese *satoyama*. The mountain village had endured a turbulent winter that year and frigid combinations of rain and sleet had kept us indoors for days at a time. As a *gaijin*, a foreigner from the American Midwest, I had no analog, no previous experience with winter that lacked snowdrifts and salted sidewalks yet still held people housebound. I had grown up shoveling driveways and sledding down hills, not hunkering under a *kotatsu*, consuming warm liquids throughout the day in the form of tea refills and *nabe* hotpots to ward off the chill. So it felt like boundless relief when Shoko, at the first sign of thaw, threw open the sliding screen doors of Michikusa House and put us to work.

The four of us stepped outside into cool, filtered daylight in rubber boots and puffy jackets. Jun and Hideyuki wandered out to the fields while Shoko and I tended to chores around the house. I was assigned to the veranda, polishing the long wooden floorboards with a wet cloth, while Shoko swept last years' pine needles from the garden, clearing the walkway around the stone lantern. We chatted while we worked. As usual, Shoko accommodated my faulty Japanese with her faultless English.

"You juggle so many tasks here and make it look easy," I mused. "The farm, the kiln, hosting people like us."

"Maybe it seems easy now," Shoko acknowledged politely, "but it took many years of trial and error. Many people cannot find work in the countryside, so they move to cities. The economy in small villages suffers, and more people leave. It's a sad cycle, happening all over Japan. For us, the farm and studio could not earn enough, but neither could my husband abandon his family home."

"What made you consider a farm stay program, of all things?" I asked.

"It has become a popular tourist option. We have so much space and so much work, and only the two of us, so we thought, why not?"

"Is it mostly people like Jun who want to learn about farming and cooking with the seasons who come to stay?"

"Some will stay a full year, like Jun, or maybe just the summer, and earn their time by working on the farm. But most people only come for a short while, a long weekend or sometimes a week."

"Then it's almost like a bed and breakfast."

"Yes, in that case, we are like *minshuku*. A home stay, or guest house. Those who stay only a short while, they usually want to try working in a real ceramic studio, or simply escape the city for some time. Others bring their own car and tour the countryside, taking day trips, then return at night for a home-cooked meal and a comfortable bed."

"How do they know about you, if you don't have a website?"

Shoko laughed. "We are so old-fashioned, so far from the city. We rely on people telling one another, saying good things about their time with us."

"Word-of-mouth? You definitely need a website," I said, thinking about the different packages they could offer: farm internship, artist's apprentice, bed and breakfast, cooking classes. I wondered which my mother would have chosen for me. Had she paid her friend to keep me a full year? Since I hadn't had any say in the decision, where I'd spend the last months of my long rehabilitation, I hadn't thought to ask.

"Ah, much better," Shoko said, standing upright to admire our handiwork. "How about we take a break? I thought today you might like to see how we harvest *sansai*."

Sifting through my Japanese vocabulary, I came up empty. "I don't know that word," I admitted.

"Mountain vegetables. Wild foods," she translated. Then she smiled. "It's more fun when you gather *sansai* with a friend."

We grabbed gardening gloves and scissors, a *hori hori* knife, and a basket each. Heading out to the road, Shoko shouted something to Hideyuki and Jun, who were across the stream at the very edge of the woods. We could see them debating how to tackle a troublesome mud slick that had claimed one portion of the planting field and would have to be releveled. Shoko waved her basket and pointed in the direction we were headed, down the road. Hideyuki waved back. Maybe I imagined it, but I thought I caught a hint of a smile from Jun aimed directly at me.

In the weeks since our drive into town, when we had confessed to troubling, painful pasts, something fresh and exciting had blossomed between us. We talked more openly in the kitchen, about our childhoods and our hopes for the future, laughing at the strange twists and turns our lives had taken. I found myself inventing reasons to be near him, passing up studio time in exchange for tasks that would place me in the kitchen. Similarly, Jun had begun making excuses to visit the studio, especially when Shoko went away on some small errand, leaving me in charge of prepping clay or sweeping up or arranging the dried pottery on the many shelves. Yet despite what I thought was an obvious desire to be close to one another, Jun had maintained—ever since that day in the truck when his fingers intertwined with mine—a respectable distance, never again coming close enough to touch. The boundary was so deliberately upheld that I started to think he might not feel for me what I felt for him. Despite his attention, I felt rejected.

"You seem far away, in your thoughts," Shoko said.

"Sorry. I am a bit, I guess."

"Is it about Nakashima-san?" she asked, striking dead center. Was it that obvious?

I tried feigning indifference, but my acting convinced no one.

"Pssh. I might be getting old, but I am not blind. You two are circling one another like—" she struggled to find an apt comparison—I prayed she wouldn't say vultures.

"Really, it's nothing," I interjected. I should have lied and said I was homesick.

Shoko, thank goodness, was diverted by a patch of familiar yellow flowers. Weeds, really. "Ah, Win-chan, look here," she said, stepping to the side of the road. "This one, *tanpopo*."

"Dandelions?"

"Yes, yes, that. The whole plant, you can eat."

"Really? They grow everywhere back home." Though truth be told, I had never seen anyone eat one before.

"Very good in salads, for making tea," she said, listing their many beneficial properties and uses. We clipped a few bunches, taking the leaves, milky stems, and sunbursts of yellow flowers, and laid them in our baskets. Moving on, our boots tapped out a syncopated rhythm along the narrow lane. Eventually, Shoko led us down the embankment toward the small stream, avoiding the most overgrown and brambly patches, wary of twisting an ankle. There, along the lazy riverbed, we found other edible plants: *yomogi, tsukushi*, and green *warabi* tendrils, none of which I recognized or had an English name for. We plucked and clipped, then helped each other back up the embankment, laughing at our clumsiness, trying with all our might not to tip our baskets. Back on steady ground, we took off once more down the lane, winding past thickets of bamboo and an overgrown *ume* plum orchard. Where our path intersected with the main road, down by the little shrine, we discovered a cluster of *obachans* in muddy boots and head scarfs working their way along the riverbank. Their baskets contained primarily the little *tsukushi* shoots, like colorless asparagus. Shoko chatted with the old women for a few minutes. She had them all giggling like girls, though naturally I couldn't understand a word they said. She introduced me as Win-chan, a friend from America. I bowed respectfully, then we took our leave, waving as we walked on.

"Those women, they taught me everything I know about *sansai* and foraging culture," Shoko whispered in English, as if the elderly women would have understood her. "So important, that wisdom. They always tell me: you get the energy of the earth when you eat fresh mountain vegetables in spring," she recited. "Animals want to eat them, too, so you have to know exactly where and when each one appears, or you will miss your chance. Spring vegetables rid the body of poisons that have built up over winter. Very, very healthy."

We connected with a muddy path leading up the mountain in a gradual slope, into the density of woods. Up we stomped, weaving between cedars, careful not to lose our footing in the mud or trip over an exposed root. The higher we climbed, the colder the air felt, as if spring had yet to visit this peak. Snow clung to the soil and discarded pine needles in pebble-sized patches. The tremendous climb made it difficult to chat. After several minutes we stopped for a rest, leaning against a boulder that seemed left there for just that purpose, to revive weary climbers. "Those women down by the river," I said. "They must go foraging together every spring. Wouldn't you prefer to be out there with them, rather than—" I gestured onward up the mountain.

"There are secret spots on this mountain they can no longer reach."

I nodded. Old bones and old joints should not attempt this risky climb. "It is only women who gather *sansai*?"

"Not always, but I think women do it best."

I might have laughed but Shoko appeared entirely serious. "How so?" I asked, feeling the cold and damp seeping through the seat of my jeans. Even so, the view from our resting spot out over the valley below, over unplanted rice fields and orchards, begged a longer respite.

"Women are better at quiet noticing. To gather *sansai*, you must notice when buds grow and swell, when berries ripen, when mushrooms push up. I am grateful for the small community of older women who still practice the old ways and who teach others, like me, who want to learn. Who do not want to forget."

"So much knowledge must get lost when families move to the cities," I mused, thinking back to what she'd said about village economies failing.

"*Hai.* Those women, they remember the old ways but have no one to share it with."

"Except you," I said. "And now me."

Shoko patted my knee. "Then I will share another bit of their wisdom. They tell me health comes only from knowledge of all parts of many types of plants: buds, leaves, roots, flowers, fruits. Women carry this knowledge," she said, nodding. "Here, we say that city people are unwise to rely on only a few cultivated plants for eating and for healing and medicine. Perhaps these same plants do not grow where you come from, but the lesson still applies. I think it is so," she concluded. This time it was Shoko who gestured up the hill. "Shall we? Not much further now."

I agreed and we continued. "Why do you think that is, that people don't eat a wider variety of foods anymore? Because they don't know where to look, or what to look for? Or because there are no *obachans* around to teach?"

"Both, I think, yes. The wisdom passed down from older to younger is so important, but that way of teaching is broken when people move away from their family and ancestral homeland. And it is easier to go to the store than climb a mountain to collect a few small plants."

"Yet here we are," I said, and we both chuckled, albeit a bit breathlessly.

"The difference is," Shoko said, resting a hand briefly against a tree trunk, "I also crave the—" she searched for the word— "the complex flavors of *sansai*. That unique, desirable flavor means there are important nutrients in the plant that are necessary for our bodies. Our bodies contain that deep wisdom. If we pay attention to those desires, we can learn to enjoy the bitterness of wild vegetables. Many of our most important medicines and stimulants are bitter, you know. That signifies potency."

Though the answer lacked the air of scientific rigor I'd grown accustomed to, being around Liam, therapists, and physicians, I sensed that Shoko and the *obachans* were relying on a different sort of wisdom. Theirs was the wisdom of hundreds of generations of women before them who had known how to nourish themselves and their families, not because they had access to grocers and nutrition experts, but because they didn't. They had learned to trust the land they lived on to provide everything their bodies needed to survive, season after season. It also made sense, then, that the little shoots and buds we gathered now in spring would be bitter but nutrient dense, arriving just in time to supply winter-starved creatures, humans and non-humans alike, with live-saving minerals, phytochemicals, and healing compounds.

When Shoko spoke again, her words echoed my own thoughts. "The culture of *sansai* gathering teaches us about eating with the seasons. In Japan, seasons transition gently. In each season there is an ebb and flow: something on its way in, then fully arriving, and finally waning. These three parts have names: *hashiri, shun*, and *nagori*. With each ingredient we gather we can follow these stages and notice the subtle shift in flavor as that ingredient comes into, passes through, and goes out of season."

"How do you know which is which?" I asked.

"I will tell you. *Hashiri* ingredients grow early and are rare. They must be taken at just the right time and are flavored with anticipation and delight. *Shun* ingredients are gathered at the peak of the growing season and possess flavors of abundance and plenty. *Nagori* is the sad feeling you get when the season has almost passed. When eating *nagori* ingredients, we taste the sorrow of parting as the season wanes. We savor the ripe, passing flavor one last time and look forward to its return in a year's time. These three elements are woven into the culture of gathering *sansai*."

We reached another gap in the trees through which a brilliant sun pierced the cold ground around our muddy boots, igniting the world's desire for spring. Ferns that grew lush and broad in summer had collapsed in on themselves in a tangled weave. Shoko drew back a clump of desiccated leaves, revealing a tight emerald bud. Others nearby had already opened to reveal a cluster of tiny flowers encased in green leafy petals.

"The first *fukinoto* shoots. Normally we can harvest them around our home at the end of winter, but up here," Shoko explained, implying at higher elevations, "the season begins later, so we can still collect *fukinoto*."

She advised me to leave the newest shoots, the smallest of the bunch, only collecting those that were well underway. The chill that still clung to the mountain worked to penetrate my layers as I knelt into the cold, damp soil. Yet as we plucked and foraged, hunting for rare green gems, I felt the warmth of satisfaction. Whether it was some primal bliss from gathering something edible after surviving another bleak winter, or simply the promise of life returning in the coming weeks, I could not say.

I felt a youthful pride, presenting my basket of jewels to Jun later that evening. Jun seemed equally delighted to receive them. Treasures in hand, I followed him into the kitchen where he placed our ingredients carefully on the deeply scarred cutting board. He chose one of the beige asparagus-looking shoots we had collected, the *tsukushi* favored by the local *obachan* brigade.

"You see these?" he said, pointing to the little skirts encircling each tiny stem. "This part is called *hakama.*

"Like the, uh, traditional garment? Worn over *kimono*?"

"*Hai.* For each stem, you remove the hakama, like this."

Jun set me the tedious job of stripping the shoots of their little skirts while he prepped a thin batter and put a shallow pot of oil on the burner to boil. The act of peeling away the hakama from each shoot, while repetitious, set my mind free to wander. Naturally, my thoughts went straight to the man standing two steps away. Lately I'd been imagining ways to recreate that moment in the truck, excuses to run an errand, to be alone with Jun. Yes, we were technically alone in the kitchen, but it wasn't the same with Shoko and her husband sitting on the other side of the noren curtain. Besides, Jun took cooking and each associated task incredibly seriously. He was at his most focused when standing over a cooking pot or at the cutting board. We could laugh and chat together one minute, then his tone would shift, and his attention would return to the essential task of preparing our meal. *What on earth is going through his mind right now,* I wondered? *Could he be hiding a girlfriend back home, like I'm hiding Liam from him?*

"When you finish you can blanch those, then season with shoyu," he said, jolting me back to the present.

"That's all?"

"Best to use simple preparations with such fresh ingredients."

"Copy that."

"Huh?"

"Sorry. That was dumb. I only meant I understood and will follow your instructions, *Senpai.*"

Jun half-chuckled. Thankfully, he seemed to find my odd phrases and awkward idioms endearing rather than completely off-putting.

"So, what happened to that girl you moved in with, after you came back from living overseas?" I asked, as casually as I could manage.

"We don't talk anymore. It was a bad relationship. There were a lot of those."

"Ah," I said, deciding I didn't need details. "In that case, I'd have thought you'd've found another one since then," I insisted.

"What makes you think I would move that fast?" Jun sounded amused, rather than offended. He took very little personally, I'd discovered. His temperament was steady and often serious, impossible to rile but, around me at least, he smiled easily. "You think I go after every pretty girl I see?"

"Don't you?"

"I had only two, maybe three serious relationships."

"And how many not-so-serious ones?" I asked, not sure whether I wanted to know the answer, whether or not the number exceeded my own.

"Win-chan…I'm hurt. You think I'm a—a playboy?" he said, struggling to find the word, struggling with the L just a little, cracking the tension I'd felt only a moment ago.

"Sometimes I don't know what to think about you," I said, meaning it.

"Then I will tell you what to think: I'm a very nice guy, but I'm not the best judge of people. I trust them too easily and allow myself to cling to the wrong ones. That, you can believe."

"I only meant, I didn't know your timeline, when you were in Sydney, when you returned, whether you had time to meet someone new."

"I started at Michikusa House two weeks before you did," he said coolly. "Before that, I spent about two years moving around, between friends and family. Not the best time to meet women."

"You're right. I was at my lowest point back then. I can only imagine what it was like for you—"

"Try not to imagine. We are not those people anymore. Here, come watch." With an outstretched arm, a gesture I hadn't expected, Jun drew me in, pulling me to his side. His hand on my shoulder radiated the most exquisite heat, it was all I could do to focus on whatever it was he was about to show me. His hand rested there for only a heartbeat, however, before slipping back to the cooking chopsticks and the vibrant green *fukinoto* buds we had gathered on the mountain. With surgical precision, Jun manipulated the extra-long chopsticks, using them to dip each bud into the light batter before dropping them into the heated, golden oil. After a quick dip, he whisked them out again, laying each perfect morsel onto a paper towel. Amazingly, very little residue remained. He drizzled one with lemon and sea salt, then lifted it to my mouth.

"Try it, before it gets cold," he said.

With the chopsticks, Jun dropped the piping hot, crispy bite on my tongue. Under the deep-fried batter, the bud tasted velvety smooth, accented by the rich bitterness Shoko had described: the promise of spring. It tasted so pure and full of new life that I felt my eyes tearing up.

"Too hot?" Jun asked.

"No, just right." I took another breath to appreciate the delicate balance of flavor, of external crunch to soft interior. "You're such a good cook. Everything you do is completely amazing, I just…" I faltered. *I could never compare*, is what I thought, what I almost said aloud. "I love it," I said instead.

"*Osomatsu.*" The corner of Jun's mouth lifted slightly, genuinely pleased. "It wasn't much."

CHAPTER 8

'Please call me. We need to talk.'

Liam's unanswered text stares back at me, taunting and distracting my already cluttered headspace. Not only do I have an interview at the cemetery in less than five minutes, squeezed tightly between classes, but today will be my last shift at the library. Next week is Thanksgiving, so the campus will be mostly empty. The days between that and Winter Break are always the busiest time at the library, with everyone wrapping up classwork and taking exams, so I told Erin I'd help out if she needed me, but otherwise to go ahead and let someone else from the very long backlist of students in need of employment take my place.

'Busy,' I reply to Liam's text, which is true, but add, *'I'll call in a bit.'*

With seconds ticking on the clock, I dash across the intersection—as fast as one can dash with a pack full of books weighing down every step. There isn't time to stop home to change, and I regret failing to select something a bit more casual and workaday this morning, rather than my usual assortment of denim and leather. Hardly screams "groundskeeper."

Hustling eastbound along Euclid Avenue, I crunch and shuffle through piles of leaves overflowing the curb, and I consider what I'll say to Liam. He is right about one thing. We do need to talk. We haven't spoken in days. Nearly a week. I suppose he's hoping for a cool resolution. Very little breaks his rigid calm. I can't even picture Liam being so beside himself with worry over the unresponded messages as to be unfocused at work, for instance. Then again, maybe he just wants to know whether he should bother showing up at my apartment on Saturday, in accordance with our established routine.

The main office sits just inside the cemetery gate. No wandering past ornate monuments today. I check my phone. Right on time. Barely. Walking towards me is a sun-dried man roughly the same age as my father, a man I recognize as the groundskeeper superintendent, the same one I spoke with at the start of term. I try hard to pull a name from my memory bank but come up blank.

"Weren't you here lookin' for a job a few months ago?" he asks, without preamble. "You turned down the offer, as I recall."

I tell him how the timing wasn't right just then, I couldn't juggle the hours, "But I'm not in school anymore so I wanted to give it another shot."

"You scheduled the interview?" he asks. "For today?" He seems to think I've made some foolish error, but if I have I don't see it.

"Yes," I confirm. "I figured I'd have to interview again."

"It's the same position," he says, with emphasis, as if he can't believe a college student would be this thick. Then again, I'm no longer a college student, so…"We have your paperwork on file."

"So…I don't need to interview?" I try, sensing this is going left, fast. God, what will I do if I don't get this job? I didn't have another in mind, nothing within my walking radius. Nothing as appealing at any rate.

"Well, you didn't seem like a total bozo when we talked last time."

Whether he's implying that his impression of me has since changed, I can't say. Instead, I press, "Does that mean I can have the job?"

"The one you turned down last time?"

Is he being deliberately unhelpful, I wonder? "I can do full-time," I try. "Weekends, too."

He sniffs hard and rubs his mustache. "You had some experience, right?" he asks, trying to recall our previous conversation. Hence the reason I scheduled an interview. "This ain't light work, you know. We got two-hundred and eighty-five acres here. The work is divided up by forty staffed groundskeepers."

"I worked on a farm for a year."

"Some kid came in here the other day, used to mow his grandma's lawn once a week and thought he could handle the work. Didn't last two days."

"I know how to operate a riding lawnmower, if that's what you're saying," I say. "And I live right over there, so I can get here early to clear snow—like me, winter's right around the corner." When he fails even to crack a grin, I press, "I never get poison ivy; I'm not afraid of bee stings or chainsaws or, you know, dead people." I shrug my backpack into a more comfortable, or rather, a less uncomfortable position.

He nods. "Well, like I said before, we keep the grass trimmed around markers and monuments, remove any dead plants, sod and seed the graves, repair any damaged structures, pretty straightforward. Also, we act as guides for visitors who get lost. We dig and fill the graves, and make sure the rules of our cemetery are abided by. Can you handle that?"

"Absolutely," I affirm.

"Alright. You can start Monday."

"Yes, I can. Absolutely."

"It wasn't a question. You're on first shift. Be here by six. Wear better boots," he says, then stalks off back the way he came.

"Thank you, I will," I call after him. The superintendent throws a dismissive wave over his shoulder but doesn't turn around.

As I hurry out the gate, I reach for my phone, eager to tell Liam the good news. It's an automatic response. Whenever I have anything noteworthy to share, Liam is the one I turn to, the first and often the only person I want to tell. This time, however, I pull up short, knowing that if I dial now, I'll not only be interrupting him at work, but I'll also have to hash out a resolution to our argument. Then again, maybe if he sees I've secured paid employment to support myself so that I can stay in my own apartment he'll relax. Either way, I might as well get it over with. I've got another fifteen-minute walk back to campus. Plenty of time to solve all our relationship woes.

I punch a button and the phone starts to ring. Liam picks up on the second tone.

"I'm at work," he says, sans greeting, as if he wasn't just texting me ten minutes ago.

"Can't you take a five-minute break?" I ask, knowing full well he can and wouldn't have answered if he was in the middle of anything important. The space in the conversation tells me he's stepping out of his cubicle.

"Alright," he says coolly. "What's up?"

"You wanted to talk," I say, deliberately pressing that button. Why do I do this? Can't I just be a little bit more respectful or, hell, simply excited to share good news with my partner?

"After work might've been a better time."

"Well, I have work tonight." How quickly the tables turn. He likes to think his work matters more than anyone else's, including mine. "Actually, it's my last shift at the library."

"Even though you still have a couple weeks left of school?"

"I'm starting work at the cemetery next week," I inform him, realizing as I say it that I told the superintendent I could start full-time beginning Monday, forgetting I still have classes to wrap up. Oh well, that's a hiccup to deal with later. "They let me have the groundskeeper job I wanted."

"Will you be earning enough?" No 'congratulations', no 'that sounds fun, glad it worked out', just 'does it pay well?'

"It'll be full-time," is all I say. Let him sort out the numbers.

"Right. No classes to contend with this time."

"Yep."

"Win…are you sure you're up to it? That's a lot of really hard work."

"I've done manual labor before, Liam. I worked on a farm for a year."

"I just don't want to see you get in over your head, is all. If it gets to be too much—"

"I don't need you to watch over me," I say, more fiercely than I intended.

"I'm not saying that," he whispers angrily, as if someone might be within earshot on his end of the line. "I don't want you to overdo it because I don't want to see you start relapsing again."

"I won't," I promise. He doesn't push it.

"Why are we so angry at each other, Win? It seems like all we do is argue."

"It's a rough patch, is all. I'm sure once I'm on my feet making my own choices and supporting myself everything will—"

"I don't think so. Reconciliation can't be some far-off goal. I care about you but you're not letting me in anymore."

I wait for an ambulance to pass, sirens blaring, on its way to the medical center up ahead. "Liam, letting you in doesn't mean you get to decide what I do."

"Are you really going to work a job like that the rest of your life? I don't understand what you hope to achieve."

"Not everyone wants the life you do," I say.

"That's what I'm worried about. I don't think we want the same things anymore."

"What does that mean?"

"I don't see a way forward from here. It's like you're pulling away from me, like you want to run in a totally different direction."

"That's not true, I just—"

"I think we should just take a step back for a bit. Let the dust settle."

"I don't—"

"Then you can do whatever it is you want to do without feeling like you need to make me happy about it, and I won't feel like I have to sit by and watch you tailspin. Maybe in a couple months we'll both be in a better place, a better mindset, and we can talk again."

"So, you're breaking up with me? What the hell, Liam?"

"I don't think either of us is happy right now. Are you? Tell me I'm wrong and I'll reconsider. Because I'll be honest with you; I'm not happy. You're the one driving a wedge between us. I don't know where you are anymore. You act like you don't need me, like you don't even want me around—"

"Stop it, Liam. That's not fair. You can't put all the blame on me."

"I'm hanging up now, Win. I can't get into this again. I've got work to do."

"So that's it, then?"

"For now, yeah. I can't deal with this anymore. It's too hard. You're making it too hard."

"Well, I certainly wouldn't want you to feel like being in a relationship requires effort."

"Don't put words in my mouth. You know what I mean. This relationship isn't fun, it's a chore."

"Okay. If that's how you feel, then…"

"It is."

"Alright then," I say.

"Tell your mom I won't be around for Thanksgiving next week, will you? I don't want her to plan on—"

"Oh, I'm sure you'll find an opportunity to tell her yourself," I say, and hang up.

When I look up, dazed, I realize I'm already standing outside my lecture hall. I manage to find my seat but focusing for the duration of the class is out of the question. I consider leaving—who cares about another absence on my record?—but the thought of going back to my studio, sitting there alone, seems unbearable. It also seems ridiculous that I should feel that way, given the fact I'd have done exactly that after class ended regardless of my relationship status. More than anything, though, I dread the phone call from my mother.

As the lecture wears on, I wonder whether I should tell her myself, as opposed to giving Liam the first strike at breaking the news. Should I tell her the decision was mutual, or that Liam had enough of me? What does it matter? In her eyes, Liam can do no wrong. Either way I spin it, the fault will be mine.

Predictably, my phone buzzes just as I'm unlocking the door to my studio. Claymore rushes out from god knows where, meowing and hovering near his food dish. Ignoring the phone call for the moment, I reach down to pat his neck, but he skitters away at the slightest touch. My mother calls back immediately and may very well keep on calling until I answer.

"Hi, Mom," I say, dropping my backpack beside the table, moving through the apartment, tidying this and that, as if to restore some level of predictability and organization to my life.

"Are you home now?" she asks.

"Just got in." I decide to hold off on the Liam news and instead launch into my retelling of the interview debacle.

"Well, at least you won't have a long commute to work," she says. Again, I sense no congratulations are in order. "I wanted to ask whether you'll be spending an overnight here next week. I don't mind either way, but if not, I'll offer the spare room to Aunt Colleen."

"That's fine," I say. "I wasn't planning on staying."

"You'll come straight from Liam's?"

There's a bump of hesitation before I can answer. "Not this year. I'll just head over to your house," I say, realizing I don't have a car or even a ride to get me there anymore. Before she can question the change of plans, the usual routine of Thanksgiving lunch with Liam's family, then dinner with mine, I press on. "Do you want me to bring anything?"

"Oh…well, if you feel like it. If not…" she trails off. I know she prefers to control every aspect of the event, not least of all the food that's served. I never bother bringing anything, apart from my emotional armor. This year, I might need both.

*   *   *

For the first time in living memory, Erin greets me with a hug. "Why do you have to go? I'm going to get stuck with some stupid freshman who can't even spell the word 'conscientious' let alone act it out."

I give her a tiny, awkward squeeze. I'm not a hugger. Nor, do I think, is she. "I'm sorry. I'll come visit," I say, deciding not to mention that I, too, was technically a freshman when I started working with her a year ago. Then again, I was also a solid six years older than my peers and classmates.

"It won't be the same. Besides. You won't have any business being on campus."

"Then you can come see me. You can visit my apartment for the first time."

As we take our respective seats, she asks, "So you can afford to stay in the same apartment?"

"I think so. I'll be working full time."

"You got the job?" she asks, the first person to express any excitement whatsoever on my behalf.

"Yep. The pay is fair. It's a good place."

"A cemetery...I can't even imagine. I mean, I can. I'd be tempted to dig up the graves, though, if anyone handed me a shovel, like an archaeologist."

"Luckily, I don't feel that urge," I assure her. "Have you ever walked through?"

"On a field trip in, like, third grade. We were studying the presidents, so we went to see the monuments and those two sarcophagi—sarcophaguses? Is that a word? You know, the two in the basement of that tower thing?"

I forgot; like me, Erin is a native Ohioan. "It reminds me of an old English churchyard."

She shrugs. "If you're into that kind of thing."

"I don't think Liam really got it—" I cut myself off. Already I'm putting him in the past tense.

"What is it?" Erin asks. "Something happened, I can tell."

There's hardly any point hiding the truth from her, since I've already been keeping her up to speed with the escalation. In fact, maybe she'll offer a different perspective on the whole, unpleasant situation.

"He broke up with me."

"Oh my god, when?"

"Earlier today."

"Holy shit, girl. How are you even standing? Why didn't you say so?"

She crosses the short expanse between us and pulls me forward off my seat into another hug. Her bony arms and wrists press thinly into my back. It reminds me of what Liam used to say when I was at my lowest weight, that it hurt whenever we were intimate because everything about me was hard and angular, digging into his body. Too sharp to touch. The reminder makes me flinch and I step back.

I think over what believable inanities I can offer. "The world doesn't stop for one miserably failed relationship."

I can tell she's trying to sift through her inner psychology textbook for a useful entry. "So, you think it's permanent? No fixing it this time?"

I'm surprised she remembers that we've been on and off in the past, Liam and me. "He seemed to think we might try again in a couple months. Let the dust settle, so to speak."

"But?"

"Maybe it will, maybe it won't."

"You sound, uh…kinda unruffled by the event," she observes.

"It's happened before. It gets old, the on and off." Though to be fair, we've been 'on' ever since I left for, and returned from, Japan. Unlike in the past, however, I didn't see this one coming. I had started to rely on Liam again, or rather his constancy. "I'm upset, but not totally surprised," I continue. "I'm tired, mostly, of being on the defensive. I want things to feel easy when I'm with him." *Like they used to be*, I want to say. *Back when we were in school together, when we did everything together, when what we did felt enjoyable, not obligatory.*

"Okay," Erin says, her voice wavering, as if to imply 'okay, well, it's your life,' or possibly 'I told you so, didn't I?'

"I thought you didn't like him," I try, just to test her reaction.

"I don't, really. He sounds like a tosser," she says. Whether she means it in the English sense, as in 'Liam's an obnoxious jerk', or in the sense he's a person to be tossed out or set aside, I can't guess. "You always seemed pretty hung up on him, is all, so…I dunno. I'm sorry. That really sucks."

"Thanks."

"D'you want a cupcake? I think you need a cupcake." She rises, as if pastries might be waiting to offer themselves to the situation in the admin office. "I'll make an Upper Cup run. It's on me."

"Um, okay. I'll just do chai then." I don't think I can stomach much else. Besides, anything too highly processed and calorie-dense reminds me of those old purging episodes. It makes my stomach churn just thinking about cupcakes.

"You sure?"

I give her a thumbs up. "I'm good."

"Alright," she says, grabbing her purse and coat. "I'll be back."

It's only a five- or ten-minute walk to Upper Cup from the library, but Erin will most likely drive. I hunker down behind my laptop to await her return and try not to think about Liam, how long our break will be this time, how I'll manage to survive the holiday events in the coming weeks without him there to bolster me. The longest we've gone without speaking was not during our breakup during our college years, but during my stay at Michikusa House. We couldn't chat online without an internet connection, and the international call rates on the Hanada's land line were so ridiculous we agreed to talk only infrequently. Even then, I think we only spoke a spoonful of times over the phone. Also, and I hate to admit it, but I sensed, even then, that I was undergoing a transformation and I didn't want any outside influence disrupting the process. Liam, I felt sure, would not have understood. Sure, he had been happy to know I was learning a lot and enjoying my stay, but he wouldn't have been able to grasp how the simple daily tasks of preparing meals, working in the studio, and gathering wild edibles contributed to my figurative growth spurt. And there was no way I could tell Liam about the most influential person in that equation, Jun Nakashima. Not without raising eyebrows or provoking more probing questions.

I'm recalling this when an idea strikes me. I open my email account and hit the button to compose a new message. I write:

Dear Shoko,

I hope you and Mr. Hanada are doing well and that you have top notch students and trainees working with you in the studio and on the farm this year. The last time I wrote, I had just been accepted into a nutrition program at a really good university, but it turns out the program wasn't what I hoped. I learned more, by far, at Michikusa House. So I'm leaving school. I already found a job I'm excited about. I'll be working at a really beautiful historic cemetery, right around the corner from where I live. I'll help take care of its trees and gardens, tidy the paths, keep everything healthy and looking nice. The cemetery is the reason I chose the apartment I live in now; my porch overlooks one of the older sections so there are plenty of beautiful old trees and songbirds nearby. I can't wait to get my hands back in the soil. I've missed that, ever since leaving Michikusa House.

Apart from sharing this bit of news, I wanted to ask whether you've heard from Jun Nakashima recently.

Here I stop typing, wondering how much to reveal about my lost connection. I decide to be honest.

Unfortunately, Jun and I lost touch after I left Japan. If you have any contact info, an updated phone number, an active email, etc., I'd really like to talk to him again.

Much love,

Winona

I hit send before I can second guess myself. At the same moment, Erin reappears in the doorway balancing two mugs and a paper bag on a cardboard drink holder. She passes the spiced milk tea to me. Then, tapping her cup of whipped cream to mine, she says, "Here's to new beginnings, or some shit."

CHAPTER 9

I spend the weekend alone, without Liam. The first in a long line, it would seem, stretching toward some nondescript future horizon. Well, not completely alone. I have Clay. And the plants, the cacti and potted palms, and herbs on the windowsills. People don't give houseplants enough credit, in my opinion. They may not talk or play, but they're living beings with dynamic needs. Learning to notice and respond correctly to their individual requirements has brought me endless fascination and has strengthened my relationship with them. They, in return, make the studio feel less lonely, add their fragrance and sometimes even something edible.

On Saturday, I take time to trim away their dead foliage. Clay finds this task endlessly amusing, chasing scraps and diving into the pile of refuse I've created on the wood floor. He's been needy and fussy lately, much more vocal than when he first arrived, so I'm happy to let him amuse himself even if it means more cleanup for me later. As he bats at a particularly fluttery frond, I'm reminded he used to be an outdoor cat, albeit one relegated to the underside of Mike Hoxley's collapsing porch. Maybe I should let him outside again, I think. No doubt he misses that wild freedom. I'd worry for his safety in this city, though, even here on this dead-end street abutting a property occupied by the no-longer-living. Nor do I want to deal with what he might bring home: invertebrates or endangered avian wildlife. Would he tolerate a harness, I wonder? I make a mental note to read up on it, then finish my plant caregiving tasks, refusing to consider how my weekend might otherwise have looked if Liam were still part of it.

*　　*　　*

On Monday, I skip my classes in order to fulfill my promise to Curtis, the mustachioed superintendent with whom I interviewed, twice. I figure, this late in the year, what does my academic attendance matter anyway? The way I see it, even if I fail my classes I won't have a degree to fall back on, irrespective of my exiting GPA. Better to land a good recommendation from my new manager somewhere down the line by starting off on the right foot. The right foot being clad in appropriate workman's attire for my first day on the job.

Most of their groundskeepers are seasonal, not full time like me, Curtis explains when I arrive in advance of the appointed hour. That means the late autumn and winter crew is sparse, compared to what it's like in summer. We're divided into shifts; each shift has a few teams handling different tasks. As he introduces me to my team, I sense the reason I was hired was purely geographical, or perhaps to meet some quota, a specific male-to-female ratio mandated by state law. According to Curtis, however, I'm the first girl they've had "since the moon landing." I assume he's joking, but his sense of humor is so dry it comes off in flakes, like dandruff. The two other guys on my crew are double my size, easy, and they make no attempt to hide the fact they're less than thrilled with the newest member of their team, or rather my weight-bearing capacity, my ability to lift and carry.

Curtis introduces them as Kyrone and Dodge. I sense the latter is a nickname, inspired by an oversized pickup truck, is my best guess. He's white—pale, actually—a bit heavy in the midsection and experimenting rather unsuccessfully with facial hair. He reminds me of Liam's younger brother, Mike, who named his cat Claymore and disappeared to the Texan outback. Kyrone is African American, lean but well-muscled, clean-shaven, and is a part-time student in technical college. He's studying to be a welder, he says by way of introduction, which sounds as terrifying as it must be dangerous. But, then again, I fired a *noborigama* kiln, with Shoko.

Curtis sets us our task for the day: replanting the beds out front of the chapel, replacing the summer set with orange mums, purple cabbage, flowering kale, and variegated dianthus. Dodge groans, but I've been anxious to get my hands back in the soil, so I'm thrilled this will be my first project. We load tools and plant pots into an open bed truck and trailer, then the three of us, sans Curtis, clamor into the front seats. I squeeze awkwardly between the two males without, thankfully, having to straddle the stick shift. Kyrone drives.

"He's stuck behind the wheel till April," Dodge grunts, then offers freely, "I'm on probation for a DUI."

"Does your mom drop you off at work then?" I ask, cool as you like. I'll need to be on my toes around this one, I can tell.

Kyrone snorts out a laugh, but Dodge is not impressed. "Better watch it," he growls, barely containing the expletive he's bursting to say.

"Leave her alone, man," Kyrone says, exasperated already, and it's barely six thirty. I decide I like Kyrone. I'll have to ask him more about welding sometime. We can swap stories about working with inferno-like heat.

*   *   *

It turns out Kyrone is in class on Tuesdays, Thursdays, and Saturdays so those days it will just be me and Dodge. I don't think Curtis, the superintendent, thoroughly thought through this arrangement, partnering a man of questionable character with a small young woman. By Wednesday, the day before Thanksgiving and my third day on the job, I already know I prefer the shifts with Kyrone. On those days, Dodge feels like less of a threat, barely a nuisance, a buzzing mosquito. Aside from being clever and funny, Kyrone is well-versed at putting Dodge in his place.

"My coworker and I frequently discuss our plans for the zombie apocalypse," Kyrone explains to me, the sarcasm well-disguised by a veil of authenticity.

Dodge is quick to chime in. "We actually have a pretty badass setup," he says, grabbing a wilted bouquet from a gravestone and tossing it in the trash bag he carries. Each of us has one, making a sweep of the cemetery to clear old offerings from grave sites before the snow hits. "We got sheds full of riding mowers and power tools. Plus, there's chainsaws and a backhoe. Come at me zombies!" he shouts, his fist hitting the sky.

I look around to make sure we're not disturbing anyone in mourning. It's important to show respect and consideration— heck, it's part of our job description to help visitors however we can. That said, I'm not overly sentimental about the dead. Everyone has to go some time. Even so, I read the names on the gravestones as we walk. *If I was buried here, I would want my name read once in a while*, I think. Then again, I don't want to be put in a box when it's my turn to go. I'd prefer to return to the nitrogen cycle, back to the earth and all that.

"Is it possible to be buried without a casket?" I ask.

Dodge seems to think I'm still riding the "zombies rising from the earth" train. "Not here, thank Christ. They'll have to bust their way out then claw up to the surface first. By then, we'll be ready for 'em." He mimes firing an automatic weapon, raining hellfire across the historic acreage.

"Seriously, though," I press, trying to direct my thoughts at Kyrone. "When I die, I'd want my molecules returned to the earth as effortlessly as possible. What's the best way to do that?"

"The quickest way would be to get cremated then spread at sea, or wherever," Kyrone says. "That or a sky burial. That's where they basically cut up the body and place it on a mountain to be eaten by vultures."

I kind of like that idea. It feels honest. Generous, even, but Dodge disagrees. "That's fucked up, man."

"No, it isn't," I say automatically.

Dodge is about to argue, a habit of his, I've discovered, but Kyrone comes to the rescue. "It's Buddhist, man. It represents the impermanence of life; you know what I'm saying?"

"And it provides food for other living things," I add.

Dodge balks. "Both y'all," he says, waving a finger gun between the two of us, "are mental." Then, slinging his trash bag over his shoulder, he veers off by himself, offering only a rude one-fingered gesture to explain his sudden departure.

"What's his problem?" I ask, meaning it rhetorically, but Kyrone sighs, shaking his head as if he really has no clue.

"Dude's off to take a nap, bet you any money," he says.

"For real?"

"He already got busted once by a family when they found him sleeping on their grandfather's plot, like a bench type of thing."

"And he didn't get fired?"

"Curtis is his uncle. I'm pretty sure he's just keeping him on as a favor."

"How do you deal with it, all his BS, day in, day out?"

Kyrone lifts a single cordless earbud from one ear, grinning. "Mostly I just ignore him."

"What do we do with these?" I ask, indicating the mini flags posted around a veteran's plot. "Do we take them out?"

"Nah. Leave those," he says, and we walk on. "I hate those flags so much. People always complain when we break them, like with the weed whacker. Those and the wire fences, like this one." He taps a short, sturdy border encircling a headstone with his boot. "My job would be a thousand times easier without those getting in the way. Just wait till summer; you'll be cursing those things. You got in at a good time. Winter's easy. Well, 'cept for burials, but our team doesn't do those."

"Why not?"

"Uh, can you imagine Dodge using the backhoe?"

"Good point," I say, and we both laugh.

"Actually, in winter, you can't just dive in there with the backhoe. You either gotta use a jackhammer or a heater 'cause of the ice and how hard the ground is."

"Huh. Things you never think about," I say, picking up and dropping a wreath in my bag. "I feel bad throwing this stuff out."

"If we didn't this place would be a dump."

He's probably right. My bag's feeling unwieldy from the weight of the refuse. "Do you ever notice certain graves that always have stuff left on them?"

"Oh yeah. We get a couple regulars. There's one guy who always comes with two cups of coffee. He pours one on his wife's grave, then drinks the other."

I can't decide whether that's sweet or passive aggressive. For a while, Kyrone and I talk about our plans for Thanksgiving, where our families are from, that kind of thing. Eventually, we make our way around to our professional choices.

"What's it like, studying welding?" I ask.

"Classes are pretty basic, basic math and English and whatever, but also metallurgy, blueprint reading, and safety training, obviously. For me, I only spend half of each day in a classroom. The other half's doing actual welding." When I admit I dropped out of university to work here, Kyrone says, "I have a friend who dropped outta Georgia Tech after three years, started welding, and now has a successful welding company. But if you want to break six-figures without sweating and bleeding and getting burned, I'd say stay in college."

"Do you like it?"

"Yeah. I like it a lot. The instructors are easy to follow and spend as much time with you in the booth as you need. It's also only three minutes from where I live; I've always been a Euclid guy, so it made sense."

"When you're welding, even with all the protective gear on, can you feel the heat?"

"Eh, not really. Not unless you set your lap on fire. Win, I ain't never known a girl so interested in welding before," he says at last.

"Not even your girlfriend?" I try, only half-serious.

"*Especially* not Jamayka. She set designated, non-breakable hours for me to talk about school stuff, that's it. This work, though, that's another story. That girl's always pressing me to tell her real-life ghost stories."

"Have you? Ever seen a ghost or anything?" I ask, not because I necessarily believe in the supernatural, just genuinely curious.

"Nah," is all he says.

"I only asked—about the welding, I mean—because I helped fire a kiln in Japan, the traditional wood-burning kind. So, we have that in common, kind of; sweltering manual labor."

"No shit? You got layers, girl."

"You have no idea," I say, mock serious.

"You're a…what, a potter? What's that like?"

"No. My mom's a pretty well-known ceramicist, but I didn't inherit that particular gene, her artistic prowess. I stayed with one of her colleagues in Japan, though, for a while. I was there thirteen months, but that week, when we did the firing, that was the hardest week of the year…of my whole life, probably," I admit, recalling the opening of the kilns across Kyushu in late spring, including the one at Michikusa House.

The spring firing happened right around the time the summer vegetables went into the ground, once the days grew fractionally warmer and brighter. Day by day, as the four of us worked to fill in the beds with what would eventually become eggplants, tomatoes, and a dozen other things, we watched the mountains fill in too, thick and wild. Ferns and vines sprang to life on those slopes, preventing anymore *sansai* foraging. Instead, we relied on the garden—the crops over-wintered there and those we had planted after the last frost—for fresh produce; green pearls and leafy tendrils, sweet and crunchy, plucked fresh each day from the kitchen garden. Although all four residents of Michikusa House contributed to the hopeful rebirthing that year, Shoko retreated to her studio more and more often. Final preparations for the firing of the kiln, a twice-yearly task that required intense preparation and management, were underway.

Not only did the opening of her kiln have to coincide with the seasonal firing happening across the prefecture, but Shoko had to prepare for the pottery festivals that occurred immediately thereafter, during the first weeks of May. After the firing, she would pack up and haul dozens of boxes of fragile pottery pieces to sell, her biggest source of income until October, when the process would be repeated. Hideyuki, too, retreated to his workshop most days, repairing some damaged or misbehaving piece of farming equipment or other. Which left Jun and I to plant and pluck, just the two of us. This arrangement suited me just fine.

"Are we going to help Shoko during the firing?" I asked Jun one afternoon. "She says the kiln has to be watched day and night."

"Sure," he said. "Though I doubt Shoko-chan will let anyone monitor the kiln for her," he said.

"I can't blame her. It's her livelihood. If it goes up in smoke, she's out half a year's worth of work."

"What do you think you'll do when you go back?" Jun asked. The change in topic threw me, but only for a moment. After six months of working together, spending hours together every day, we'd gotten used to talking without reservations. Nothing was off-limits anymore.

"I've been trying to come up with a plan," I said, but without much enthusiasm. "Am I allowed to say I don't want to go back?"

Jun's eyes flashed up at me for a moment, then back down again. He placed a sprout in the little dent he'd made in the earth, then gently patted it in, like covering a child with a blanket.

When he didn't respond, I asked, "What about you? You said you hated the restaurant business, but you still want to be a kaiseki chef. How do you reconcile that?"

"I am hopeful that traditional apprenticeships, training under a master chef, will be more beneficial. Less toxic."

"Where will you go? Back to Kumamoto?"

"I haven't decided," Jun admitted. "Maybe someplace else

would be better. Too many bad memories and people I don't want to see in Kumamoto, I think."

"I feel that way when I go home—to my parents' house," I admitted. "I always end up running into people who remember how I was before."

"Can I ask you a question?"

"Another one? Golly, you're full of 'em today," I teased. He waited. "You don't need my permission to ask."

"Then, you don't have to answer if you don't want."

"I think that's the subtext to all our conversations." The joke didn't appear to register, so I said, "Really, I don't mind. Ask away."

"You talk about how you were 'before', when you were unwell, but still, you look—" he stopped himself suddenly, second guessing his decision to ask.

"I still look unwell?" I tried, going for lighthearted, but the potential truth hidden in that statement, his question, what he saw in me...I felt myself shrink fractionally.

"No, no, not like that. You look very healthy," he was quick to assure me. "I only meant, you are quite thin...what I mean is, were you very big before you tried losing weight? Was that the reason?"

"I already told you, the *reason* was because I was self-conscious, then I was lonely," I said, but we both knew that didn't answer his question. "It might sound dumb," I tried again, "but I've always looked exactly like this—except for, like, one year when I was in college I got really, really skinny. I don't gain or lose weight easily. That's why I had to basically stop eating, otherwise I stay exactly the same size, regardless of what I eat or whether or not I exercise, or whatever."

Jun took a minute to let that sink in. "You were already

looking like this when you tried to get smaller? I don't understand. You look just right to me."

I smiled, facing away, so Jun wouldn't see how happy the little compliment made me. Whether or not his assessment ought to have that effect on someone supposedly "recovered," well...I dropped another sprout into the earth, patted it in. "For what it's worth, it took me ages to understand it—mostly that's all I did during my recovery, after I dropped out of college. I read everything I could to figure out why I ended up the way I did and how to get myself out of that cycle. The doctors were only there to help break the habit, make sure I kept eating, but they didn't give me any helpful context."

"Well, don't do it again," he said, a mild reprimand. "And...I know it doesn't matter what I think, but I don't think you have to change anything to look pretty." We hunched over the earth, silent for an eager, palpitating moment, until Jun broke that shimmering bubble, saying, "But your cooking, that still needs a lot of work."

I recovered quickly. "Then it's lucky I still have you around to coach me, for a few more months."

Suddenly, we had come full circle, discussing where we would be when this idyllic year ended. The fact our time at Michikusa House would eventually come to an end eclipsed the lovely things Jun had just said, laying a shadow over the otherwise sunny patch of ground on which we labored. I think it was that moment I realized I didn't want us to go our separate ways. I spared not a thought for Liam, my parents, or the life I had waiting for me back in Ohio. None of that carried an ounce of significance. All that mattered was clinging to whatever this was that felt so right, here with Jun. Jun, who seemed to accept everything I shared with him without judgement or condescension, who listened easily, who always wanted to know more, not about America or our cultural differences, not specifically that, but about me and my life. Each day we gathered more pieces of each other's puzzles, building the images slowly, over time, over shared meals and cooking pots and muddy work boots.

At that time, I had nearly reached the halfway mark in my time at Michikusa House. We had just over six months left together, Jun and I. What would happen in that interim? What would happen after? I decided not to plan too far ahead, to live only in the moment and enjoy whole-heartedly what I had found in Jun: a friend and confidant unlike any I'd had or could hope to find again.

That night, over a dinner of steamed rice, miso soup, homemade pickles, and sauteed mushrooms, Shoko announced we would begin loading the kiln the following morning. She would need help moving the unfired ceramics into the kiln, a tunnel so big you could crouch and move around inside its different compartments. Once the pieces were inside, she would organize them within each chamber. She would spend about three days packing her work inside, settling them in just so, in just the right configurations to help achieve whatever look she desired for the finished pieces. Close packing would reduce contact between flame and pots and the amount of ash that glazed the surface, while the opposite was also true; it all depended on the final look the potter hoped to achieve. So much depended on positioning, but also on temperature control. This would be our second task. Shoko would need our help to maintain a steady influx of kindling, wood she'd split and dried or purchased throughout the year, literally a ton of it, two tons maybe, an entire wall of it. We would have to stay awake for several days after the firing commenced, monitoring the burn and adjusting the heat by manipulating the wood and the charcoal to keep the temperature within a specific, relatively narrow range. Raise the temperature too fast and the pottery might crack or even explode, destroying half a year's worth of work. Fail to heat it long enough and the pottery wouldn't seal or hold up over time. For one potter, the work is lengthy and exhausting. In years past, Shoko had only her husband to assist in these essential motions, unless she hired help. This year, however, she would have twice as much assistance at every stage. Between Hideyuki, Jun, and I we would have a full working crew to make lighter work of such a massive undertaking.

As predicted, we spent three days preparing the kiln for its seasonal firing, placing nearly fifteen hundred unfired pieces in the three chambers of the kiln. Once the kiln was packed, the three of us, Hideyuki, Jun and me, waited while Shoko lit a small fire in the fire box. As the temperature rose, the kiln seemed to come alive with a voracious appetite for wood. It breathed fire through open pores, called blowholes, though to me it looked less like a whale and more like a heated dragon ready to defend its lair.

She had said so already, dozens of times, but Shoko repeated herself once more. "To ensure the temperature rises properly, great care and attention must be taken not to over or under-stoke the fire. We can divide the work into shifts. I want to pair us in groups of two, more experienced with less experienced. Nakashima-san will work with my husband," she decided, which made absolute sense since Hideyuki and I were completely unable to communicate without hand gestures. "Win-chan and I, we will take the first watch."

Early on, we had to stoke the fire every twenty to twenty-five minutes, using the blowholes to give us an indication of pressure inside the kiln. The process intensified until we were stoking every ten minutes or so, me on one side, Shoko on the other, working in parallel to feed logs in through side openings, laying them directly between rows of pots, glowing red hot. Working that way, we maintained a balance in the firing process. Logs were inserted by hand, wearing thick gloves, but even so I felt the intense heat. Not for the faint of heart. During the rapid downtimes, we monitored the seven or so thermocouples, keeping track of temperature changes in a notebook. Every detail was observed and recorded. This work, after all, amounted to half a year's income. The pressure to get it right was enormous.

A small cot was set up in the studio where Shoko would sleep until the firing ended, so she would be only a shout away in case anything required her immediate attention. Indeed, sometimes she would lie down only to be woken by the slightest shift or gentlest breeze. The days were cool, so we brought each other tea and warm meals, eating together in the light of the burn.

Once the first chamber was brought to top temperature, stoking ceased in that chamber and commenced in the second, which would take nearly twelve hours to fire. Upon completion of the second chamber the process was repeated in the third. Our energy poured into the kiln, minute after minute, hour after hour. The physical and mental demand was unlike any I had experienced or expected. My mother, the only other professional ceramicist I knew, did not produce work the way Shoko did. She fired her pottery in small batches using an electric kiln provided by the university and was assisted at every stage by a swathe of graduate students. She could even fire pieces individually, if needed, to accommodate a single customer, commission, or gallery.

After the third and final chamber had been fired, the kiln was sealed and left to cool. Then we slept, for days it felt like. Shoko alone remained vigilant.

Firing with wood fuel creates a unique expression in the

pieces. It's said that no matter how skillful the potter is, the firing cannot be predicted. Finally, after one week of eager anticipation, the sealed doors of the kiln were broken open to reveal the result. Shoko crawled inside while the three of us awaited her assessment with bated breath.

"Still warm," she called out to us, handing the first piece within reach to her husband. A tall, elegant pitcher with her signature light-hued glaze.

"*Sugoi*," Jun marveled.

"Amazing!" I agreed.

One by one the items passed from Shoko's hands into Jun's, Hideyuki's, and mine. Carefully, oh so carefully, we transferred each object to tables as wide as barn doors and shelves reaching to the ceiling. Like moving house, emptying the three chambers took nearly as long as setting the items inside.

In the days that followed, Jun and Hideyuki returned their attention to the farm and kitchen, while Shoko and I remained in the studio, packing dozens of crates. Each contained items destined for different festivals, shops, and small gallery spaces across the prefecture, including Toho Village, her hometown. Given how much focus was required to wrap and store each piece individually, I found I had little time to think about Jun. It was only in the evenings, after the day's work came to a close and we'd said our "*otsukaresama desu*" and settled down to dinner with an "*itadakimasu*", it was then that I realized how much I missed spending time with him, in the sunny garden or the tiny kitchen. In the presence of Mr. and Mrs. Hanada, we couldn't laugh or talk as openly as we would otherwise, it wouldn't have been polite or proper.

"I will be attending the Toho Village pottery festival for three days," Shoko announced, translating for my benefit. After that, she would be away for an additional two weeks. I looked up to gauge Jun's reaction to this news, but his eyes remained fixed on his rice dish.

"Will you have time to visit your family?" I asked out of politeness.

"*Hai.* I will be staying in my parents' house," she said. "Afterwards, I will spend much time transporting things," she gestured in a circle around the table, indicating the circuitous route she would take to deliver her wares to their respective destinations. I asked a few more well-mannered questions, whether she got to arrange her own setup in the shops and how often she would have to replenish them, whether she had any plans to open a gallery space inside her own studio. But my mind remained firmly hooked on Jun. Without the prying eyes of the lady of the house, would anything happen between us... finally? I had wondered whether Jun's hesitancy had been out of respect for the Hanadas. With Shoko gone and Hideyuki most often running errands or occupying himself in his workshop, the house, studio and grounds would be more or less empty. If Jun made an advance, would I reciprocate? I had thought about it, about him, us for so long...at least it felt like a long time. It had been months since we held hands—Christ, that sounded so childish.

Shoko was still talking, something about how she'd considered a small shop on the property, wondering how on earth anyone would ever find it—but she stopped abruptly, as if she could sense not one of us was actually listening. Her husband, of course, could not understand English, and my mind was decidedly elsewhere. But Jun? He, too, seemed preoccupied.

"Well, be sure to keep up with the garden while I'm away," she said, ending the conversation.

Shoko left before we woke. Or rather, before I woke. Jun had risen early to prepare a simple breakfast and a bento lunchbox for Shoko to take with her, just in case. I found him seated at the table. I joined him, pouring myself some tea.

"What a week," I said, requiring no confirmation, although Jun mumbled some sort of agreement. "Did Hanada-san head out already?"

"He will be gone most of the day. He had errands to run, I think, and wanted to stop by a friend's house. Something like that."

"What's your plan? Did he leave you with an assignment?" I asked, wondering whether I could make myself a part of it.

"No, he said nothing else. I was thinking we could visit that soba shop, if you want." He said it so casually, so confidently, I felt like I'd been tipped off-center.

"Oh! Yeah. Sure. You, uh, pointed it out that one time we drove into town," I said, recalling our midwinter drive, that day in the truck.

"It's not far. We could walk," he suggested.

It looked like a beautiful day. Through the window I could see the grasses by the roadside glistening with dew. And I couldn't deny I liked the idea of spending whatever time it would take to get there on foot alone with Jun.

"I'll agree on one condition," I told him.

"*Nani?*"

"You have to order for me; no making me speak in Japanese," I said, trying hard to sound entirely serious.

He laughed, smiling beautifully. "You got a deal, *gaijin*," he said, a word that basically translated to 'foreigner' or 'outsider', but lately he had started using it as a term of endearment. At least that's how I interpreted it. "I have some work to finish up," he said with a nod behind him, toward the kitchen, "but I will come find you later."

He rose, leaving me to my breakfast. I considered looking for something to read while I sipped my tea, drawing the meal out deliciously past seven, but I knew I wouldn't be able to concentrate. It felt like the evening before a first date with a high school crush. My stomach did a somersault, but not from girlish butterflies. My high school crush had been...my *current boyfriend* was...But no, this wasn't a date. I was perfectly allowed to go to a restaurant with a person, no, a co-worker of the opposite sex. The only difference between me going to lunch with, say, Hideyuki instead of Jun was the fact that the latter was my age and was, I had to admit, outstandingly attractive.

I consciously tried to spend very little time or effort getting myself ready. Jun was used to seeing me caked in varying forms of earth—mud and clay—so making too much of a show might raise eyebrows. So instead, I donned my favorite jeans, a plain white t-shirt, and my usual leather coat. Then I took a cup of tea and a book I'd brought from home—thinking, naively, that I would have plenty of time to read at Michikusa House—out to the garden. It really wasn't warm enough yet to sit outside for long stretches, but the tea soothed my churning stomach, and the book made me appear preoccupied. Jun materialized not long after, wearing a smart wool coat I hadn't seen on him before.

"You want to finish that?" he asked, indicating my cup.

"Not really. Just gimme a sec." I emptied the tea over the gravel path, then popped in through the kitchen door that overlooked the small herb garden, which had plumped nicely in recent weeks, and dropped my cup and book inside before making a quick pit stop in the bathroom, making sure my bladder was absolutely empty. Nothing's worse than an urgent need to go when you're nowhere near anything resembling a toilet; nothing so primitive would interrupt my attention, not today.

When I returned, I found Jun scrolling through images on his phone. "Are you connected?" I asked, assuming he'd magically gotten online somehow.

"Huh? Oh, no. I was deleting old photos. I want to take more while I'm here, but I keep forgetting."

He pocketed the phone and we headed down the sloping drive, toward the narrow lane. We walked side by side, chatting about this and that, about our hosts mainly. Wondering whether Shoko was having much success at the festival, who Hideyuki's friend might be.

"I haven't seen much of Japan, but I think I like this corner of it best," I said, admiring the burgeoning green hillsides and blossoming orchards. Lavender wisteria and wild thistle accented the verdant green of adolescent growth surrounding us. Insects stirred in the branches, hidden in the leaves and fronds by the wayside.

"I thought Tokyo was everyone's favorite. That's why it's the biggest city in the world, right?"

"Guess I'm not everyone," I said.

"That's true."

"I'm going to take that as a compliment."

Jun inclined his head, neither agreeing nor disagreeing.

"Okay, so what about you?" I asked. "You grew up in a big city, you've been to Sydney…"

"There are things I like about both, and things I dislike. Not having internet, for example," he said, and I didn't disagree. "In the city," Jun continued, "there's so much to do you can never be bored, assuming you don't run out of money."

"What about here, then?" I asked, like a challenge, though honestly, I wanted to know what he thought about rural life.

Jun had a ready answer. "In the countryside, you get to know one piece of land, one tiny part of the world, really, really well. Like a friend, or a sibling. You spend enough time together and you can almost read their thoughts. That's what I like about this place. I don't know it that well because this isn't my home, but I see from working with Hanada-san how that can be possible someday. He knows his family home as well as he knows his wife. Maybe even better," Jun said, breaking into that cockeyed grin of his.

"So, maybe you won't end up back in Kumamoto?" I wondered aloud.

He shrugged, but it felt like a sigh, like trying to dismantle a weight from his shoulders. "The more I learn about growing food, the more I think I could never be a chef in the city. I need to be close to where food grows. I need to be—" he searched for the right words— "part of the weather and geography and seasons of one place. Now that I know these things, I could never use products that come in plastic bags, shipped from places so far away that I know nothing about them."

"Well, when you're a kaiseki chef I plan to come back to Japan and eat at your restaurant," I said, realizing the statement implied, first, my leaving. I think Jun read something similar in it.

"I hope so," he said. "You can be my first guest, then maybe I won't be nervous."

What is he saying, I wondered? *That he feels calm around me? That in five, ten years he hopes I'll still be part of his life?* "You've never struck me as the nervous type," I responded coolly, ensuring he sensed nothing of the happy excitement he'd sparked.

"That's only because we get along so well."

"Well," I said, trying to think of something witty to add, and failing. "I'm glad you're never nervous around me."

"I wouldn't say never," he said, again with the cockeyed grin, the one that flipped my stomach. The funny thing was, though, I didn't feel nervous around Jun either. Excited and eager, maybe, but not like I had to work hard to impress him or, conversely, be on my guard. At Michikusa House, the art of conversation and a strong work ethic spoke more loudly than appearances, thanks in part, I think, to the aforementioned perpetual layer of earth covering hands and clothes alike.

It took a quarter hour at a leisurely pace to reach the soba restaurant. Like Michikusa House, the restaurant sat on a slope, a short step away from the main road. From the outside, it looked like a traditional farmhouse, wood aged the color of black coffee. The covered veranda overlooked the narrow road and a triangular rice paddy beyond it. Any day now that paddy would be flooded and planted. Jun stopped to take a picture, then we climbed the slope and let ourselves in.

"*Irasshaimase!*" came the warm welcome as we slid open the door.

Given the age of the place, I had expected an interior a bit more care worn. Instead, and to my surprise, the owners had taken considerable effort to renovate the space while keeping the updates in the traditional style. Fresh woodwork was accented by cream-colored plaster on the walls. A hanging scroll with a bold calligraphic print graced a small tokonoma. The traditional alcove also displayed a minimalist flower arrangement, delicate blooms plucked straight from the roadside and set in a ceramic vase that might very well have been one of Shoko's. A raised *tatami* platform and three low tables polished to a high sheen faced a wide window, overlooking the rice paddy across the road. One of the three tables was already occupied by a group of older men, the husbands, perhaps, of the *obachans* I'd met picking *sansai*. They turned to look at us, at me, as we entered. I smiled as warmly as I could, though the acute aware-ness of being a foreign oddity struck me like a slap to the side of the head. Jun, too, sensed the mild disruption we'd caused, so he went ahead and greeted the men politely, apologizing for...I couldn't tell what. They spoke too fast for me to catch any but the most common of formalities.

"Everything alright?" I asked, drawing his attention back to me.

"I think so," he said, which seemed like an odd thing to say, because why wouldn't it be? Even so, I let it slide. Better not to make a big deal of it. After that, Jun and I sunk into easy conversation as effortlessly as ever, though he seemed to be keeping a close watch on the neighboring table as they ordered another round of sake.

Although I was accustomed to the practice at Michikusa House, it felt odd to remove my shoes in a public place in order to step up onto the *tatami* mat, but we settled in comfortably enough. The restaurant, Jun explained, was run by a father and son duo. The elder managed the kitchen while the younger greeted guests, brought out dishes, and generally kept the ser-vice running smoothly and efficiently. Soon an array of small plates were offered and tea was poured. There was no ordering to be done, after all, only a daily rotating menu, so my fluency, or lack thereof, was not put on display.

Soba noodles were the main entree but were preceded by seasonal dishes, whatever the neighborhood farmers and lo-cal rivers had to offer. We dined on house-made pickles, fluffy *tamago* egg, grilled eel, tempura, a light kombu dashi broth, peanuts the size of marbles presented in-shell, and finally the house noodles served with grated wasabi and a savory dipping sauce. Everything from the presentation to the setting to the company was perfect.

As we sipped on green tea, letting our food settle in, I said, "This is where you should work, a place like this. It's exactly the sort of restaurant you always talk about." Jun didn't disagree, though neither did he chime in. "I can't believe we didn't eat here before now."

"I came with Hanada-san soon after I arrived."

"Then you should've brought me sooner."

"Then you never would have wanted to eat my food again," he said. "And we couldn't have that."

"Pssh. Your cooking," I said in a whisper, "is easily this good."

"Liar."

"Cross my heart." Jun raised an eyebrow. I translated. "I only meant, I promise I'm not lying. Your cooking is outstanding."

"I'm glad you think so, but I couldn't work here. Not here, exactly. This is a family business, passed down from father to son."

"That's common here, isn't it?"

"Mm, especially for *shokunin*, I think."

I searched my word bank of Japanese nouns. It took a minute, but Jun waited patiently for me to find it. "Craftsmen, right? Artisans, maybe is a better word."

"*Hai.* Though there's maybe a bit more to it than that," he said. "*Shokunin* use the highest quality raw materials and create something with pride and precision to the utmost of their abilities, striving to improve on previous efforts."

"That sounds like you," I said, meaning it, but Jun only shook his head. I didn't want to upset him by trying to peel back layers of a culture I could never fully understand, so I let it pass.

He finished his tea. "You ready?"

When I nodded and went for my purse, Jun held up a hand and insisted on paying. As he dug cash from his wallet, the men at the neighboring table spoke again, louder this time, and in our direction. Naturally, I couldn't understand a word they said, and they knew it, but I could read their laughter and sense the rancid, lopsided energy wafting off them like a foul breeze. The one who had laughed the loudest mimed grotesquely, a gesture no one, not even a flimsy American tourist, could misinterpret. Jun stepped forward, standing in front of me, as if to defend me from the vile, albeit imaginary, projectile. Jun's moderately raised voice, when he spoke, alerted the server, who hurried into the dining room, ready to break up an argument.

I tugged on Jun's arm. "Let's just go."

Jun dropped a wad of bills on the table, then ushered me through the exit. The poor waiter was left dumbfounded in our wake.

"What was that about?" I asked, more than a bit dumbfounded myself.

"Nothing. Don't worry about it. They drank too much, is all."

"They didn't insult you, did they?"

"Not exactly."

We were walking slowly, quite close to one another, along the midline of the road. So few people drove out that way. All you could hear for miles was the chirping of birds and insects. I breathed in the scent of spring, wet earth, and new life. Suddenly, I felt the back of Jun's hand brush against mine. Intentionally? I couldn't be sure. Then, with startling tenderness, he interlaced his fingers between mine, holding me there.

"A lot of Japanese people, they don't like seeing couples who aren't the same," he said.

I blushed inadvertently. Since when had we become a couple? *God…what about Liam?* I sensed I was digging myself into a hole I would have a difficult time climbing out of. Then again, at the end of my stay at Michikusa House, I would return to America, no two ways about it.

"That sounds…old-fashioned," I said, thinking of the American civil rights era, decades in the past. Maybe some stigma remained, but I'd never dated anyone outside my own race, let alone my own culture.

"They have their reasons. Even some young people still think it's a bad thing."

"But not you," I said, feeling his hand, very warm in mine.

"I lived in the West for two years and dated a girl who was not Japanese. She was like you. A French girl. So I've had experience with both, Western and Japanese, and I prefer this." He let go of my hand, wrapping his arm around my shoulder instead. He pulled me in close and kissed the top of my head. "Because I can do that. I like Western-style relationships better. It's easier to be honest about how you feel."

"Is that so?" I said, snaking my hand around his waist. When was the last time Liam and I walked like that? How often had he wanted to be that close to me? "Tell me then: how do you feel?"

"I feel," Jun began, "that I like myself better when I'm with you. You give me confidence," he said. "For a while, I thought I would never have that again. So those guys back there, they can laugh and make a scene. I don't care."

I bit my lower lip, trying hard not to appear girlishly thrilled. Working to steady my expression, I straightened my features. I was ready; he'd made the first move, and now it was my turn to close the gap. But just as I prepared to lean in and show him how I felt in return, a car horn sounded behind us. I jumped. Jun pulled me to the side of the road, both of us laughing so hard we hardly noticed the little green *keitora* pickup sailing past.

CHAPTER 10

As Erin and I pull into my parents' driveway, I think not of what awaits me and the arguments sure to come, but of a Thanksgiving two years ago. That November after thirteen months spent living independently in Japan, I moved back into my parents' house. This house. Did that sudden loss of freedom prompt me to make a hurried and rash decision? I enrolled as a university undergraduate the first chance I got, choosing a course in nutrition science set to begin the following autumn. Now that I've unenrolled, I'll be damned if I lose my apartment, the last shred of freedom I can cling to. I will not move back in with my parents, I promise myself, no matter what.

Erin says, "You okay?"

"Yeah, why?"

"You've been seriously spaced out. Good thing you didn't drive."

"I'm fine," I lie. "Thanks for the ride."

"No prob."

"How did I not remember you lived out this way?" I ask as I gather my belongings, and my wits, about me.

"My parents moved after I started college. The empty-nesters wanted a place near the lake. They're super middle class."

I decide not to ask where they moved from, in which community they ended up, or anything else so mundane, because frankly I don't care and have more urgent matters on which to fixate. Like the fact I haven't seen my parents in person since the night of the Faculty Art Show and my big announcement. Instead, I say, "You don't mind swinging by again on your way back?"

"My dad'll turn down the heat by eight. That's always our cue to G-T-F-O."

"The earlier the better, far as I'm concerned."

"Sure you don't wanna ditch this crowd? My parents wouldn't mind. I can't promise my brother won't hit on you or try to get you to smoke weed with him out on the dock, but," she shrugged, "might be an improvement. Alternatively, you could come as my girlfriend, then my brother will leave you alone, that's for sure, damn homophobe," she added, sotto voce. "But since I haven't technically come out to my parents, I can't completely predict their reaction to that plan." The offer, it seems, is genuine. Oddly, I'm reminded of how much younger Erin is than me. A couple years my junior, but I can't recall how many just now. Five sounds about right.

"Tempting," I say. "But I'll pass. Text me when you're on your way, alright?"

"You got it, chika."

I climb out holding a covered pie plate.

"Break a leg." She waves, and I slam the door shut.

As I march resolutely up the drive, I refuse to look back or watch Erin leave, my last chance at escape. Instead, I gaze in through the familiar living room window of my childhood home. Inside my family, aunts, uncles, cousins, their kids, are chatting and mingling, carrying small plates of appetizers or glasses of wine, like it's a cocktail party. Knowing the interrogation I'll face the moment I open the door without Liam beside me, I wish for a drop of that liquid courage. Thankfully, with a ride back to my apartment, I won't have to survive this sober.

Just as I'm bundling myself in an extra layer of willpower and mental fortitude, my phone buzzes. The email alert shows I have a message from Shoko. Will she have a response to my questions about Jun, his whereabouts?

Balancing the dish in one hand and my phone in the other, I tap over to the note, and read:

Dear Win-chan,

So good to hear from you. It has been too long. I'm happy you are well and have found a job you are excited about. Doing work you love makes all the difference, don't you agree?

We are well also. The website has been a great success and now we have many helpers and guests, but I remember fondly your time with us as you were one of our earliest (and longest stayed!) guests. I remember that year with great joy and happiness. Perhaps you can visit again some time. You are always welcome at Michikusa House.

As for your question about Nakashima Jun, we have not heard from him in many months. In fact, I think he contacted us only once. He asked for a letter of recommendation, which I happily supplied. You may remember he wanted to train to become a chef. If you like, I will try to find out where he is now. I am curious about what happened to him, myself, and would like to wish him well in whatever position he found.

Please give my love to your mother and tell her I think about her often and hope she is still having great success with her work. I will call her again soon; it's been far too long. As I send this to you now, I think it might be Thanksgiving Holiday in America, is that right? If so, I hope you are spending this day with family.

Best wishes from your friend,

Hanada Shoko

花田 祥子

I type out a quick response, thanking her for her note and saying I'm about to drop in on my parents now.

...I'll send them your good wishes. And please do let me know if you find or hear from Jun.

Much love,

Winona

Then I climb the front steps and ring the bell, which feels odd. Ringing the bell to my own house, like I no longer belong here.

My mother answers. The first thing she says is, "I heard what happened with Liam."

"Happy Thanksgiving to you, too," I say, holding out the covered dish in place of an embrace. She takes it and I step past her, into the foyer.

"Oh, for god's sake, Winona," she hisses, shutting the door, her eyes fierce. "What on earth were you thinking? First your education and now Liam? My god, I hardly know—"

I figure I'll never know what degree of disappointment she was about to project because at that moment Aunt Colleen, my dad's sister, rushes in. "Winona! Oh my word, last time I saw you you were skinny as a zipper! Who am I kidding, look at you? Even in that coat you can't weigh more than a carton of eggs," she laughs merrily. Already a few glasses into the punch bowl, I see. I refuse to correct her estimation or draw further attention to my current size and weight. Besides, she's on to the next thing before I can get a word in. "You don't mind me stealing your room from you, do you?"

"I'm not staying," I say, as I watch my mother drift back into the crowd bearing my pie plate. "I really don't mind."

"How is she?" Aunt Colleen asks, mock-quietly, then carefully sips from her glass. Her dark lipstick leaves a wine-colored stain on the rim. She means my mother, I presume. "She seems," her hand wavers side to side. *Unbalanced? Drunk? Is that what she's implying?* "Upset," is what she says.

"Probably. Let's just assume it's my fault," I say, and step aside, going in search of my father. I pass through the living room, dodging small, screaming children running circles around the couch, diving under the grand piano, flying past rows of built-in bookshelves containing both academic tomes and priceless family heirlooms. A young mother not much older than me steps in, grabbing one of the youngsters by the arm, scolding him harshly for getting too near the fire in the hearth.

"Next time I see you over there you'll get a time out," she warns.

Do I even know this woman? Who are half these people? My mother's graduate students, maybe. Husbands and wives of distant cousins. Friends of friends, even. Too many people, whoever they are. I maneuver into the kitchen. Dad's standing at the island, its surface laden with plates of fancy hors d'oeuvres, little skewers and toasts and things of that sort. Noticing my approach, he ends his conversation with his other sibling, my Uncle Jerry, and opens his arms for a hug.

"Sorry to hear about Liam," he says. "Think you can mend it?"

"He said he wants to take a break for a while, so...I don't know."

"How'd you get here?" he asks, suggesting that he knew I didn't have a ride but didn't intervene, whatever that means. Keeping a polite distance? Pretending not to be in the know?

"I had a friend from school drop me off. She's picking me up again later."

"You should've asked her to stay."

"Her parents live out this way," I explain, pouring myself a full glass of the spiked red punch. I don't even like drinking. Not really. The taste is off-putting, and the smell reminds me of sticky college parties, but I down the glass holding my breath, like swallowing a potent medicine, and taste nothing. Dad's talking about the latest family gossip, recent job changes, births, retirements. My grandparents on both sides are deceased so everyone in attendance is roughly my father's age or younger, but really I couldn't care less about the fluctuations these people have endured. Instead, I wonder what Liam's doing right now. What did he tell his mom? Hell, I even wonder whether Mike came home for the holidays. Is he missing his abandoned cat? I think of Clay at home in my apartment, curled up, asleep on the bed, and wish I could be there with him, be that relaxed ever.

My mother drifts in and notices me standing with my father. "Thank you for the lovely dessert," she says, trying to act neutral and polite, as if she doesn't want me to start something or make a scene. I figure I can play along to that tune, until she says, "Where did you buy it?"

"I made it," I correct her.

"Oh, really? She did this lovely lattice pie crust," she explains to Dad. "It looked so, I don't know, professional. I just assumed..."

"Ah, what kind?" Dad chimes in.

"It's an apple cranberry pie. The fruit came from the co-op near my apartment. I wanted to make something seasonal," I explain, wishing they knew or could at least understand how much my time in Japan changed me, my way of thinking and eating, and living.

My mother says, "I didn't know if you could eat dessert now."

I can't retreat to my bedroom and lock the door. I'm not sixteen anymore, nor is it my room. It's been redecorated to accommodate guests, like Aunt Colleen, who, I discover, has unloaded the contents of her suitcase and toiletry bag on the bed, in the closet, on the dresser. Instead, just as I did at the art show, I retreat to the bathroom. Twisting the lock into place, I recall the days when that simple act was forbidden, when I had to shower and sit on the toilet with the door ajar. Through the closed door—such a small but meaningful privilege—I can hear music playing downstairs, not through the speaker system but on the piano. Most people in my family play an instrument of some kind, though it was my maternal grandfather who typically graced the family with off-the-cuff concerts. As I try to catch my breath and reign in my thoughts, someone tries the door handle.

"Someone's in here," I say.

A child responds. "I really gotta go!"

"Go downstairs," I suggest, willing him to leave.

"Uncle Jerry's pooping in there. He's taking too long."

I forsake the upstairs bathroom and retreat to my parents' bedroom, closing the door behind me. No one will try to enter this space. I flop down on the four-poster bed, an antique masterpiece of wood carving inherited from my grandparents. It's not the only ornate piece in the room, either. The dresser set, the walk-in closet and changing room, the pedestals reserved for my mother's wild ceramics, all of it seems so extra. Compared to the minimalist simplicity of the rooms at Michikusa House, this bedroom feels overburdened.

Eventually, I did see all the rooms at Michikusa House, including the one Jun occupied above the studio.

The first time, unsurprisingly in retrospect, was the same day we went to the soba restaurant. We walked home hand in hand but were quick to return to our chores once we realized Hideyuki was there waiting for us. He suggested, via Jun's translation, that I go tidy up the studio, but I wasn't fooled. I heard the quiet reprimand Jun received, even if I didn't understand a word of it. Jun was unusually quiet that afternoon and into the evening. He insisted on preparing the evening meal alone, without my help. Dinner was a subdued affair.

That night, troubled by Jun's silence, I lay awake on my futon, wondering what Hideyuki had said to chill Jun so completely. Had the older man chastised him for going out to lunch when he should have been working, fulfilling his obligation to the farm? Or, like those men at the restaurant, was he against the idea of inter-racial relationships? I supposed a man like Hideyuki could harbor old-fashioned opinions on any number of topics. Then again, maybe it was simpler than that; maybe he assumed Jun had been taking advantage of a young woman he had no business intermingling with.

I sat up in bed, concerned that if I didn't act this stony silence would perpetuate until November. I didn't think I could bear it. That's when I noticed, through the window, a light on in the room above the studio. Without hardly thinking, I slipped on a pair of jeans and a coat over my sleep shirt, an oversized, overworn T, and tip-toed downstairs. Every step I took I stopped to listen to make sure I hadn't disturbed Hideyuki in his sleep.

Finally, I passed through the kitchen and exited through the side door, slipping on my rubber work boots as I went. Heart racing, I slid across the gravel drive as quietly as a shadow, not daring to look back.

There's an inexplicable thrill that comes from throwing your life away. I understood that recklessness well, the familiar pleasure that precedes a terrible disgrace. If caught, I would fool no one. If discovered, the sin would fracture the only stable relationship I had ever cultivated. No one worth having would forgive a girl who tosses aside the earned trust and respect of another as carelessly as she would yesterday's rubbish. The shame would infect my parents, too, I had no doubts about that. Yet plenty of people choose this path, I told myself, avoiding the glow of light passing through Jun's upstairs windows, as if invisibility could protect me from the oncoming wreckage. That was the word for it. Wrecked, as in beyond repair. Hadn't that always been my preferred method of muddling through life? Self-destruction, it seems, had come to infect me again.

The ceramics studio was unlit, quiet and still. I slipped inside and, for the first time, ascended the staircase that would take me to Jun's private living quarters. The door at the top of the staircase was closed but light shone promisingly underneath the threshold. The barrier to a room set aflame. I removed my boots and set them on the step beside Jun's. I knocked twice, quietly. If he had fallen asleep, I wouldn't wake him and that would be that. I would return to my futon, pretending I had given no thought whatsoever to tossing myself over this particular cliff, into yet another poorly considered decision. If he answered...

The door slid open. Jun stood there wearing nothing but grey sweatpants. "Win? What are you—" he began, but neither of us really cared about the question, because we already knew the answer. I stepped inside, barefoot, and he shut the door behind me.

I don't remember the exact details of that night, only the sensations. The intensity of my craving for Jun. The months of build-up practically blinded me to the exotic newness of him. The way he touched, kissed, it wasn't like it had been with Liam. He wasn't even like the people I'd slept with through college. Jun enveloped me completely, his scent, his body, his need... the energy of it, it wasn't slow and sexy, like people might expect a first time with someone new would be, or ought to be. It felt almost...angry. He was intense and passionate. Every time I would relax and drift off, he'd wake me again. Again and again, until the sun came up. Only then was Jun exhausted enough to rest. Sweating, we lay atop of his futon, panting, spent. Steam practically rose off our bodies in the chill room. As he lay on his stomach, his eyes drifting shut, Jun turned his head to look at me.

"I'm sorry," he whispered.

"For what?"

"Did I hurt you?" Wriggling one arm free, he laid it over my waist, resting his hand on my bare hip.

"I don't think you could," I assured him, and he kissed me one last time. Before falling fast asleep, I said, "Remind me how you say goodnight, in Japanese."

"*Oyasumi,*" he said slowly.

"*Oyasumi,*" I repeated, but Jun was already asleep. I rose and dressed. It was nearly six. Hideyuki could wake at any time. I returned to the house as quietly as I'd left it. As silently as I could, I slipped back in through the kitchen, leaving my boots at the door. As I parted the *noren* curtain separating the kitchen from the dining room, however, I saw Hideyuki sitting there, already dressed. He had made rice and green tea, a simple breakfast.

"*Ohayou*," he said, not bothering to look up.

"*Ohayou gozaimasu*," I said. Then, "I think Jun's not feeling well." I'd said it in English, willing him to understand, to not ask questions. He replied in Japanese. The only word I caught was "*gohan*," meaning rice, or possibly just breakfast. "*Arigato. Sumimasen*," I said, figuring I couldn't go wrong with a "thank you" and an "excuse me," probably the two most useful words in the whole Japanese lexicon.

Just then the phone rang. Hanada-san rose to answer it in the hallway. "*Moshi, moshi, Hanada desu*," is all I heard before he appeared again, motioning me forward. I stepped into the hall, bewildered, and he pointed from me to the phone. Shoko, perhaps? No, he would speak with his wife before passing the phone to me.

I picked up the receiver and Hanada-san returned to his breakfast. "Hello?" I said, knowing it could be only one of three people.

"Win, I'm so glad I caught you," Liam said, and my heart plummeted into my stomach like a heavy stone dropped into a dark pond.

"I told you, mornings are super busy here," I said.

"Aren't you even a little happy to hear from me?" I could tell he was genuinely hurt, though he was trying hard to play it off coolly.

"Of course. And I miss you. Every minute," I said, knowing in my gut, knowing instinctively that was only half true.

I'd never had other crushes, not once throughout middle or high school or even in college, those two years of dizzying experimentation. Sure, we had tackled a few hills, Liam and I, but each time he'd gone and trotted ahead Liam had always turned and come straight back to me. He had proven his quality as a friend and as a partner. Most recently, as my cheerleader and confidant, a supplier of comforting words during the worst hours of my recovery, two years of physical and mental hell. Or, more accurately, purgatory. Even over distances spanning state lines, Liam remained a mere phone call away. In the worst throws of my desperation to escape the tsunami of pain and long-suppressed emotions that never seemed to break, Liam had talked to me, sometimes for hours, long past reasonable expectation.

Why couldn't I do the same for him now that I was the one who had gone away? I had suspected my mother's motivation for sending me off so soon after Liam graduated had been partially motivated by his employment at a prestigious, well-paid engineering company. Her way of giving each of us time and space to settle into our new lives. Such a strange turn of fortune. If I had never ended up in Japan, if Jun hadn't chosen Michikusa House, if he was fifteen years older and dumb as a brick...

Dear god, I just slept with another man. I really am the worst kind of person imaginable, aren't I? There was no excuse for my betrayal apart from altered priorities. Sunk up to my neck, that's what it was, so deep it felt life-threatening. Liam didn't deserve my hard-heartedness. He deserved better than me, a broken, weakened, skill-less excuse for a partner. And yet...the way Jun looked at me, the way he treated me, like a wonderful gift rather than a weathered trinket one keeps in his back pocket. No one, not even my myriad therapists, had ever listened to me the way Jun did. No one marveled at my eyes, compared them to beautifully smooth river stones, or caressed my hair as if handling fine strands of rare silk.

We chatted only briefly, Liam oblivious to the sickening tempest of guilt raging inside me. Levelly, I told him about the firing of the kiln, how Shoko was off selling her wares, how the garden was coming along.

"Anyone else there with you?"

"Shoko's husband, it's his family's farmhouse where I'm staying, and there's another farm hand this summer."

"Guess I do remember you saying that. Well, I won't hold you up. I've gotta head out, myself. I'm meeting some of the guys from work for drinks"

"How are you liking the new job?" I asked.

"I think it's going to be good for me. It's testing my limits, but in a good way."

"Well, then I'm happy for you. Keep up the good work," I said. We exchanged our goodbyes and "I love you's." All the while I was looking over my shoulder, but Jun didn't appear, or rather, overhear. I didn't see him until lunch, in fact, when he emerged looking entirely refreshed. When he spotted me hunched over in the herb garden, selecting the choicest leaves to season our meal, he smiled, that slightly cockeyed grin of his. I couldn't resist and smiled back.

"Look at you," I said. "Not so mopey anymore, by the look of it."

"Thanks to you," he said, carefully stepping along the row until he reached me. With one hand, he cupped the back of my head and drew me in, kissing me briefly as if Hideyuki might materialize at any moment.

"He's out in the workshop," I said, reading Jun's thoughts.

"So, you're saying we've got time for—"

"You wish. I'm starving. Get your butt in the kitchen, *Senpai*. We only had rice and tea for breakfast thanks to someone's absence. Hardly enough to rebuild a girl's strength."

"I'm on it," he said, disappearing through the kitchen door.

I watched him go, willing myself not to chase after him.

How could being with Jun feel so good and right when everything that defined my moral compass told me it was wrong? I had betrayed Liam and lied to him by omission. What kind of person did that? A cheat and a coward, that's who. Sure, I could stay in character, act an innocent when I was half a world away from Liam and didn't have to disguise my emotions. What would happen six months out? If Jun wanted to part as friends, so be it; that would be a reasonable outcome. I would return home with a vulgar secret as my one souvenir, stashed behind a blockade of resolve. But if Jun wanted to remain more than friends, then what? Could I make myself choose, assuming neither ever learned about the other? Who would I choose, if it came to that? This thing with Jun felt fresh and exciting and I was eager, more than eager, to find out where it went. On the other hand, Liam was the steady, predictable choice, the partner I was "destined" to end up with. My best and only friend. It was wrong, I knew, so terribly unfair and wrong, to betray him, betray his trust, the way I had. But I'd already crossed that threshold. And if Jun came back for more, I knew I wouldn't say no, because I didn't want to.

The truth was, Jun made me feel like a different person, a person I actually liked exactly as I was. I felt smart, capable, and unselfconscious when I was with him, not as if I constantly had to strive or impress or compare or live up to certain standards, like I always had with Liam. Unshakable Liam, so responsible and clear-headed. He did things by the book, followed the rules, which is why he succeeded. People trusted him and relied on him. Me? Well, no one besides Liam had liked me in a long time, including myself. Until Jun.

*   *   *

When I sit upright on my parent's bed, I feel the trail of tears snaking into my hair. I wipe away the damp, sniffling like a wronged child. I dug my own grave, I know that, and I lost both of them. I have no one to blame but myself.

I don't want to return to the festivities, but my absence will be noticed. Dinner is a lighthearted and jovial affair thanks primarily to the husband of one of my mother's graduate students, a man who missed his calling as a standup comedian, it would seem. I'm given not the slightest bit of attention, and for that I'm grateful. At eight-thirty, when my phone buzzes announcing Erin is on her way, I rise to fetch my things and say goodbye to a few choice members of the family. Most guests have trickled into the living room to chat and play parlor games, or have left, taking the youngest home to bed before tantrums have a chance to arise.

"You have a ride?" my mother asks, coming up behind me as I fish my coat from the assortment of dense black and grey fabrics in the hallway closet.

"A friend from the library is picking me up," I say.

"We'll get your dish back to you sometime."

"I'm sure it was yours to begin with."

"Sorry we didn't have more chances to talk this evening."

"I didn't know you'd invited the whole art department," I comment, but it comes out sounding more ungracious than I had intended.

"I get so many international and West Coast students these days," she says, by way of explanation. "Win-chime, I'm sorry about Liam. Try to work it out, okay?" she says, and I sense the kindness in it. If there's any self-interest in her counsel, a sense of losing a friend and potential son-in-law, she doesn't show it. Instead, she hugs me and watches from the door as I hurry out to meet Erin.

"You survived," she says, as I pull the door shut.

"You as well," I reply.

"Your mom's pretty," she says, waving at her from the driver's seat. My mother, from the open doorway, waves back. Erin pulls away from the curb, circles the cul-de-sac, then we're off. Rather than discuss my mother's many refined qualities, I recount my first week at my new job, working with Kyrone and Dodge, which Erin finds hilarious, especially Dodge's plans for the zombie apocalypse. "What kind of name is Dodge, anyway?"

"Maybe it's a warning."

Back at home, in my apartment, I spend the remainder of the evening playing with Clay and reading online reviews for cat harnesses. Finally, after selecting one and making a purchase, I allow myself two lapses in judgment. First, I text Liam.

'Hope you had a nice time with your mom. Tell her I miss her. My mom misses you, I can tell. I don't mind if you still want to call her or whatever.' I sign it 'XO' and hit send, telling myself I won't be surprised if he doesn't respond. After an hour, during which I allow myself another lapse in judgement, scrolling endlessly through the @j.nakashima.j account, I figure I must have been right. Liam's gone. This time, probably, for good.

CHAPTER 11

Winter chickadees flit from stem to branch, enjoying the relative quiet of the cemetery. Their cheeriness and constant whistling remind me I should smile more often, if only for the simple joys and pleasures the day brings, even now as autumn dissolves. It may be bitter cold, with the sun weak and low in the sky, but the birds who overwinter here manage to sing even on the dreariest days. I enjoy their company while I work, preparing the cemetery for its winter hibernation. Unlike these tiny birds, however, who benefit from layers of feathers, stores of winter fat, and an advantageous body volume to surface area ratio, I survive the long, cold hours outdoors bundled in thickly knitted sweaters and extra layers of wool socks crammed inside my work boots. Also, unlike these small, feathered beings, each day after my shift ends at two, I can rush home to a cup of fragrant, steaming tea and a hot bath. Today, though, I'm off to the co-op. I stop home only to change out of my work clothes and don a heavier jacket. Its puffy weight reminds me again of the chickadees, their plush feathers a downy barrier against the wind.

Clay follows me to the door, weaving around my ankles, anxious for a walk—he took to the harness like a fish to water, and now all he ever wants to do is go out and explore the big world that is our neighborhood—but that will have to wait. Erin more or less invited herself over for dinner. Or rather, she suggested we meet up; I suggested coffee; she said, "How about dinner?"; I thought noodles in Coventry, or pizza in Little Italy, sounded reasonable, both being within walking distance of my place; she said she wanted to see my apartment and play with Clay, so here we are. Now I need to acquire ingredients and decide, based on what's seasonally available, what I want to make. I shoo the eager feline aside, then slip back out into the gusty cold afternoon.

A frigid wind hits me hard, looking for gaps in my layers, anxious to steal my well-concealed heat. It's the second week of December, and we have yet to see snow, but I sense it's on its way. Any day now the cold air will gather the comparatively warm water as it sweeps over Lake Erie, then dump inches of white precipitation across Northeast Ohio. Every year lake effect snow wipes out power lines and snows people in for days, canceling school and keeping people off the road. Unlike schools, however, the cemetery remains open three hundred and sixty-five days a year, albeit on reduced staff, so it will be up to my small team and me to keep the paths and stone steps and parking places clear once the real Cleveland winter finally arrives. There's no holiday for mourning.

It's a fifteen-minute walk to the co-op from my apartment, which isn't insignificant when carrying heavy produce. Still, the season is winding down and only the hardiest root vegetables and greens remain. Nothing like the full, twenty-pound summer watermelons I hauled home in a wagon. I find turnips and kale and cabbage at the market now. Potatoes, too, are sold in ten-pound bags, which I couldn't possibly carry, not that far, not without the wagon. There's another section of tantalizingly red and orange orbs, apples, bell peppers, and tangerines, each imported from Holland, Puerto Rico, or wherever else. My eyes might be drawn to their lustrous colors, but my taste buds won't be fooled. Instead, I make my selection from the table of locally grown options and load my basket, imagining what sort of brilliant concoction Jun would have come up with using these seemingly lusterless vegetables. I palm one of the white turnips. Maybe he would have cooked them down in a light dashi broth until soft enough to puree, drizzling olive oil and sea salt on top to make a simple but elegant soup. We would eat it with brown rice, cooked low and slow until tender and chewy. Jun would, of course, serve the dish with homemade pickles. The meal would be light and sweet, the courses complimenting each other perfectly when served on Shoko's beautiful ceramics. On my way to the counter, I spy trays of mushrooms. At the last minute, I bag half a pound of the grey oyster and wood ear varieties, imagining a sauteed dish with shaved carrot and hijiki seaweed mixed with rice—a bit too unfamiliar for guests, but I can save that one for later, just for me.

I lug the groceries home and begin my preparations, flipping through the notebook of recipes I jotted down all those years ago, while working alongside Jun Nakashima in that tiny, foreign kitchen. I had brought the moleskin from home, thinking—foolishly—that I might start a diary while living abroad. Instead, I only pulled it from the bottom of my suitcase midway through my stay at Michikusa House, realizing I wouldn't have Jun's intuition to rely on once I returned to the States. From that moment on, I wrote down every "recipe" he ever shared, from that first *nabe* hot pot to the—probably useless outside Japan—homemade *tsukemono* pickles, using the traditional fermentation method.

"What are you writing?" he asked the first time I brought the little black notebook into the kitchen, laying it open on the wooden cutting board. Jun had moved the cylindrical ceramic pot containing *tokozuke*, the pungent fermenting mixture of rice bran and kombu-infused brine used to make homemade pickles. The concoction had to be mixed daily, by hand, to prevent spoilage. Since his arrival, Jun had taken over this essential process, kneading and aerating the ferment. Beside the pot sat pre-salted, bite-sized turnips and baby cucumbers, vegetables we'd plucked that morning and planned to pickle for dinner.

"Your recipes," I said. "I want to remember how to make them."

"You could just ask," he said.

"Then, in the unlikely event you're ever unavailable at a moment's notice six years from now, I'm writing them down so I have something to reference," I said, continuing to jot notes on quantities, ratios, sequences, and timing.

He laid a hand over the open page. "Win-chan, cooking is not this; cooking is about confidence. You cook with your whole body: listening for the moment the oil splatters, feeling the temperature of sushi rice, knowing the smell of a freshly caught fish is not a fishy smell. Cooking is something you feel."

"*Sōdesu ka?*" I asked, meaning "is that right?" Meaning, I have to start somewhere, don't I? A recipe, even a rough guide, seems as good a place as any. I don't think he caught the sarcasm. Changing the subject, I asked, "Shoko's supposed to come home tomorrow, right? Feels like it's been ages since she left."

"Win-chan...we should probably be more careful...once Shoko-chan returns," Jun said. "People in Japan, they are not used to Western-style relationships."

I knew what he meant. The Japanese are traditionally more reserved in their affections, especially in public. I hadn't spent much time in heavily populated areas to know from personal experience, but based on what Jun described, couples rarely hugged, kissed, or even held hands in the presence of others. After moving to Sydney, it had taken Jun a while to grow accustomed to what Western girls expected from a partner. Eventually, he came to prefer the more unabashed version of love, a preference that clung to his shirttails when he eventually returned to Kumamoto. Our relationship—for want of a better term—blossomed rapidly thanks to Shoko's absence. Ever since her departure, Jun and I had had plenty of privacy. For whatever reason—and maybe we were it—Hideyuki was spending more and more time in his workshop, running errands, visiting friends, leaving Jun and I to manage the regular farm chores and, frankly, be as intimate as we wanted. As long as the world could not see us, the rules did not apply. We had spent hardly an hour apart since that first night we slept together. We hadn't, however, talked about how that might have to change once Shoko returned. Would I be able to sneak into Jun's room at night, and sneak back again before sunup? If Hideyuki noticed anything after that first encounter on the road, he hadn't said so. Shoko would most likely be a keener observer. And much more likely to confront us about it.

"What do you think we should do?" I asked.

"*Shiranai,*" he said, as clueless as I.

"You think I shouldn't come around anymore?" I hovered over my notebook, giving him a sidelong glance.

Jun's crooked smile appeared. "I'm not saying that."

Shoko returned the following day looking spent but unburdened.

"*Tadaima!*" she called from the genkan, joyfully announcing her return.

"*Okaeri!*" Jun called back, welcoming her home. Jun and I had just begun prepping lunch, so we hurried through the dining room and into the entry to meet her.

"Welcome home," I seconded. "Have you seen Hanada-san yet?"

"*Hai.* In the workshop." Wearing a long khaki skirt and striped t-shirt tucked in at the waist, she looked almost youthful. Refreshed, certainly. She tucked her sandals into their cubby, handing her floppy straw hat and purse to me. "Going to take a bath."

"You should have time," Jun said. "Lunch will be some time yet."

"Win-chan, will you—"

"I'll unload. You relax," I said.

Afterward, looking considerably rejuvenated, Shoko joined us on the veranda for tea, a vibrantly green *gyokuro* brew, and a light lunch of cold *somen* noodles, pickled vegetables, and broiled fish. By then, cool mornings had given over to hazy afternoons that buzzed with the songs of insects. The warm air practically vibrated with the rattling trill of cicadas, the quintessential sound of a Japanese summer. We chatted at length about the pottery festivals, the people she met there, and the galleries she had toured.

In the days and weeks that followed, Jun and I kept our affair quiet, though secrecy only intensified our passion. We slept together with the windows in the room above the studio thrown open, enjoying what little coolness pervaded the dark hours, evaporating with the rising of the sun. Each morning, I left as the songbirds began their chorus, before sunup. We reached mid-June without so much as a peep from Shoko. I was beginning to think we were in the clear until one day she appeared in the kitchen doorway while Jun and I were preparing lunch.

"I could use your help," she said, holding a basket of eggplants. The harvest was in full swing and every day we brought in a bounty of ripe, richly-hued produce. I donned my boots and followed her into the steamy afternoon sun. Working side by side to cut the purple *nasubi* and bright green *piman* peppers from their hardy stems, she said, "My husband called while I was away. He had some troubling news to share." I hadn't the foggiest idea what she could be talking about, so I waited for her to explain. "I would have mentioned it sooner, but I wanted to see for myself, and I see now there can be no doubt." Again, she paused, as if waiting for me to chime in, but I was completely at a loss. "I know you and Nakashima-san have been... seeing one another," she said, at last.

What had she seen, I wondered? We had been so careful. Apparently not careful enough.

"You don't deny it?"

"No," I said. "I think Hanada-san saw us walking together one day."

"He saw more than that," Shoko replied, her voice stiff. "Win-chan, it isn't my place to tell you how to live your life, but you need to be careful. So much could go wrong. While you are here, it is my responsibility to keep you safe. I considered sending Nakashima-san away, but I don't think that is the right answer."

"Don't punish him on my account," I begged her. "He really wants to be here, to learn about—"

"I know. That is why I will let him stay. He is a good worker. You both are, but you cannot carry on this way. What if," she placed a hand on her belly.

My shoulders slumped. Was that all? She was worried about a possible pregnancy? "You don't have to worry about that. I'm always careful. I've been in relationships before; I know what I'm doing."

"It's not only that, Win-chan. I don't want you to get hurt." This time she moved her hand to her heart.

"We both know I'm going back at the end of the year," I said, returning to my task, forcing myself not to consider too deeply ending things with Jun.

"Do you know for certain that is what he expects? Japanese people are not like you, in America. We expect different things from relationships. We don't date, date, date, date, anyone we like. There is an expectation for marriage. Whether he says so or not, that is his culture."

"I don't think—"

"Stop, Win-chan, and listen to me carefully. Nakashima-san went away to a Western country and had a great time for a brief, fun period. I know what it feels like. I did the same thing and thought I could not go back to my home country after living in America. Some people spend the rest of their life trying to get back that feeling. But you know what? Living overseas after you are young, once you turn thirty, thirty-five, forty, you will find you have no family, few friends, most of your co-workers will be more concerned with their own lives and have no interest in you. Building and holding onto a social group is hard enough, harder than learning a foreign language." She took a breath before the monologue continued. "And that is assuming you could find a job here. Without speaking Japanese, you can teach English. That is all you can do." She spoke louder, loud enough to be heard through the kitchen window. Perhaps that was her intention all along. "Even if you learn to speak Japanese very well, you will always be considered an outsider. Or worse, an odd *gaijin*. Right now, you know only the most basic things about Japanese manners and customs. To most Japanese, you will seem awkward all the time, even if you can use chopsticks. Even if you live here twenty years, you will struggle to rent your own apartment, you will struggle with driving on the opposite side of the road, if you can even pass the difficult driving test. And it will be just as bad for Nakashima-san if he goes to America to be with you. But," she said, speaking slowly, deliberately, "I won't prevent you from seeing him…because I don't think I could. That doesn't mean I think it is a good idea, or a responsible way to act."

"What about Hanada-san?" I asked, my voice wavering, like a trembling leaf.

"I will handle my husband. You worry about yourself."

It seemed there was nothing else to be said. No one on either side of the earth, in Japan or in America, would approve of my relationship with Jun. Not the Hanadas, not my parents, and surely not Liam. God…Liam. I bit my lip, hard, willing myself to say nothing. I crouched low, working fast to move along the planted row of vegetables, to put distance between myself and my, presumably, well-intentioned host. Even so, I'm sure I failed to hide my emotions from Shoko.

That night, as Jun and I lay side by side, I confessed. "Shoko knows." That's all I said, and it was enough.

"I heard," he said. "That was her intention all along. She can't tell you what to do, but she's trying to give me a chance to do the right thing, by pointing out all the barriers."

"It seems like we're pissing a lot of people off."

"*Shouganai,*" he sighed. "One older couple, who else?"

He couldn't know what I meant, the people I was thinking of, the ones he'd most likely never meet, the ones I had betrayed just by getting close to him. "She was talking about marriage, implying that was the only logical outcome. It was so awkward." He said nothing, which worried me. "What's all this coming to, Jun? In November, I go back home. How do we—" but he cut me off.

"Win, are you happy? Right now?"

"You know I am," I said, hurt that he might think otherwise.

"Then enjoy it, being together. Who cares about what might happen six months from now? I could get in a tractor accident tomorrow and then what?" I gave him a pained look. He remedied, "What I mean is, we don't know what's going to happen in two weeks, let alone half a year away. Can't we just—" he sighed, pulling me into him. I rested my head on his shoulder. "I just want to stay like this as long as we can, however long that is."

How long would it be, I wondered? Until he grew tired of me? Until Liam found out? Until I flew back to the opposite side of the world, is that when it would be over? Not one of those endings sounded appealing, but I wouldn't sacrifice the contentment of now for the sake of preventing the possibility of future unhappiness.

*　　　*　　　*

I realize I've been daydreaming. The smell of scalded soup and a whining cat brings me back to the present. Cursing myself, I turn off the burner and check the damage. Unsalvageable. I drop the saucepan in the sink. *Dammit.* There's less than an hour until Erin arrives and I still have to shower. *College students don't eat vegetables, anyway,* I tell myself. I'll just order take out from the pasta place up the road and call it an evening.

Unaccustomed to strangers, or any visitors for that matter, Clay hides the moment Erin arrives.

"I figured you'd need someone to talk to," she says as her opening line. Nothing about the apartment she wanted to view or the cat she planned to entertain.

I'm baffled. Has someone died that I don't know about? "I have no idea what you're talking about. Oh, no shoes, please."

"That girl he's seeing?" she says, slipping off her Converse high-tops. "Who is she, anyway?"

"Which 'he' are we talking about?"

"Wait…you really haven't seen?" She can tell by my expression that I'm totally lost. "Liam's new arm candy! You really… wow, you haven't noticed?"

"What…do you mean?" but she's already pulling up various social media accounts. "Wait…Are you—?"

"Uh, yeah, I've followed him for, like, a year." I'm about to ask another inane question but she's flipped her screen around to face me. It's a selfie, two faces, their cheeks pressed together, grinning as if they've never been happier. Liam…and Fiona Justice.

"Are you kidding me?!" I explode.

"Oh, I know. The guy's got some nerve. I mean it's been, what, two weeks since he broke up with you?"

I am literally dumbfounded. I can't think of a single thing to say.

Erin sits herself down at my table, scrolling through more photos of the two of them together. "Yeah, there's like a dozen of these."

"Bastard," I growl. I can't help it, though I know I'm nothing close to innocent. "Didn't take him long to test out a new ride."

"I'll say," Erin agrees. "I mean, she's hot. I'd do her." I give Erin a scathing look. "Sorry; not helping. But, yeah…I assumed you knew, but clearly…you did…not."

"We only ran into her—Fiona Justice, I mean—at that art show. I bet that's why he was so eager to cut and run."

Erin doesn't disagree. "Well, you know how men are. I try to avoid 'em as a habit. Do you wanna talk about it? You can cry if you want to, I don't mind. I need the practice, dealing with other peoples' feelings."

What's there to say? Liam has very clearly moved on and there's no getting him back this time. Karma come to bite me, and I deserve it, but I don't want to explain my past transgressions to Erin. There is one person I do want to tell though, about Liam: my mother. She has a right to know.

"I'm not crying," I say, pointing at my eyes, proof that my mascara isn't running.

"Suit yourself. Smells super good in here, by the way," Erin says, and I present the pasta from the place up the road, which we fully enjoy. Over dinner we chat about our respective holiday plans, and I tell Erin a bit more about my new job and my coworkers, how much creepier Dodge is than the cemetery itself. Through it all, I don't even think about Liam. Or Fiona. *And* Fiona. It's not until after Erin leaves that I crumple and let the tears flow.

CHAPTER 12

"You know, I've seen people try to dig up graves with their bare hands," Dodge says. We, Dodge and I—no Kyrone today—are dealing with a particularly thorny patch of invasive buckthorn over by the reservoir. I never feel safe with him waving his loppers all over the place, so I've been working to keep some distance between us.

"I cannot imagine why," I say, loud enough to span the gulf.

"They're after the bodies, but mostly they just end up wanking over the graves."

"That's disgusting," I say, the only possible reply. I consider, not for the first time, requesting a lateral move to another team—the gravedigging squad, the graveyard shift—but neither option sounds terribly appealing. I took this job so that I could play a small role in maintaining the property's grand Victorian-style gardens, not play watchdog overnight. This is not the only horror story Dodge has shared regarding certain transgressions that occur within the cemetery after dark. Dodge has always been very explicit in that respect.

"I've had to call the cops on half a dozen of them fuckers."

"Why don't you work the night shift anymore?" I ask. Playing guard dog feels much more Dodge's speed than pruning hedges.

"Ain't got a ride," he says.

Ah, yes. Ye olde DUI.

After that, thank god, we lapse into silence. When Kyrone accompanies us, I feel comfortable listening to music or a book on tape while we work. Whenever it's just the two of us, however, just me and Dodge, I prefer to keep my ears open and my wits about me. On days like today, it's always a relief to run into other workers, other teams, during a shift. Today, though, we haven't seen a soul for the better part of three hours. Just as I'm about to suggest Dodge go ahead take a nap, I notice the superintendent lumbering our way, his truck parked a couple yards behind.

"Winona," Curtis calls. "Need you guys over in Section nine. Lot fourteen's been trashed again."

"Aw, hell, no!" Dodge whines. "That plot's creepy as shit."

"Don't be such a baby," I say, loud enough so even Curtis can hear.

"Get your butt over there, Dodge. And don't make Winona do all the work. If I hear you're sleeping on the job again you are outta here, you hear me, son?"

Dodge grumbles something in response.

"What's that, boy?" Curtis yells.

"Nothing," Dodge says.

"Leave your gear. You can come back when you're finished. I'll drive ya."

Curtis drops us in Section nine with a pair of trash bags, then drives off to check on another team, leaving us to contend with the garbage left at the foot of one the cemetery's more cult-famous residents. Not former Presidents or wealthy men of industry, but the Haserot Angel. That's not her real name, but it's less chilling than her actual title, the "Angel of Death Victorious". The larger-than-life bronze statue sits on a marble throne, staring straight ahead. She holds an inverted torch in her strong hands, a symbol, I think, of life extinguished. Wings outstretched, death's guardian appears to weep black tears that drip from recessed eyes all the way down her neck. It's only an effect of the aging bronze, but consequently, people also refer to her as the "Weeping Angel". Though she's quite popular among tourists and ghost hunters, she's by far the least popular among the groundskeepers. People claim all sorts of weird happenings near her; hearing the sound of concrete scraping against stone, screams late at night, that kind of thing. As for me, I believe there's an organic cause behind every paranormal experience, ranging from bizarre weather to chemical imbalances in the brain. Meaning, I don't mind cleaning up after the high school vagabonds who leave crushed beer cans and cigarette butts at her feet.

I grab a trash bag and walk toward her. Dodge lingers close to the road while I do the dirty work, sifting through the ivy to score every last piece of abandoned rubbish.

"Why do you even work here anyway?" I ask. "You clearly hate this job."

"Fuck you," Dodge says, his go-to response when he has nothing intelligent to say, which is most of the time. "Why the hell do you care?"

Because I have to work with you and your lousy attitude; because this is a site of historic significance; because the people who reside here deserve a modicum of your respect, is what I think, but I know better than to poke the cranky bear. "Forget it," is all I manage. Then, "Where are you going?"

"I need a cig, alright? Christ. What are you, my mom?"

"No, thank god," I mutter.

I finish tidying the site, apologizing to the angel and the family she oversees for the disrespect their plot receives. Then I make my way back to the buckthorn patch on my own.

Unlike most weeding we do, this task is best left until winter. Buckthorn is one of the last to lose its leaves, staying green until they drop off, usually mid-December. Even after the snow falls and leaves vanish, the thorny silhouette and sulfur-yellow heartwood make for easy identification. Now that Dodge is away, I can relax more completely into the work. This is where my zen lies, working closely with the plants. Not so much the grass mowing or replanting the flower beds but in identifying and interacting with individual species.

As I work, I'm reminded of a bit of wisdom Shoko shared. For millennia, she explained to me once, humans survived thanks to such intimate, holistic relationships, not only with individual species but with land and sea, entire ecosystems. Fishermen, farmers, people who know how to observe the weather and seasonal changes to maximize harvest, who understand the varying needs of seeds and soil and the importance of timing. Nomadic tribes who follow grazers across harsh northern landscapes; traditional healers who know the benefits and uses of individual herbs, flowers, berries, roots, and bark; even cooks, those who provide our daily sustenance, know—or used to know, in ages past—how to prepare meat, grains, legumes, and potent seasonings to enhance nutrition and digestibility. Today we benefit from their gifts, that collective knowledge, built over generations, handed down through centuries of survivors, those who withstood the harsh realities of the eat-or-be-eaten cycle. That's why I think it's hard-wired into my brain to love this work, getting to know one specific parcel, the land's topography, habitat, and occupants. It's a practice I share with humans throughout history.

When my shift ends at two, I realize I haven't seen Dodge since he took that "smoking break"—guess that's what he's calling it now, these regular disappearances. Tossing our combined equipment into a wheelbarrow, I decide to leave it where it is, figuring the guys on second shift will be picking up where I left off. I trek back to the office to clock out. Curtis catches up to me before I can make my exit.

"You seen Dodge?" he asks. "He didn't come back with you, did he." It's not a question.

"He said he was taking a smoking break after we finished Section nine. I haven't seen him since then."

"That son of a bitch," he grumbles. "Gonna have to do something about that little shit-for-brains."

I figure it's not entirely my place to agree, so I tell Curtis I left the equipment over by the reservoir and take my leave. The walk home is brief, but brisk. I'm anxious to hop into a hot bath and comb the leaves out of my hair.

The moment I open the door Clay rushes forward, working to squeeze past my ankles, anxious to get outside. "We'll take a walk in a bit," I promise. "Just let me thaw out first." He drops his haunches to the kitchen floor, staring up at me. "Hi," I say, and he yawns widely. While I soak in the tub, Clay wanders between the front door and the bathroom, yowling each time he finds the former blocking his exit, then coming to see whether I've risen to help him open it. "For heaven's sake," I say. "Why are you so fussy today?" I towel off, dry my hair, and re-layer myself in winter wool, down, and leather. Clay allows me to fit his harness, knowing it's his ticket to an afternoon of adventure, then we clamber down the fire escape.

Walking a cat is nothing like walking a dog. It mostly involves me standing in one place, scrolling through my phone, while Clay investigates a particularly interesting leaf pile or stares up into the trees at creatures that I, with my limited human vision, cannot see. Today, he's noticed a rustling in the leaf litter, built up where our dead-end road meets the cemetery wall. He crouches low, eyeing it intently. I, meanwhile, refuse to let my mind wander to Liam or Fiona Justice. Instead, to distract my-self, I revisit the @j.nakashima.j account. The page continues to expand, one new photo uploaded each day. I haven't checked in a while, so it's fun seeing what new images have been added. The theme still appears to be "water", but as I scroll, I no longer feel the same sense of serenity that overtook me when I first discovered the account. Something's different, shifted.

The most recent post shows a view through a train car window. Dappled with rain, the scenery beyond is obscured, but a line of yellow trucks along a single-lane road is still visible. The next photo shows the ocean, its waves crashing against a rocky shoreline with a factory of some kind in the far distance. The next, a puddle reflecting a rusted shop sign. A plastic bucket, half buried in grass, overflowing with rainwater. An abandoned fishing boat, floating cockeyed on open water at dawn. A rain-soaked graveyard with headstones strewn so haphazardly they look more like books toppled from a shelf than heavy marble and granite blocks. Then I find one that doesn't feature water at all. Instead, the image shows a Japanese high street so overgrown with weeds they're buckling the pavement. In the foreground, a semi-dismantled sign spans the road. The letters, a combination of kanji and hiragana characters, have been removed but their dusty shadows remain.

My first clue? Maybe.

I take a screenshot, as if the image might actually disappear at any moment. I'll try translating it later, that sign over the street, when I can sit down properly at my laptop. Most likely, it'll mean nothing—nothing useful to me, at any rate, but still…

Clay makes a dive for the leaf litter at the same instant a chipmunk darts out the far end. It runs headlong down the passage defined by my neighbor's house and the cemetery wall, disappearing moments later. The cat lunges after it, testing the limits of his harness. Thankfully, it holds. Knowing the startled creature already made a safe escape, I give Clay the chance to follow. We wander along the passage, Clay pulling hard, until we reach the spot where the chipmunk vanished. That's when I see a familiar silhouette standing quite still on the sidewalk the next street over.

Dodge, with his hands jammed in his pockets, appears to be looking for something, or someone. Did he follow me? God, does he know where I live? If it was anyone else, Kyrone or Curtis, literally anyone other than Dodge, I would step out and say hello. Instead, I scoot backwards, slowly, until I'm ducking behind my neighbor's giant recycling bin. I try tugging on Clay's lead to pull him back into the shadows, but he resists, his attention locked on the tiny hole in the ground. I hope my coworker doesn't notice him, the cat on the leash, and wander over. Dodge seems like the type to throw rocks at small animals.

What business would he have in this neighborhood anyway? Does he know someone who lives here, other than me? Or did he simply get turned around on his way to grab a late lunch in Little Italy? I've never known him to stick around after a shift. Maybe his ride didn't show. Still, that wouldn't explain why he's wandering the streets. More likely he would wait for Uncle Curtis to take him where he needs to go.

Carefully, I peer around the side of the bin. He's gone. No sign of him. Must've moved on. I bundle Clay into my arms and hurry home. Feeling more rattled than the event probably warrants, I decide to text Liam. In the time it takes to compose a message, however, my fear dissipates. I delete every word, figuring it will sound like a desperate cry for attention—*Oh, Liam, I've got a stalker, please help!* No, he already ignored the message I sent on Thanksgiving. Vowing I won't be the one to make contact again, I search for an activity to distract myself. The screenshotted photo comes to mind. I pull up the image, the one of the dismantled sign overhanging the abandoned street. I consider trying my hand at translation, but the idea of digging through a kanji dictionary requires more effort than I can muster.

Considering my options, I settle on a different tack and upload the photo into Google's image search. It bounces back results for "traffic light," despite the fact there are no traffic lights in the original image. Next, I try posting the photo on a popular forum in the "translator" subcategory. The tagline reads, "[Japanese>English] Please help me translate this street sign." Amazingly, within minutes, several people have responded. Some claim the characters are too faded to read, others post which characters they think were on the sign. After about thirty minutes, another commenter, using the bot-assigned name of u/Engimatic_Carrot, contributes the most helpful response:

'That sign is at the entrance of Futaba. It says, "Nuclear Energy for a Bright Future". They took down the letters after the Fukushima disaster. This is what it looked like before:' The commenter adds a link to an article in a well-known international news publication. The photo underneath the headline shows the same street view, this time with the sign intact and readable, though the street over which it passes remains empty. The subtext reads, "The entrance of Futaba town, which has been empty since the radiation leak at the nearby Fukushima Daiichi nuclear power plant in 2011."

Immediately, more responses roll in.

'Wow! Talk about ironic. No wonder they took the words down.'

'Why not dismantle the whole d*** sign?!?'

'Nobody wants to spend a second longer than they have to in a radioactive wasteland. OBVIOUSLY!'

'*Poor Futaba.*'

'*Can't believe they haven't cleaned it up yet. It's been like a decade. WTH.*'

The thread is closed by a moderator shortly thereafter because the original request has been fulfilled, the sign successfully translated. Even so, I feel more confused now than enlightened. If this is my Jun, then why is he in Fukushima Prefecture? The disaster site is almost a thousand miles from Kumamoto, his hometown. That would be like driving from New York City to Milwaukee, or from here to Florida. It's not the sort of place anyone would go for a vacation or for casual sightseeing, either. Not now.

The nuclear disaster happened years before my stay at Michikusa House, but like everyone else around the world, I had seen the footage. The tsunami rolling in, consuming everything in its path. I became only vaguely aware of the consequences of its aftermath. Like most average college students, I expect, I primarily had myself to think about and gave any news outside my immediate circle very little attention. In fact, by that time, I was already drowning in my own dark place.

I scan a few articles. Unsurprisingly, given the scale, the disaster has not yet been resolved. The photos alone are harrowing. Towns, left to grow over, abandoned to wild boars and other wildlife, to those unafraid or unaware of the lingering radiation. Some villages have reopened, but those who returned to them are generally older and their numbers are few. Evidence of radioactive hotspots keeps most evacuees away. Some efforts have been made to rebuild, but the new towns appear sterile in comparison. Cookie-cutter houses, cheaply and swiftly made. Little of the rich cultural heritage of that unique region remains. Japanese people, even now, it seems, are reluctant to purchase food, especially seafood, sourced from the Fukushima region.

Even so, residents in surrounding towns are trying hard to recover.

All of which is interesting and noteworthy from a world news perspective but what, if anything, does it have to do with Jun Nakashima?

By the time I glance up, evening has turned the glass over-looking the porch into a mirror; my face, a fogged echo. The *furin* wind chime on the porch sounds. Its cheerful, summery song now seems to announce my whereabouts. I step outside and take it down.

*   *   *

As the sky fades from violet to navy-hued darkness, I find myself peering out once again over the porch railing. The dead-end street remains quiet as ever. What few neighbors I have at this far end of the block return from work, park their cars, and disappear into their homes. A few reemerge wearing running shoes or trailing a dog on a lead, but otherwise I see nothing—no one—that could be considered unusual. No one suspicious lurking in the shadows, far as I can tell. Still, I feel on edge. Distracted. That near run-in with Dodge earlier...the more I think about it...That's the problem with having my afternoons and evenings free. Instead of wandering the cemetery, like I used to, I find myself losing that time to meaningless activities, to wonderings and rememberings. I have no friends to see, no boyfriend to chat with, and without either cooking loses much of its flavor. It can be hard to summon an appetite when you always eat alone. That said, I'm conscious of that slippery slope, one that could easily stimulate old habits. To help prevent even the imaginings of relapsing, I stick to a schedule. Regardless of whether I feel inspired or not, I prepare dinner for myself, from scratch, and eat by seven. Afterward, Clay and I play for half an hour or so, then I sink into the couch with a book. It's unchanging, but I take comfort in the routine. Finding ways to anchor myself in measured, predictable ways throughout the day helps me avoid the sort of anxiety that, in the past, would trigger impulses to search out immediate gratification—or immediate numbing. Whichever.

But this time is different. Maybe I am lonely, but I'm also nervous. Not anxious or antsy, but genuinely fearful. Without considering the decision too fully, I make a call. Not to Liam, as I normally would, but to my mom.

"Hi, Win-chime. Everything alright?" Her line reveals how little we talk outside our weekly routine calls. "Can you hear me alright? I'm in the car."

"Where you off to?"

"Your neighborhood, actually. I'm giving a special presentation at the Museum of Modern Art this evening."

"You should've told me. I'd have come."

"Actually, it's geared more towards fundraising. Nothing you'd enjoy," she says, though I expect she means it's not a talk I'd be permitted to attend. Not without a trust fund.

"Are you busy afterward?" I hear myself ask. "I, uh, want to talk to you about something."

"I can be," she responds, her surprise unveiled. "What's up?"

"I'd rather just tell you in person," I say.

"You're not pregnant, are you?"

"Mom, oh my god!"

"I had to ask."

"Well, it's not that," I say, meaning it. Is that really the first thing that comes to mind when I call out of the blue?

"Alright. Honestly, not one of these idiots knows how to use a turn signal…"

"When will you be done?" I press. "You don't have, like, a banquet afterward, do you?"

"Not this time. I planned on having—Oh, Christ Almighty, he just ran the light!"

"Planned on what?"

"This is why I never drive on this side of town. I should've made your dad chauffeur."

"Okay, well, I'll let you focus then," I say.

"Alright. See you in a bit, honey."

"Bye." I hang up, then consider what I'll do for the next however-many hours. I need to get out of the house, if only to keep myself from checking over the balcony for Dodge every five minutes. Maybe I will take a walk after all. Not around the cemetery, but in the opposite direction. I could have dinner someplace then meet Mom near the art museum.

Decision made, I bundle up, throw a book and my laptop into my old school bag, say goodbye to Clay, and head out. Flakes dance before my eyes in light flurries. They've scarcely begun to stick to the ground, but I think of Mom having to drive back to the West Side in potentially bad weather. She's a distracted driver at the best of times. Personally, I don't miss the burden of car ownership. After returning from Japan, having lived a full year without one, I never wanted to go back to driving again. Unlike most American cities and neighborhoods, designed not for people but for cars, where I live now a car-less existence is possible because everything I need is within walking distance. That, or it's deliverable.

I dart between the cars scooting along Mayfair, everyone looking in vain for parking, then dodge over to Murray Hill

Road. It's not exactly closer to my mother's location, but there's a corner coffee shop I love up ahead. I haven't stopped in since beginning my new job. Even so, the barista recognizes me, I can tell. He nods familiarly and takes my order. I choose a seat in the back, far away from the drafty front door, then set up my laptop.

The @j.nakashima.j account remains open, staring back at me. What to do? Should I wait for Shoko to track down Jun's whereabouts, or do I…? *Hell with it,* I think, and click on the photo taken in Futaba. In the comments section I type *'I hope revitalization efforts are helping the people of Fukushima to recover,'* then click enter. My post appears as the first and only comment. Whether or not this photographer knows me, and irrespective of his or her English fluency, the sentiment is genuine. I decide not to think too hard on the possible outcomes of this small action. Better to expect nothing of it, then I can't be disappointed. But who am I trying to fool? Myself? Of course, I want this to be Jun, the Jun I care about so very, very much. Of course, I want him to respond, to welcome me back into his life, to tell me he's been missing me all this time as much as I've missed him. Of course, I want this one small ripple to change everything, to change how we parted ways, to be the start of mending everything between us, fixing what went wrong.

I close my laptop because I know if I don't, I'll keep refreshing the page, willing a response. I try to read, but end up staring through the pages of my book, thinking…

By the time my mother calls, I'm considering ordering a third pot of tea. I give her my location. Minutes later she's blustering in, turning heads. Without stopping at the counter, she drifts straight over to me. Customers and staff stare. Wherever she goes, without fail, she draws attention. It must be an energy, a kind of pure, undiluted feminine confidence. She folds her wool coat over the back of the chair opposite me and sits.

"This is a nice place," she says, readjusting the bangles encircling her narrow wrists.

I ask if she wants something to drink and am surprised when she asks me for a recommendation. "Depends on what you like. I've been drinking silver needles. It's lighter and more refreshing, rather than toasty," I explain.

"Sounds fine," she says. Rather than approach the counter, however, she raises a hand to wave one of the staff over to our table. My face flushes, mortified, but the young man in the beanie doesn't seem to mind being beckoned by my mother. "We'd like a fresh pot," she explains, expecting him to remember what his patrons are drinking, I suppose. "Also, a plate of bread, and whipped butter if you have it," she asks, items not specifically detailed on the small menu, but he nods and goes off to make it happen.

"You should've gone to the counter," I mutter.

"But I was already sitting. Oh stop, Winona. I'll leave him a good tip. For crying out loud." She rummages through her bag for her lipstick and refreshes its color, no doubt wondering how she raised such a pushover. "How've you been?" she asks.

"Fine. How was the fundraiser?"

"Oh, same old." She offers nothing else, which is fine since I don't especially care what her affluent friends and colleagues are spending their money on these days, which, despite being patrons of the arts, is basically the sum of their whole existence. Or so I've been told. "So, what did you want to talk about?"

The barista brings our teapot on a laden tray: cups, saucers, and my mother's bread and butter. "Give it another minute or so," he instructs.

I smile in thanks, but he doesn't notice. I turn back to my mother. "It's about Liam."

"Oh, I hope you've spoken to him, worked this mess out somehow."

"Uh, not exactly. Have you?" I ask, though I think the answer is obvious. Then again, Liam might still call my mother without revealing the fact he has a new belle.

"I haven't heard from him since, gosh, the night of the Faculty Art Show, I think? I can't remember," she waves it off and pours herself a cup of the light brew.

I wait until she's tasted the tea before revealing, "Well, he's seeing someone else. I know that much."

My mother stops, sets her cup carefully. "Please tell me this is a joke, Winona."

I scoff. "Why would I lie?" I feel my throat tighten. I should have known she'd blame me. Willing myself not to cry, I beg, "Please...don't be mad at me." I speak each word as steadily as I can manage, but my voice quavers, just a little.

"Oh, honey. I'm not mad at you." My mother reaches across the table and lays a hand on my arm. "I'm so sorry."

Tears leak from the corners of both eyes, despite my best efforts to hold them back. My mother produces a packet of tissues from her purse, and I dab my eyes and blow my nose. The momentary respite helps me rebuild some composure. "I found out on social media. He posted pictures. Posing with her."

My mother sighs, as disappointed as any mother might be in her own son. "That's awful," she agrees. "Are you sure it's not just a misunderstanding? Liam's such a good guy—"

As she talks, I pull up the photoset on my phone, which he's taken no effort to conceal. I flip the screen around to show her, the same way Erin did for me. My mother takes the device and swipes through the images, her brows knitting together. I'm grateful she doesn't point out any of Fiona's more attractive qualities. Actually, they're a lot alike, now that I think about it, Fiona and my mom: artistic, independent, ambitious, self-actualized. Given Liam's respect and regard for my mother, it's hardly a wonder he chose someone like Fiona over me.

She hands the phone back.

"So, yeah…" I say. "Not a whole lot to misunderstand."

"Well, give it time. Maybe he'll get tired of her. You two have always been such close friends. I bet—"

"Mom, stop."

She acquiesces, takes a bite of the bread. She offers the second slice to me, but I have no appetite whatsoever. "Are you eating?" she asks.

"Yes."

"You promise?"

"Yeah. This new job is sort of helping. The work is hard—it's physically demanding, I mean—so I usually have a strong appetite."

"That's good. Are you liking it?"

"Mostly. I like the work itself. The cemetery—it was that view, walking around there, that's why I picked my apartment—and now I get to spend every day over there. I love spending that much time outside. Definitely an improvement over a stuffy classroom." I wait for some acknowledgment, but I guess it's still too soon. "The only downside is that one of the guys I work with is kinda sketchy."

"How so?"

"I thought I saw him wandering around my neighborhood earlier today." I explain my misgivings, try to give her an overview of Dodge's particular quirks, then wait for her to respond. When she doesn't, I add, "It's probably nothing. I'm probably just lonely," or feeling vulnerable, I think, "without Liam."

Again, she rests a hand on my arm, but the level of comfort I need, I don't find it there. Somehow, I feel more isolated than ever. I'm in a room with a dozen other people but I'm so, so alone. My mother, Erin, Liam, none of them come close to matching the level of connection, the solace I found in Jun. Even here, amid everything else going on, I find the strength to hate myself for losing his friendship.

My phone buzzes, rattling against the tabletop. I glance at the notification. Someone responded to my comment on the @j.nakashima.j account, the Futaba photo. My heart skips so wildly I have to catch my breath.

"Everything alright?" my mother asks.

"I'll check it later. I might have to get going soon, though. I need to feed Clay and—"

"I forgot you had the cat."

"You've never seen him, so..."

'And whose fault is that?' is, no doubt, the thought we're both having.

"I'll drive you," my mother offers.

"You don't have to."

"I won't come in. I'll just pull up and—" she waves a hand— "drive off."

Beyond the wide storefront windows, the snowfall has intensified. That, and I'm still picturing Dodge lurking near my apartment. I feel that familiar knife edge of loneliness acutely. I accept the ride. Mom leaves two twenties under the tea tray.

The drive takes all of two minutes.

"Don't drive too fast on the highway," I suggest before hopping out.

"Shoot, I forgot to ask you about Christmas."

I'm standing in the road, getting pelted by fat snowflakes, so I suggest we talk about it later.

"I'll call Thursday," she agrees.

I wave her off then hurry up the fire escape. Once the kettle's on and Clay's been fed, I unpack my laptop. The @j.nakashima.j account tab remains perpetually open on my browser now. I open the Futaba photo and there, under my comment is a response...in English.

> Win__chime: I hope revitalization efforts are helping the people of Fukushima to recover.

> j.nakashima.j: Regular citizens do a good job. The government is trying to hide how bad it really is. Radiation levels are still high in places, but authorities say otherwise. Water and soil are polluted. It will take years to recover. Also please forgive my English is not good. I used a translation app.

I reread the response several times before realizing I've been biting my hand. It's not that the words themselves carry any significant weight—any outsider would see this as a purely formal exchange between strangers—but underneath there are layers of substance.

For one thing, this photographer claims they're not fluent in English—whereas my Jun very clearly was—but that could have two meanings. Perhaps this Nakashima J— simply can't read English. Speaking and writing in a foreign language, let alone an unfamiliar alphabet, are two completely different beasts, and I wouldn't be surprised if Jun had mastered the one but not the other. The other question is why this Nakashima J— would be in Fukushima. Are they a tourist, or a journalist maybe, who took a single trip years ago, collected enough photos to keep on posting one a day ever since? I can't say for certain, but I don't think so. They write about the region as if they're there now. Or, at least, the photographer was there recently...assuming nothing was lost in the translation.

I need to respond. I type out a few versions of what I want to say, nothing too complicated, then settle on asking a question.

Win__chime: *Have you gone there to document the recovery work?*

Again, the question itself isn't especially remarkable. This is a deliberate choice. While I'm genuinely interested in the answer, whether they know anything about what's happening in Fukushima and how people plan to revive their land and waterways, the point is to keep Nakashima J— engaged in the exchange. If this is my Jun, it's the first time he's responded to any attempts at communication since I left Japan. Even if he didn't take a closer look at my profile, if it is my Jun there is no way he doesn't know @Win__chime is me. He knows my nickname, that it's a riff on Win-chan. He was the one who picked out the *furin* wind chime, the one I hang on the porch, on what I guess would be considered our second formal date.

It was in July.

Michikusa House hosted a number of other guests that summer. A photographer traveling solo; a young couple from Kitakyushu who were hiking sections of the famous Kunisaki Hantou Minemichi Long Trail; another couple who preferred the Buddhist iconography and various folk rituals on the Kunisaki peninsula. I also recall a trio of college students, three friends who stayed for four weeks over their summer break to work on the farm. There were even foreign tourists, a cyclist from Germany, and a writer of undetermined origin who left his room only at mealtimes and spoke to no one. It was around that time that Shoko, despite the added burden, suggested Jun and I do some sightseeing, too. She said something along the lines of not wanting to disappoint my mother by keeping me trapped on the farm. We made the polite protestations dictated by common courtesy, but inside I was eager, impatient even, to escape the rural perimeter that had described the last seven months. Especially if it meant an entire work-free day with Jun as my only companion.

"Why not take her to one of the summer festivals," Shoko suggested in English one afternoon while we were setting salted *ume* plums out to dry, a process that tenderizes the flesh and softens the skins, improving the texture. "So many to choose from, but the seaside Ocean Fire Festival in Beppu might be best. Not too far, but very, very good. Dancing, music, food vendors selling local specialties; yes, you should go."

And so, it was decided. On the day of the festival, Hanada-san drove us in the little green keitora pickup to Tateishi Station, the same station with the red vending machine where he'd collected me all those months ago. From there, the train ride took us through several agrarian towns where other passengers, many dressed in yukata, boarded the train destined for Beppu. I, on the other hand, wore nothing quite so special, just my usual dark jeans, slip-on tennis shoes, and a navy silk V-neck care of my mother's forced shopping spree. It felt light and airy, not too revealing but accommodating for Japan's hot, humid summers. From our comfortable seats on the train, I spied farmers in their picturesque fields sweating under the midday sun. In late July, waves of high heat, known as *doyo*, blaze day after day, as unrelenting as the cicadas' roar. Despite the oppressive heat, a childlike grin appeared on Jun's face, remembering, perhaps, a fond memory from childhood that began on a day much like this one.

"What is it?" I asked.

He rested his arm over the seat back, not on me but still close, protective. Three girls in yukata, sitting across from us, whispered behind their hands. "It's going to be a good day," he said.

Beppu, from afar, appeared to be smoldering. Steam rose in great billowing clouds over the city thanks to the many natural hot springs. A sign at the station exit informed us there are over two-thousand hot spring sources in Beppu that release an impressive eighty-thousand-something liters of water every minute. The abundance of these natural hot springs have made Beppu one the most popular *onsen* resort towns in Asia. Various buses leave from the station throughout the day and travel directly to a collection of the most impressive *onsen*, called Jigoku Meguri, or Hell Tour.

No more reading was accomplished, however, because the buoyant music and clamor of the festivities drew us into the sunlight. A beer garden immediately outside the station sold alcohol and snacks, but we bypassed those stands knowing we had a full day and night of sampling ahead of us. Jun led the way, pointing out stalls, some selling Japanese specialties like *karaage* fried chicken, and American ones selling cotton candy and caramel apples. We stopped long enough to watch a duck race, and Jun obligingly took a photo of me with one of the feathery contestants resting in my arms. After that, an energetic traditional group dance called *yosakoi* caught my attention. Jun seemed perfectly happy standing back, watching me marvel at the unfamiliar sights and enormous sounds: taiko drummers, rock music, hula dancing, a haunted house set in an actual temple.

After an hour or two, we took a break from the crowds to wander through quieter residential and shopping streets. I'd had no time to play tourist, so every tiny alley and storefront plucked at my attention. I wanted to investigate each one, sample food from every restaurant smaller than my parents' garage, ask Jun to read every random bit of signage to help anchor me in the culture, the ebb and flow of the neighborhood. We discovered so many tiny doors and twisting staircases leading to invisible upper levels. With each turn around a corner, tantalizing new sights and smells emerged. Honestly, I preferred this adventure through the rambling mishmash of incongruent streets that somehow fit together in a perfectly mesmerizing whole, to the bustling excitement of the summer festival.

"Why on earth would you ever want to leave a place like this?" I asked Jun, stopping to admire the potted plants outside a home older than my country's Constitution. "It's incredible."

"Whatever you grow up knowing, eventually it seems boring. That's what I think."

"Except every city in Japan, each region has its own kind of flavor. Where I'm from, every city and suburb is more or less a replica of all the others."

"Huh?"

"I meant, there's nothing much to differentiate between them. Sometimes you get a sense of, I don't know, a few remnants of authenticity, or history, but mostly everything we've created is uniform. Which seems unimaginable to me considering that America is such a melting pot. You'd think we would have the most unusual, the most experimental, diverse human-built environments on the planet, but..."

"But?"

"But that's not the case. Most of what's built there these days looks about as eye-catching as a cardboard box."

We turned down a covered shopping street, its storefronts more shuttered than not. "Japan is becoming that way, too, in some places," Jun said. "It's cheaper than keeping the old buildings or designing different ones every time a new store or apartment complex opens. Always about money...and earthquake preparedness," Jun said, grinning.

"I don't get it, though. If I lived in this area, I'd much rather shop in this arcade than drive to some big-box store."

Jun wrapped an arm around my shoulder. "Don't get so upset, Win-chan. You shouldn't be sad about everything all the time. The world is what it is."

"That's a poor excuse for not trying to make things better."

"Sure, always try to do better, but focus on improving only your small piece of a very big puzzle, not the whole thing all at once."

"Thank you, sage teacher, for your words of wisdom."

"I think you mean *sensei.*"

"You've graduated from *senpai*? When did that happen?" I didn't want to sink into a sulky mood, not on an idyllic day like this, lost in a foreign city with a man I loved, with, let's be honest, hardly a care in the world. I should have been thrilled, but the grey wave of generalized worry and disappointment threatened to overwhelm me anyway.

"Hey, I have an idea that will cheer you up," he said, sensing the shift and kissing my temple warmly.

"I'm really turned around."

Jun pulled out his phone, a device I had forgotten we could use again; I'd grown so used to life without one. It took less than a minute of Jun poking around on the screen to locate a serviceable destination. We did not, however, return to the main festival corridor. Instead, we ended up at the bus depot on the backside of the train station. He bought two round-trip, open return bus tickets, then we boarded the Noguchibaru/ Asia Pacific University Line for Kannawa. The higher it ushered us into the mountains, the less compact the streets became, offering space for palms as tall as houses to thrive alongside lush, verdant greenery. Twenty minutes later we disembarked in the foothills outside a traditional Japanese building, white plaster with ornate blue-grey roof tiles. Its small parking lot accommodated only three cars but seven very large billboards, all unreadable to me. Any hint of what the building contained was further concealed by a stone wall and dense shrubbery bordering the property.

"Can you tell me what we're doing yet?" I asked.

"You'll see," he said, repeating the same line he'd used repeatedly on the bus.

At the ticket desk inside, Jun paid for two tickets at 2,000 yen each, the equivalent of about twenty bucks per person. We didn't linger in the building to view the various exhibits. Instead, we pushed straight to the back, out into brilliant daylight. I actually gasped when I saw it, the majestic garden with the pale turquoise hot spring at its center, sending clouds of steam billowing toward the sky. The trees reached so high they blocked out all images of the streets and modern conveniences beyond, transporting visitors into a time long since passed. A stone path lined by rhododendron bushes in full bloom encircled the hot spring, encouraging guests to wander deeper into the lush, leafy garden. Innumerable lichens, mosses, and ferns had made this oasis their refuge and thanks to the steam, the humid air, each one felt soft and supple with moisture. Thanks to the popularity of the summer festival, we competed with few tourists for open viewing space.

"I can't believe I didn't think to bring a camera," I moaned, and not for the first time that day.

"Here, use mine," Jun suggested. "I'll send them to you."

"You don't mind?"

"I wouldn't offer if I did."

"You don't keep scandalous photos of past lovers on here, do you?"

He handed me his phone. "Not anyplace you could find," he said, with that cockeyed grin of his.

The first and only photos I took during my time in Japan were of nothing more or less spectacular than living, breathing water. The steaming hot springs of Beppu, their colors ranging from the purest aquamarine to rust orange to bubbling, grey-ish mud, were unlike anything I'd seen before, places seemingly better suited to storybooks and fairy tales.

"You like this more than the festival," Jun said, observing the phone screen over my shoulder.

"Maybe," I agreed.

"Then I've got one more thing to show you."

"How do you know so much about this city?"

"I can read the signs."

After a slow, luxurious circuit around the more popular hot springs, we returned to the bus stop and boarded the same APU circuit line. After several minutes, however, I realized we were not heading in the direction of town. "I think we boarded the wrong bus," I whispered to Jun. "Should we get off at the next stop?"

"Trust me," he said. "We're going the right way."

Soon, all signs of human settlement vanished, giving way to dense forest on both sides. Eventually, these too disappeared, leaving only flat mountaintop prairie.

"This is it," Jun said, and we exited to what, to me, appeared to be an uninhabited, middle of nowhere, roadside. Leading off the main thoroughfare, however, was a narrow lane lined with signage, easy to spot in bright blue and yellow, but naturally I couldn't read a word printed on it. We were the only ones to disembark at this stop, so I felt strangely wary of venturing too far. That, and being entirely at the mercy of Jun and his whims felt both exciting and unnerving.

"This way," he said.

Ahead stood boxy buildings and tall radio antennas. "Jun… are you sure this is the right place?"

"Win-chan! Do. You. Trust. Me?" he asked, feigning exasperation.

"At least there's vending machines," I murmured, as we passed a set of three tucked under a thicket of scrubby pines at the roadside. Despite my reservations, however, the scenery was quite lovely. Red and pink azaleas, interspersed with leafy ferns and tiny white blossoms, lined the quiet roadway. Long green grasses leaned carelessly in every direction. Jun stopped to buy a bottle of water from the vending machine, then chugged half in one go, offering the remainder to me. After I had emptied the bottle, we carried on, passing between two of the buildings each with its own red antenna standing sentry, only to arrive at a parking lot. "Jun, what the hell?" I actually laughed, albeit nervously.

Behind me, hands on my shoulders, Jun pushed me forward. "A little further."

We crossed the small lot, and then I saw it; green hills rolling over each other all the way down to the city of Beppu, its arms reaching wide to hug the aquamarine bay.

"That's Mount Takasaki over there on the right," he said. "And that's Asia Pacific University on the left—see it, down there—and way out that way is Shikoku Island."

"Jun, why'd you scare me like that?"

"How did I scare you?" he asked, his face a shipwreck. "Win, what's wrong. Don't cry. Hey."

"I don't know. It's scary, sometimes, to be in a place with no one around you can talk to if you need help."

Jun bundled me into his arms and once again I felt safe. I wiped my eyes, laughing. "Oh my god, I'm such a baby."

He gave me a solid squeeze then turned me around to face the open expanse of the bay.

"Do you like it?" he asked.

"Mm."

"What are you thinking?"

"What it would be like to be a bay. To do so much good, support so much life."

Jun rested his chin on top of my head. "*Aishiteru.*"

"Hm?"

"That's what I'm thinking."

"What's that mean?"

"It means...I have another idea for making you smile."

"Oh really? Not another surprise, I hope. Please spare me."

"A souvenir. To remember."

"This is where we should've watched the fireworks from," I said, as Jun took my hand and we headed back to the bus stop.

"You will get tired before the fireworks."

"Hey!"

"Too much fun for one day."

"Can we at least get something to eat?"

At some point on the bus ride back into town I fell asleep. Jun bought me a shaved ice outside the station, then told me to wait on a nearby bench while he ran inside a shop for something. He returned after a few minutes holding a wrapped box. "Open when you get home," he said, handing it to me.

"Like, home-home?"

"Later." He held a hand out to me, pulling me back onto my feet.

"I'm tired," I admitted.

"I told you."

"Besides, I'd rather eat your cooking," I admitted. "Festival food hardly compares."

"Alright. Let's get you back," he said.

"Fireworks another time."

"It's a date," he promised.

Jun didn't keep that promise, but I kept mine. I didn't open the box he'd given me until Christmas. Back in my old room in my parents' house, out of sight, I peeled back the gift wrapping and carefully opened the lid. Inside, packed neatly against white tissue paper, I found a *furin*, a glass wind chime.

CHAPTER 13

At first, I think it's the silence that wakes me, the world growing quiet, blanketed by white. With eyes half open, I notice the streetlight in front of my apartment illuminating each flake as it falls, slowly. Still dark out. I check the time: 4:45. The comforting thought of another thirty minutes under the duvet lulls me back toward sleep until I hear my phone vibrating. Squinting at its irritating brightness, I notice there's a call coming in. From Curtis. Of course: it's snowing.

I answer. "Hello?"

"Rise 'n' shine, chucklehead. Time to plow your first snow."

"Alright," I say, sounding garbled even to myself.

"See ya at half past."

How is he so awake right now? "Five?"

"Yes, five. Half past five. It'll take longer than ya think, and I gotta show ya the ropes, so get movin'."

"Alright," I say again, and hang up. With effort, I force myself to sit upright. Clay lays coiled like a conch shell at the bottom of the bed. He doesn't stir, even when I rise. One good thing about this job is that I don't have to shower beforehand or put on makeup to look presentable. Nor do I have to commute. I can leave two minutes before my shift starts and still arrive on time. I put oatmeal in the rice cooker, then start my day off with some quick stretches while breakfast heats up. Afterwards, I have a cup of strong tea and well-spiced porridge, pack my lunch, then bundle myself into my warmest layers. By then, Clay has risen to see me off. "See you this afternoon," I promise.

My fire escape proves less treacherous than expected; not icy, only snow-covered, like stepping on freshly fluffed pillows. On solid ground, I dust off my gloves and head in the direction of the cemetery's north gate. It's still early enough that the sidewalk is lit only by streetlamps and my boots are the first to compress the freshly fallen snow on these quiet back streets. The plows haven't reached us yet and for now even the overwintering birds and the squirrels remain tucked snuggly in their nests.

Curtis meets me at the gate, the truck parked and running behind him. "You'll be down a man today," he says.

"Oh. Is Kyrone making up a class?" I ask, jumping into the truck and slamming the door behind me.

"Nope. Dodge has moved on to bigger 'n' better things."

"Oh," I say, not fully comprehending.

"Had to let him go," Curtis explains, maneuvering the vehicle slowly on the fresh snow toward the winter equipment shed. "You'd hear about it soon enough. No point beating around the bush. Not like it was any big secret what a dumb, bullheaded little shit he was."

I don't disagree but am surprised by the severity of the language. He parks and we climb out. A middle-aged man I don't recognize waves from the driver's seat of a snowplow as he maneuvers it from its parking place out onto the winding cemetery road. Curtis waves back and then opens the shed.

"Shovels're there. Salt's there," he says, pointing. "Without a license, ya can't operate the plow, so yer on sidewalk and staircase duty. Each of the major chapels and what-have-you's need to be cleared," he says, and loads me plus the gear into a truck. Although I don't own a car, I can drive and keep my license up to date, so I drive myself to the south gate, starting with the community mausoleum. While I work, shoveling paths and spreading chunky salt crystals, my mind repeatedly wanders to Dodge. Just as well he's gone. Not only was he a pain to work with, if you can call what he did working, but his attitude, morals, and opinions left a lot to be desired. A man of questionable character, no doubt about that. At least now I won't have to worry about him creeping around my neighborhood.

Curtis was right, it takes me a full three hours—well past when the cemetery opens at 7:30—to finish clearing the major chapels and monuments, but I still have other sites to attend to, and even more snow has accumulated. I meet Kyrone at the north gate and drive the both of us back around to check and make sure the myriad stone steps and walkways aren't harboring rogue ice sheets.

"You heard about Dodge?" I ask, grateful for the warm air blowing from the vents, warming my fingers and melting ice from my eyelashes.

"What happened?"

"Curtis fired him."

"It's about time," he says. "Wonder where he'll end up."

"Prison, if I had to guess," I say.

Kyrone nods. "One freaky ass dude."

"I saw him wandering around my neighborhood the other day. Was that just yesterday?" *Feels like a long time since then.*

"For real?"

"Yep."

"What the hell?"

"That's about what I thought."

"Can't think of any good reason he'd be over there."

"Me either," I agree. "Had me kinda spooked last night."

"Yeah, that's exactly what it is. Dude gives off a bad vibe, you know what I'm saying? Like bad BO."

I park at the roundabout behind the main presidential monument. We clamor back out into the snow, bags of salt and shovels in hand, and climb the sandstone steps to the entrance. The elderly greeter welcomes us inside as we wipe our feet on the mat. Kyrone makes polite small talk, mainly about changes in the weather. After thawing out for another minute, we make our way, single file, up many flights of stairs to the upper balcony. On a clear day, you can see all the way to Downtown Cleveland and the shores of Lake Erie. I've even been able to pick out my apartment once or twice. Today, though, snow and thickly padded cloud cover prevents a view beyond the cemetery's walled perimeter.

"Wonder if we'll see him around again," I say, trying to sound casual.

"Nah. Dude can't drive, right? How'd he even get his ass back over here?"

"Good point," I agree, feeling the knotted fist in my stomach loosen. Twenty-four hours of held tension decompresses, like a dammed river finally releasing its flow, and I feel fractionally better.

The rest of the day progresses uneventfully as we work to keep pace with the snowfall, but otherwise our landscaping duties are essentially done for the season unless a branch falls. No more planting or trimming or pruning until March. Kyrone, at one point, mentions he might take a break from the work entirely until then. He's saved up a good bit and could use the time to put toward his certification.

Curtis pulls up alongside us, plow on the front end lifted. The roads circumnavigating the cemetery are clear now so he must be on his way back to the garage. He leans from the open driver's side window and waves us over. "Win, you can shove out early. See ya tomorrow. Usual time," he says, then drives off.

"I'll drop you at the gate," Kyrone offers.

"I don't mind walking."

"I gotta use the facilities anyway. Come on," he insists. This time, he drives. We whip back around to the north end of the cemetery, the exit closest to my place, and say our goodbyes.

"You're not in tomorrow, right?" I ask, as we exit the cab.

"Nah. Maybe they'll put you on a new team," he muses, which makes sense. Otherwise, without Dodge, I'd be working solo. Not that I'd mind the change in company.

"Guess they'll have to, if you're not coming back."

"We'll see," Kyrone wavers. "Catch you later."

"*Otsukaresama desu*," I say, before I can stop myself.

"What?"

"Nothing!" I wave, then turn left out the gate. At the same moment a male voice behind me says, "Hey." I turn and see Dodge approaching, stumbling up the sidewalk, exactly as if he's been waiting for me. He's wearing a camo hunting jacket, a neon knit cap, and the same heavy boots he wore to work every day. "Gotta bone to pick with you," he says, the words a slurred mudslide. Doesn't take a genius to tell he's been drinking.

I'm so stunned, I don't immediately process the fact I might be in real danger. I've never confronted men like Dodge before, not like this, not when they're angry and drunk and their target is me. Instead, my first and only thought, strangely, is of his use of such a ridiculous cliche.

"You lost me my job, bitch," he says. "I'm a good worker, never get in any trouble. Then alluva sudden, you come along and then, you know, alluva sudden I'm gettin' bitched out by Curtis day in, day out."

I ignore what he's saying. It's irrelevant. What I watch—closely—are his hands, twisting and squirming inside the deep pockets of his hunting jacket.

"You think you're so smart, but you're an ugly cunt, you know that right? I wouldn't fuck you with a ten-foot pole."

"Dodge. Whatcha doing here, man?" Kyrone says, more conversational than I could've managed under the circumstances.

"This bitch lost me my job, man," Dodge says, his voice tremulous, his movements unsteady. "Came back to teach her a lesson." From his pocket he pulls a knife; when he presses a button, the long blade swings open with a snap.

"Whoa, man. Hold up," Kyrone says, standing his ground but raising both his hands. "Let's just figure out what's going on, alright?"

"I know what the fuck's going on, you piece of shit. You're as bad as she is. Both of you, y'all make me sick."

I can't tell if my mind's racing or slowing down. I can't think or react. I should run, right? But what about Kyrone? Could we outrun Dodge together? There's a police station less than a hundred yards away, right past the corner where I turn towards home. Maybe I should scream. Would they hear me from here if I did?

"Goddammit," I hear someone else say. Another male voice. This time it's Curtis. "Put it away, Dodge. For God's sake, yer a grown-ass man," he says. "Waving that thing around, ya think you'll solve anything that way? Use yer words, boy, and yer brain. You got one, don't'cha? Christ Almighty."

"Fuck you, old man!" Dodge shouts at his uncle, just as a police cruiser pulls to a stop across the street.

"Don't try to run," Curtis tells Dodge automatically, who appears ready to do just that. "You'll only make it worse."

Dodge hesitates, wavering and unsteady on his feet, as if trying to make up his mind. Curtis puts out a hand for the knife. Another moment, pregnant with possibilities—few with happy endings—and Dodge, to my amazement, hands it over. I'm so relieved I feel sick. Meanwhile, the officer exits his car, the tallest, burliest Black man I've ever seen, like a former heavyweight champion. He holds up a hand to stop traffic easily, then crosses the road.

"Hey there, Curtis," he says. "Haven't seen you in a minute. It's usually Lloyd we get calls from 'round here, middle of the night."

"Hey, Gabe," says Curtis. "Thanks for comin' over."

"You got a problem, I take it?" Officer Gabe says, hand on his holster, eyes darting between Dodge and Curtis. A minute later, backup arrives from the station at the end of the block. I don't remember anything else, the questions they asked, how long it took, only that they cuffed Dodge and took him away.

Next thing I know, the cops have cleared out and me, Curtis, and Kyrone are sitting in the office break room sipping some god-awful coffee. The taste—and texture, as a matter of fact—reminds me of dirt, grainy and bitter, but the liquid heat revives me somewhat.

"Sorry 'bout that," Curtis says, rising to grab a refill. "We'll get a restraining order, whatever we gotta do. That little prick won't be back. You hear me, Win? He won't bother you again."

It must've come out during questioning that I'd seen him in the neighborhood. "Helluva day." Curtis drops back into his chair.

"You doing okay?" Kyrone asks me.

"I think so," I lie. I've never felt so shaken in my life. I can hardly grip the mug. The muscles all along my back and arms keep spasming; I can't make it stop.

"Good thing you were there," Curtis says to Kyrone. "I'd hate to think what that sonuvabitch would'a done."

"I was heading for the bathroom when Win was leaving. I saw Dodge cross in front of the gate, like he was following her. Knew that couldn't be a good sign so I ran back to the truck and radioed you," Kyrone tells Curtis, likely repeating the sequence of events for the third or fifth time by now. "Then I went right over to see what was up. The real miracle is I didn't piss myself in the meanwhile."

Curtis snorts, but I'm not ready to laugh.

"You must've called the cops—"

"While driving over, yeah," Curtis confirms. "It's usually Lloyd, our night watchman, who has to give 'em a ring, but I've had my share of whackos come through over the years. When you said Dodge wandered back over, I just assumed the worst. I wouldn't trust that dipstick with a tape measure." Curtis shakes his head. "His mom'll be thrilled, I can tell ya that much." The boss's eyes shift to me. "How 'bout I drive you home," he suggests.

"I live...right there," I protest weakly.

"Yeah, but ya don't look so hot right now, kiddo. Gotta make sure ya get in okay. You good?" he asks Kyrone.

"I'm good," he confirms.

"Alright," Curtis says, as if that settles it. He rises and motions me to follow. On autopilot, I trail him to his truck. "You got somebody at home? Anybody you wanna call?"

My brain clunks like rusted gears, trying to piece together a coherent thought. It comes up with Liam—I should call…but, no. He's not…he's with…"I think I'll call my mom," I say.

"Good idea."

Curtis doesn't invite himself into my apartment. Instead, he suggests we wait in his truck until my mother arrives.

"It'll be an hour till she gets here," I tell him.

"That's alright," he assures me, and I don't protest. He switches on a country station, which normally I wouldn't prefer, but today the mellow vocals and acoustic strings soothe my frayed nerves.

"How do you think he got here?" I ask. My mind's reliving the event, like a tape rewinding itself, over and over. Every time it replays, I imagine all the ways it could've gone differently, gone very, very wrong. If Kyrone hadn't been there; if he'd gone straight to the bathroom instead; if he hadn't thought to call Curtis; if Curtis hadn't answered; if anything any of us had said set Dodge into a tailspin; if, instead of handing over the knife, he'd lunged.

"Probably borrowed a friend's car," Curtis replies to the question I'd already forgotten I'd asked. "Might be good to take some time off."

I don't know what to say. I've barely started this job.

"Winter's our slow season," he adds, as if I won't be missed.

How much time does he mean? I'm hourly—if I don't work, earn the wages, I can't afford to stay in my apartment. I can't afford to fail at this job after less than a month. I won't let Dodge, of all people, take this away from me. "I'm fine."

"Up to you."

"I need the hours," I say, and he nods, understanding.

When my mother appears, stepping out in a wool coat the color of milk tea offset by a navy cashmere scarf, Curtis nods to me. We meet her on the sidewalk. Curtis explains what happened while I stand silent, staring into the gutter. The two of them chat briefly. I try not to listen, a child standing between two adults in conversation. My mother thanks my boss. He leaves and the two of us make our way inside. She's never seen my apartment. I chose it alone and, with Liam's help, moved myself in.

Over Clay's crying—he expected me home hours ago—I register my mother taking in the single room, but I'm too numb to care about her initial impressions. I pry open a can of wet food for Clay and tip the contents into his bowl.

"I see what you mean. About the view," she says amicably.

I need something to do with my hands and decide to make tea. "Did you ever drink *kamairicha*?" I ask. "While you were in Japan?"

"Hm?"

"It's produced in Miyazaki Prefecture, right next door to Oita and Kumamoto."

"Oh. I...don't recall."

"It's a unique preparation for green tea," I say, blabbering, aimless. Anything to talk about, other than— "It's pan roasted, rather than steamed or fermented. Shoko sent it to me."

"Win, I think you should move back in with us," my mother says.

"I'm not...going to do that."

She sighs. "For god's sake, Win. After what happened today? This neighborhood—"

"I can't live with you forever."

She has no response to that.

"I'm doing a job I like. I like living here. I can walk everywhere. My work is two minutes away and, apart from today, it's actually really...I don't know, peaceful. Can't you just be on my side, for once?"

"When am I not?" she demands, exasperated.

It's been a terrible enough day as it is. I don't want to fight. I carry the tea things over to the small table. She takes a seat. I pour. We sip. Clay appears, licking his lips.

"Friendly cat."

"He didn't used to be. When I took him in, I'd hardly see him. But he feels safe here now. We're good buddies." Clay investigates my mother's bag, then retreats to the bed to clean himself.

"Liam doesn't want him?"

"He didn't want Clay from the start. That's how he ended up with me. And I don't want to talk about Liam."

"I haven't spoken to him either," my mother offers. "I do wish you two would make up."

I pour another round.

"Where did you get all these plants?"

I shrug. "Adopted them."

"Well...now I know what to get you for Christmas."

"Another cactus?"

"And a taser."

"He's not coming back," I say. Whether I mean Liam or Dodge, it doesn't seem to matter.

"Your boss seems like a good guy."

"I like him. He knows a lot about plants. This job has been really good…for me. It reminds me, sometimes, of being in Japan," I say. *Of being happy.*

Her phone buzzes. She fishes around in her bag until she finds it. "It's Dad," she says, then answers it. They talk for a few minutes, my mother reassuring, giving only the most superficial details. "An incident at work," she explains, levelly. "Everything's fine. We're having tea, then I'll be home." When she hangs up, she says, "So, I forgot yesterday, to ask you about Christmas. Dad can drive if you want to come. We'll figure out a time."

"Yeah. Thanks. That sounds good."

"You could make that pie again if you have time. That one you brought over for Thanksgiving." She stands, picks her bag off the floor. "Or not. I know you're busy."

I don't know about busy, but at least it feels like I've done something by the end of the day.

As she's slipping on her coat and boots, she says, "I'm sorry if it felt like I didn't take your worries seriously yesterday. I didn't realize—If I'd known there was a real threat—"

"I know, Mom. It's fine. It all happened so fast…I wasn't really expecting anything to happen." But that's not true, and we both know it. It's the reason I called her, wanting to meet up: my gut instinct warned me that I was in danger, but both of us, both Mom and me, we ignored it. Still, it's not like this was the first time either of us pressed the "ignore" button when my body was screaming that my life was in jeopardy.

"Next time, maybe in the spring, you can show us around over there," she says, glancing out the window in the direction of the cemetery gardens. "Bye, honey. Glad you're okay."

"I'm fine," I assure her. "Be careful on the stairs."

From the porch, I watch her leave, then scan the road and sidewalks for Dodge. Nothing. No one. I can't tell whether the numbness I feel is the first sign of calm or exhaustion in its purest form. The fact I find myself, hours later, still clad in my work clothes, sprawled on the bed, lends itself in support of the latter. I wake only long enough to undress and crawl under the covers. I don't wake again until well past dawn.

CHAPTER 14

I call in sick. Curtis doesn't push me for an excuse. "I'll be in tomorrow," I promise. I half expect him to update me on the Dodge situation—whether he spent the night in a cell, behind bars, or is on the lam—but he doesn't. When I hang up, I realize I have an open day ahead of me, free of any plans. I begin with laundry and do two loads, carrying baskets down the fire escape and into the basement. Clay helps me sort socks, shows me which drawer to put them in, and generally occupies each space I need to complete any of my tasks. I give up on folding after he rolls over a set of black t-shirts, leaving a hairy mess on the clean fabric.

"Alright, you win. Let's go out." I throw on some extra layers and fit Clay into his harness. "Do you even like snow?" I ask, as I take him under one arm and descend the stairs. The day arrived bright and crisp. The snow, still fluffy, mounds every surface in gleaming white. I set Clay into it, up to his shoulders. No doubt he's seen snow before; he spent enough time outdoors at the house of his former owner, but he seems momentarily stunned. "Well?"

Clay paws the snow and a small clump collapses. This, he decides, is great fun, and continues to dig, creating an ever-widening circumference. When a neighbor exits her home, he completely ignores her, doesn't even react when she starts her car and drives off. He is transfixed by the simplest pleasure of the season. When I was little, I used to play like this in the snow, usually with a neighbor or two who lived on our cul-de-sac. Back then, we must have looked like astronauts, padded heavily in water-resistant nylon and neon snow pants, the puff balls on our hats bouncing as we ran across each other's yards. We used to hollow out forts in the snow piles along the driveways, mounds as high as our chests from shoveling a season's worth of accumulation. Back then, I never felt the cold. We could stay out for hours, our cheeks and noses bright red, ice on our gloves, and still beg to play longer. I don't remember what we played at, what games we invented—heck, I don't even remember where those kids ended up after middle school. We grew up and, as expected, went our separate ways. By the time I met Liam I didn't play in the snow anymore. Then, as my body mass diminished, as if reversing the process of growth, I felt the cold more acutely. I spent more and more time in front of artificial heating sources, a requirement to regulate my body temperature. Even now, I sense the cold underneath my boots. It knows how to creep in through the narrowest cracks, where scarf and neck meet, under the cuffs at my wrists. What was the turning point, I wonder, where snow was no longer a friend, but a foe, a chore, a hassle?

What a sullen mess I've become, I think, savagely. I need to correct my attitude before I sink into a miserable rut, brooding over an unalterable past and the men who transformed it—Liam, Dodge, Jun—for better or worse. What to do? My mind shifts to the only woman I know who doesn't amplify my inferiority complexes with pointed personal critiques.

'You free?' I type, and I hit send.

Erin's reply comes back almost at once. A single thumbs up.

'Can we do something fun?'

'Wanna go sledding?'

I actually laugh and send her a double thumbs-up in return.

'Pick u up in 1 hr, k?'

Perfect. That'll give Clay enough time to exhaust himself from his outdoor adventure and me to finish folding laundry. I send another thumbs up, then add, *'I don't have a sled.'*

'No prob,' she says. *'We got extra.'*

She's not exaggerating. A cavalcade of college undergraduates, primarily from the Psychology Department, gather at the top of a steeply sloping hill in a park not far from campus. It's the first time I've seen Erin wearing anything other than Converse. Her rainbow-striped moon boots—red on the toe, yellow at the ankle, then jade and aquamarine—rise to calf height and award her dozens of complements from the youngest sledders, several of whom rival her in both weight and stature. Erin whizzes down the hill as if she's weightless, her orange sled intermingling with the other large plastic petals, each one the color of midsummer flowers. After my fifth run, and after scrambling back up the hill equally as many times, I'm sweating and have to remove my hat and gloves. So, this is how we managed to stay out for hours as children. Playing is hard work!

"Hey, I'll race you," Erin says, and side by side we mount our sleds. She counts down and we push off, passing a boy who leans too far forward and tumbles off his sled and rolls the rest of the way down with aggressive determination. Erin and I level out at the bottom simultaneously, but her sled keeps going, practically skimming over the snow's surface. "I win!" she shouts, gathering her sled under one arm and running back to the starting line. Her ebullient energy, the swell of buoyant cheerfulness holding the entire sledding party in its embrace, has, I realize, lifted my mood considerably. When I reach the top of the hill, I feel my phone buzzing in my pocket, nonstop. No one ever calls me. Thinking it might be Curtis with an update on Dodge, I'm stunned to see not my boss but Liam's name broadcast across the screen. I consider whether to answer, but only briefly.

"Hello?" I say.

"Win, where are you? It's really loud. Are you at the mall?"

I step aside, away from people shouting with laughter. "When have I ever spent time at a mall? I'm out sledding...with a friend."

"Sledding? Like, down a hill?" he asks, but I know what he's really wondering: *What friend? You never had any other friends.*

"What do you want, Liam?"

"Well...you've probably seen the news, about me and Fiona."

"Yeah." *So? Did you call to gloat? Go ahead, rub it in my face.*

"I wanted you to know..." he hesitates, and my heart leaps ahead two or three beats. *She's pregnant, isn't she. That's what he's going to say.* "The thing is...okay, here it is, I'm just going to say it: I proposed to her, and she said yes."

My insides plummet six stories. "Are you kidding me?" is the first thing that trickles between my parted, wind-chapped lips.

"I just wanted you to know before we, you know, make the official announcement."

"Wow," I say. "That didn't take long."

"I'm sure it must be kind of a shock."

"You think?" *We were together seven years; we've been friends for over a decade.* "After less than a month of dating another woman, you're getting engaged."

"Look…I hope you and I can still be friends."

"Uh…really? I wouldn't count on it."

"What can I say?" he pleads, but the act isn't convincing.

I think you've said plenty, I think, sensing a frightening, unstoppable urge to fight back, to fling hurt, to wound as deeply as I've just been wounded. "Liam, I cheated on you," I say. "When I was in Japan. Actually, no, I fell in love with someone else. I came home wishing I was still with him." *I did it out of hunger, I think. I was starving for connection.*

Liam scoffs. "Well, that explains a lot. Jesus. I knew it. It was that guy on the phone, wasn't it?" He utters a few choice expletives.

"Yeah. It was," I confirm. "Now you know."

"Great, well…good luck, Win," he says. We don't even say goodbye.

I feel sick and have to sit down. I manage to find a bench. Eventually Erin appears.

"Win, you okay? What's wrong?"

"Liam just called."

"Ugh. You need to stop talking to him. He always does this to you, making you miserable."

"He's engaged," I say. "To her."

Erin's eyes widen comically above the wrap of her knit scarf. I lean forward, covering my face with my hands. She sits beside me, wrapping an arm around my back. Her head rests comfortingly against my shoulder.

"You wanna go home?" she asks, and I nod. I can't participate in this communal display of joy or find fun in playfulness anymore. She tells her friends we're leaving then loads our sleds into her trunk. On the drive home, I recount the events of the past two days, my various run-ins with Dodge, and the reeling aftermath I've been suffering since.

"It's been a pretty shitty week," I conclude.

"Well, the good news is it really couldn't get much worse. Not unless someone dies," she says, though the sentiment doesn't feel especially comforting. "What're you gonna do?"

"About what?"

"Can you still work there, after what happened?"

"Yeah. It's fine. Plus, I don't have a car, so..."

"That is a limiting factor," she agrees. After a bit, she adds, "I'm sorry."

"Not your fault."

"Not yours either. Promise me you won't beat yourself up over it."

"That's a weird thing to say."

"Just promise. It's in our nature, as women, to blame ourselves for things that happen. It's conditioning, you know?"

"Okay."

After a long pause, she asks, "You want me to stay over?"

I consider the offer, the options, the implications, then agree.

"Let's swing past my place then," she says.

I've never seen Erin's apartment and don't know what to expect, either clinically sterile or a dumpster fire would be my guess. Oddly, though, her place falls comfortably between the two extremes. Borderline hippie with a dash of Victorian-era flair. We enter through a small, makeshift kitchen that opens directly onto the living room. The walls are painted a tiger lily orange with cream accents. Tall ceilings, built-in bookcases, a no-longer-functional fireplace, and an actual chandelier are testament to the building's age and character. A faded set of Persian rugs cover most of the narrow wood floorboards. An antique couch that must've been reupholstered—red velvet with gold trim, wooden claw feet—feels, bizarrely, perfectly at home in this century-old apartment. A record player graces an oriental cabinet in one corner. The place isn't clean, but what messes there are appear well-contained. Used dishes clutter together in the sink. Unalphabetized DVD cases occupy several rows of bookshelves.

"Do you live with a roommate?" I ask, thinking not a single item in the space makes me think of Erin.

"Yeah. Devin. We met freshman year, at Allies," she explains, diving through a beaded curtain that separates the living room from the only bedroom, outfitted with two twin beds with matching brass frames.

"That's gotta be awkward," I say, with a nod to the shared sleeping arrangements.

"Not really," she says. "Devin spends most nights with his boyfriend, whenever he doesn't have class the next day."

Erin rummages through a tall wooden dresser, pulling out a few items of clothing that she stuffs into a canvas tote. Next, she disappears into the bathroom at the back of the apartment. "Alright, let's go," she says, fishing a packet of namkeen snacks from the cupboard on our way out.

Back at my place, we take turns playing with Clay, order takeout, then lounge on my bed watching Japanese anime, a genre I have never indulged before, and I surprise myself by recalling the meanings of many common words. Although the slice-of-life story follows the characters through meandering Tokyo neighborhoods, the pleasant softness of the animation and the curated musical accompaniment add a degree of distance from reality that I find soothing. Clay joins us, curling into a ball at the end of the bed. Eventually, as we're falling asleep, I mutter, *"Oyasuminasai,"* and Erin, lids heavy, responds, *"Oyasumi."*

*　　　*　　　*

I wake, still laying on top of the comforter, to the sound of my alarm. Cursing myself for not having gone to bed earlier, I change into my work clothes and leave a note for Erin on the table: 'Back at 2. *Stay as long as you want.'*

As I approach the sleepy cemetery, milky daylight begins to awaken the neighborhood, igniting lamps behind curtains and drawing dog walkers from their warm dens, wrapped in thick layers to withstand the frosty morning chill. I breathe deeply, imbibing the wintery notes on the air, and march beyond the gate. Curtis, I discover, has reassigned me to a new team for the remainder of the season. Kyrone won't be returning for the foreseeable future, he says. Whether his decision to stay away has anything to do with Dodge, that whole catastrophe, Curtis doesn't say, and I don't ask. Similarly, my new team members sidestep questions concerning that particular event. In fact, they say very little to me, directly, but whether it's out of courtesy or mistrust I can't say.

At noon, I discover I forgot to pack a lunch and use my thirty minutes to trudge back to the apartment and prepare something hot. Erin is still there but has moved from the bed to the couch.

"You're home early," she says.

"Forgot my lunch."

"Want some ramen?" She slurps a noodle wetly, then wipes her chin with the back of her hand. I find a second soup packet on the kitchen counter and prepare a bowl for myself before joining her on the couch. "Hey," she says.

"No classes today?"

"Winter break."

"Oh. Right. Obviously."

"You gotta go back?"

"Fifteen minutes."

"Mind if I stay?"

"Stay as long as you want," I tell her, repeating the sentiment I left in the note.

"Tonight?"

"Sure."

She slurps a few more noodles. "You doing okay?"

"Good as can be expected."

I drain my broth. It's too salty. Jun wouldn't approve. He didn't mind the noodles that came in dried rectangles, but he would have made his own broth using a bonito and kombu base, then saved the flavor packet for enhancing a curry or sauces.

We stare at my computer screen. Erin has another animated show playing, dramatically different than the one we watched together last night. Tender conversation and gentle, flowing music have been replaced by explosive battles between Samurai warriors.

"You went there, right?" she asks, pointing at the screen, at the Edo-style shopping streets, the men and women in geta sandals and indigo-dyed yukata. For whatever reason, the topic never came up yesterday evening.

Assuming she's accurately differentiating between feudal and contemporary Japan, I confirm her suspicions, saying, "Yeah, a long time ago."

"If I turned off the subtitles, would you know what they're saying?"

"I only know a few phrases."

"Bummer. So, what, did everyone talk to you in English?"

"Pretty much, yeah. I stayed on a farm owned by my mother's friend." I decide not to reference Jun, if only to minimize confusion. Besides, there isn't enough time to get into all that, how things ended at Michikusa House. "I gotta go," I say.

"See ya," she says, then settles back under my throw blanket to finish the episode. Or, more likely, the entire season.

As I walk back to the cemetery, I pull out my phone, wondering whether @j.nakashima.j responded to my question about the recovery work taking place in Futaba. I open the app and navigate to the conversation. And there, underneath my last question, is a response.

j.nakashima.j: When I first arrived to take a picture, no one lived here and the city was a completely deserted place. There is no water, no electricity, no infrastructure. Now some people are back. I have helped with soil removal and restoration. I want to help the farms return to a healthy working condition, but things are still very bad. From the photos, you can't tell how bad it really is. Broken glass at the storefront covers all sidewalks. Goods from the shelves are everywhere on the ground and are covered with dust and dirt. Only a few blocks of the city are open. The rest is too dangerous. Those streets are sealed behind the gate. People don't want to go back if they can't go home. When people can't go back, there are no grocery stores, hospitals, or schools. Everything is miles away. There are so many towns in Fukushima like this.

I feel my fingers twitch inside my gloves, as if eager to type out a response. I must have missed the notification, the response, sometime during all the chaos of the last few days. I have so many questions but...where to start? What do I say to keep the conversation moving?

Win__chime: Are the streets sealed because of radiation contamination? You mentioned that it's still high, but the government is trying to reopen anyway. How can both be true? High contamination and reopening?

Just as I'm entering the cemetery, puzzling over the question in my own mind, my phone buzzes. An answer, already? It's past midnight in Japan. But, sure enough, there it is:

j.nakashima.j: Radiation is still a big concern, but everyone who comes back is old. They want to die in their hometown. Radiation levels have dropped as people have been cleaning since the accident. They put it in bags and landfills, but also because of the natural decay of radioactive particles. However, there are still many hotspots, as some types of radiation can last for hundreds of years. Radiation monitors are everywhere, including parks, train stations, and roadsides. People use a Geiger counter to test the radioactivity in the soil and all foods. When people put science in their hands, governments and so-called experts cannot fool us or hide the truth. Another concern is wild boars roaming the streets.

This response makes me think, momentarily, of the other account on this site, that of the scientist, Professor Okabe Nakashima of Kumamoto University. Could this be his personal account? Researcher by day, photographer and soil conservationist by night? Seems like a stretch. I know my team has already returned to work, but I can't help myself. I type:

Win__chime: Citizen science at its finest! Sounds complicated, especially since the radioactive particles would've contaminated plants as well. That means they end up in the food chain. Removing the soil doesn't sound like a long-term solution. If you strip the soil, you skin away the layer of earth that gives life to plants. I worked on a small farm for a while and my mentors condemned modern agriculture for that reason, how it hurts the soil and causes it to erode away, so I guess I have strong opinions on the subject, too! Are there other solutions?

I can't say why I included this personal flourish. Subconsciously or otherwise, perhaps I hope J— will say "me too."

I pocket my phone and hurry to catch up with my crew, jogging the rest of the way to our work site by the Memorial Chapel. I don't want to give the wrong impression on my first day with a new team, though it's possible I've already done that, what with the rumors likely circulating about Dodge and me, whether I was responsible for his termination, his public retaliation, or the police intervention. Luckily, I'm the first one to the site and get to work clearing a patch of slick ice near a leaky drainpipe.

Snow and ice removal keeps us, me and five others, occupied until the second shift crew arrives, but the moment I'm off the clock I check my notifications. Amazingly, there's another response from @j.nakashima.j. While there's no mention of previously working on a farm, the sentiment the account owner describes ignites memories of the Jun I once knew.

j.nakashima.j: The government recommended putting various minerals and chemicals in the soil to absorb the radiation. However, some people do not want it to worsen the soil. Some farmers tried to flood the fields to get rid of the pollution. So far, there is no complete fix. We are trying to be a better soil expert. Now we call ourselves amateur geologists, microbiologists, mycologists, whatever you can think of, we strive for ourselves. Even if you are not a farmer, you want a flower garden and an herb garden. People want to resume their lives, but you are right. Life begins with the soil. We believe that Fukushima must be revived from the ground.

This time I know exactly what I want to ask. Time to put the pressure on and turn up the heat.

Win__chime: Why did you choose to stay and help? - if you don't mind me asking.

*   *   *

Erin stays another night. Her company feels companionable, chaste, and pleasantly intrusive. Her positivity and humor slap me, repeatedly, out of moody internal wanderings. Yet still I cannot sleep. I lie awake. Time passes. I give myself over to insomnia.

Late at night, I remember water, the season when heavy rains began across Kyushu. Downpours lasted hours. Whenever the rains paused their roaring to take a breath, the air felt dense and swampy. During the rains, time slowed. Chores were put on pause. Guests stayed home. Those of us who remained year-round sat together on the veranda, watching the sky deliver buckets of water. Somehow, the earth drank it all up.

CHAPTER 15

In those days, I would go to sleep in Jun's bed, then trickle back to my own room in the farmhouse through a dewy, periwinkle cloud. Daylight, fine and misty, took longer to wake. Insect chatter softened, as subdued as the warmth of those early autumn days. The change in temperature and the slanting of daylight changed us, as well. Like the birds and squirrels, we began the process of sequestering stores for winter. Neighbors' rice paddies were drained in preparation for harvest. Seeds dried on their stalks, turning to golden tassels. When their weight bent them low, *inekari*—the rice harvest—began. A time for reaping what had been sown. We basketed root vegetables, pickled greens and eggplants, preserved *ume* plums, dried persimmons, and gathered chestnuts. Competition for the meaty sweetness of chestnuts was particularly fierce, a delicacy craved by humans and wild boars alike. Jun prepared them cooked in rice, a seasonal delicacy celebrating autumn.

Jun's taste in food, I had come to learn, was highly demanding, but also incalculably sensitive. His father, he told me once, called it *urusai*, fussy or noisy. Jun wouldn't eat anything that wasn't perfectly delicious, preferring a homemade meal, cooked to perfection, over a mediocre restaurant dish. But there was more nuance to his palate than taste alone. His exceptional skill in the kitchen was underpinned with knowledge of individual ingredients and seasonal specialties, traditional preparations, and the aesthetics that combine color and texture. Jun embodied a pure sort of relationship with food, and I am grateful he passed some of these unique subtleties on to me.

In October, the kilns reopened, and the grand process of firing was repeated. Jun and I spent those hours in the presence of that hungry furnace reminiscing about the first firing, back in May...a first for a lot of things. Autumn, meanwhile, went about its work wilting the flowers and curling the leaves, yellowing the fields, drawing life back into the earth. Even the insects retreated to their winter burrows in the soil, in the fissures of tree bark. The frenetic energy of summer quieted, giving itself over to the calm crispness that precedes winter. The kiln raged on, heating one chamber after another. We wrapped ourselves in sweaters and hunkered down by the kiln, its fires hot enough, even from a distance, to warm our hands and faces.

When the kiln was sealed and left to cool, more guests arrived at Michikusa House. Weekenders and artists and one young man, a poet, who spoke some limited English. Though his poems were written exclusively in Japanese, he enjoyed expanding his English vocabulary by chatting with Jun in the kitchen, sometimes over a pot of boiling soup, or standing beside a simmering frying pan. It was on one such day, with Shoko out distributing her wares across the prefecture and the poet seeking refuge in our company, that the phone rang. Hideyuki must have been at the neighbor's again because the poet offered to answer the call. With sleeves rolled up and hands busy with ingredients, neither Jun nor I protested. In fact, the moment the poet slipped through the *noren* curtain, Jun turned on me, pressing my low back into the countertop, pressing his hips against mine. His scent, his body, intoxicated me and I kissed him with the wild passion that so often ignited our secret affair.

"Meet me upstairs," I whispered in his ear, then slipped out of the kitchen. Through the garden, across the gravel drive, and up the stairs to Jun's studio. Figuring it would only take moments for him to make his excuses to the poet, it surprised me when, minutes later, he still hadn't appeared. I watched for him through the window, eyeing the kitchen door. Maybe he took the call, I thought, or got stuck chatting with that insufferable poet.

Finally, I spotted him emerging from the front door of the farmhouse, but by then I'd lost the longing that had provoked this meetup. Easily remedied. I peeled off my top and jeans and lay back on his futon. Just as I felt myself begin to awaken, Jun entered.

"What took you so long?" I sighed.

Rather than join me, however, Jun stood immobile in the doorway, his face as stern as I'd ever seen it. "Who's Liam?" he said.

My body froze. Any pleasure or anticipation I'd felt a moment ago vanished. "What?"

"Some guy named Liam was on the phone asking for you. When I wanted to know who he was, he told me."

I sat up, feeling vulnerable and exposed. My face and chest flushed. Neither of us moved a muscle. I had to say something, but...what on earth could I say? I reached for my sweater but didn't have the guts to press pause on the conversation long enough to get fully dressed.

"Liam's my boyfriend. Back in Ohio."

Jun folded his arms over his chest.

"I didn't expect things to go this far," I explained.

"*Kuso*," he swore under his breath.

"What's he got to do with us?" I tried. "I just…I didn't want to complicate things. I figured it didn't matter."

"How did you reach that conclusion?"

"Because I have to go back! I don't get to stay here. I don't have a choice about that."

"And what choice do I get? What say do I have in this?"

"I thought we were just having fun," I said, weakly.

"Well, I don't agree, and I bet Liam wouldn't either," Jun spat.

"Whatever happens between me and him, that's my business."

"You've made it my business, too." Then under his breath, "*Mendokusai*."

"Jun, I don't know what to say. I—"

"Ah! You white girls are all the same, think you can do anything you want to anyone and get away with it. You act so—" he was waving his hands, struggling to find the English word. Finally, he roared "*Jikochuu*! So selfish! You make me sick." And then, Jun was gone.

Despite my endless attempts at apology and reconciliation, right up until my last day, Jun refused to speak to me. He gave me no attention whatsoever except for the barest and most necessary formalities. I stayed away from the kitchen, knowing I wouldn't be welcome. I half expected him to leave Michikusa House, but with barely a month left in his internship I guess he didn't much see the point in disrupting the arrangement he had with the Hanadas. I think, too, it was his way of saying I didn't matter enough to alter the course of his life. I don't remember what happened to the poet. I don't even remember his name. All I remember of those last weeks in Japan was the intense loneliness I felt, the quiet, wordless days and the cold nights. I stopped eating again, briefly. Shoko guessed what had happened, that we'd broken up. She didn't act surprised, or especially sympathetic. She had warned me, and I'd foolishly ignored her advice. When I joined her in the studio we talked mainly about my plans for the future, what I would do when I returned home. "Finish school, I suppose." That's what I told her, and it made sense. That would be a sensible decision.

When I returned home at Thanksgiving, Liam met me at the airport, seemingly none the wiser. He had his own apartment by then and we spent two days together. Having endured a full year apart, we should have been basking in the relief and gladness afforded by each other's company. I blamed my lack of enthusiasm on jet lag. I never knew that all this time he suspected, but never said, never asked. I guess we both thought I had put Japan behind me.

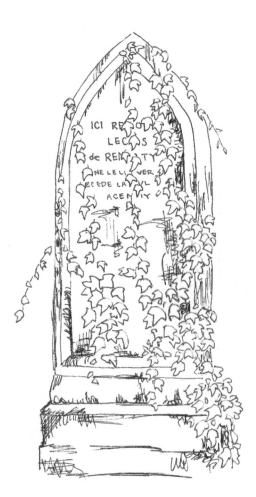

CHAPTER 16

Unexpectedly, I find a padded envelope waiting for me on the dining table when I return from work on Monday.

"Open it!" Erin insists. The postmark is from a local bookstore. Odd. I didn't order anything.

Inside, I find, unsurprisingly, a book: Diversity of Life in Man-Made Places. I flip to the back cover and read the synopsis. "...there are as many interrelationships to be uncovered in a backyard flower bed as in a meadow, in a cemetery as in a forest." I smile. I have repeatedly second-guessed the way in which I'm now spending the greater portion of my time; first arguing with Liam, then my parents, and everything that happened with Dodge. Reading the back cover of this book, however, restores some of my confidence in my choice. When I fold back the front cover, I also discover a small envelope with a message, typewritten on an actual typewriter, each individual letter depressing the paper fractionally. It reads, "I thought you could use an early Christmas present. Maybe this will help you at work. - Mom"

"What's that?" Erin asks, taking both the book and the note from me. "Guess I didn't know you were so into this stuff."

"What do you mean, 'stuff'?"

"Like, nature stuff. I don't know—the cemetery and everything."

Her tone irritates me. "Yeah. I care about the things that live where I live. We're not the only ones here. It's important stuff," I say, more harshly than necessary. I'm not sure why I'm so angry with her, but I feel oddly defensive of the gift. "You're becoming a psychologist to help people, right? Well, I'm trying to learn about this stuff so I can help beings that aren't people," I say, sensing, not for the first time, the age difference between us.

I picture Nakashima J— somewhere in Fukushima, helping to restore contaminated soil to a healthy, functioning eco-community supportive of rich life. Have I been unconsciously comparing myself with them and the important work they're doing?

"Alright. Jeez," Erin says, dropping the book on the table.

"Sorry," I say, half-heartedly. Maybe it's her constant company that's wearing on my nerves, like an itch behind my eyes, somewhere I can't reach. "I'm not used to being around people all the time."

"Yeah, definitely a loner," she murmurs, rolling her eyes toward the cat. I let her have that one. "Look, I can get out of your hair. I just didn't want you to feel, you know…I don't know… threatened? Is that the right word? Plus, with the whole Liam thing…"

I tell her—insist I'm fine. And, honestly, I'm tired of avoiding how I feel. I'm ready to let myself be depressed or angry or sulky, prepared to sink into a hole of self-indulgence—narcotics, starvation, anything to purge whatever dark feelings that sit, unwavering, just below the surface. I want to feel numb again.

We say our goodbyes and promise to get together again in the new year. Once she's gone, I look around the apartment. It's craving a good, deep clean. An orange namkeen dust smear adorns one arm of the sofa; the throw blanket somehow got tangled around the leg. Half my book collection is scattered to the far corners of the room. Clay chases a cat-fur-tumbleweed under the bed. The kitchen floor is stained white with salt residue. I'm afraid to tackle the bathroom drain, all that hair.

Instead, I collapse onto the couch and stare straight ahead, through the windows overlooking the porch. From this angle, I can only just make out the cemetery wall and the trees it envelopes. I pull my feet up onto the cushion and rest my head against my knees. It feels like the first time I've been allowed to wallow. The edge of numbness, like a tantalizing mirage off in the distance, suddenly feels dangerously close. It's in perfect stillness that I recall how sorrow tends to follow me like a shadow.

Liam, with Fiona Justice.

Dodge on the loose.

Jun...

Maybe months of therapy finally kick in—whatever the reason, I recognize the symptoms, the mindset, and know I can't let the waves crash over me. Otherwise, I will drown and there will be no one—no more Liam—to drag me back to the surface. I need some momentum, I think, one small step to propel me from that dangerous edge. My gaze drifts to the unblemished new book on the table. I can't reach it from the sofa, so I rise and drag myself to a chair, pulling the book toward me. Automatically, I flip to the table of contents. Amid chapter titles that include 'Backyard Places,' 'Food-Growing Places,' 'Sacred Places', and 'Waste Management Places,' I spy exactly what I hoped to find, a chapter titled 'Burial Places.'

"Burial places are often surprising sources of life," the chapter begins.

"On every inhabited continent on earth, special places devoted to burial practice and ritual support extraordinarily high species richness. The role of these plots in biodiversity conservation is emphasized by the fact that most were established in ancient times when the extension of natural habitats was continuous. Thanks to their cultural and spiritual importance, many burial places have remained relatively undisturbed for centuries, preserving, sometimes, the last remaining remnants of a species' culture.

"From Romania to Mongolia, burial mounds known as kurgans often represent the last guardians of steppe vegetation. Steppes are characterized by naturally treeless vegetation dominated by perennial grasses and herbs. The flat top of the kurgans is covered by drought-tolerant species, while the slopes and foot host rare loess, alkali, or sandy grassland species. Currently, steppe vegetation is most often restricted to places unsuitable for ploughing, such as kurgans. Despite their small size, therefore, kurgans act as biodiversity hotspots and harbor many red-listed species. In Ukraine, for instance, kurgans host nearly 15% of all known flora in the country. Remarkably, this extraordinarily high species richness is present on scarcely two square kilometers of land, which corresponds to 0.000002 % of the nation's land area."

The next section strikes a familiar chord, reminding me of my earliest days and talks with Kyrone, who knew a surprising amount about burial practices for being "just a groundskeeper".

"In the mountainous Tibet Autonomous Region," it reads, "the tradition and custom of sky burial is known as *jhator,* meaning 'giving alms to the birds.' Arguably due to the relative scarcity of timber resources for cremation and to the barren, rocky, and often ice-covered Himalayas which is unsuitable for most crops, let alone burial, disposal of carrion by scavenging birds became customary. Approximately two-thousand sky burial sites are distributed over the Tibetan plateau, receiving fifty-thousand corpses per year. This quantity has been estimated to feed a population of approximately twenty-thousand vultures. It is therefore possible that sky burials contribute almost 20% of the total food intake for Tibetan vultures. But they are not the only benefactors. In valleys full of prayer flags, Mani stones, and crushed bones, sparrows, red-billed choughs, magpies, ravens, hill pigeons, and others clean up the vulture's leftovers."

I scan the paragraphs that follow, describing the sacred groves of East-Central Africa; the Hopi cliff-dwellings at Bears Ears; the ancient cloud forest city of Kuelap in pre-Columbian Peru; the Madjedbebe rock shelter of the aboriginal Mirarr people in Australia; the tree burial customs of the Cavite people in the Philippines. I promise myself to read each section more carefully at a later time. What I'm most curious to read is the section on conventional, Western-style cemeteries, like the one I've come to know so well. Not because those cemeteries hold more significance, but because it seems unlikely they would harbor and provide shelter for as much wildlife as, say, a protected world heritage site.

"In close proximity to urban areas, cemeteries become islands of vegetation and repositories of urban biodiversity, home to unexpected, beautiful, and sometimes even undiscovered species. For decades, they have been recognized as refuges for birds, lichens, mosses, rare mushrooms, herbs, and endangered plant species. Trees supported by cemeteries' protected status live to be significantly older than in surrounding areas. In the United Kingdom, the Fortingall Yew, which lives in a Perthshire churchyard, is believed to be the nation's oldest tree, between 2,000 and 3,000 years old. The ancient yew is so large that funeral processions are said to have passed through the arch formed by its split trunk. Old trees play a vital role in their environment. Over their long lifespans, they offer important habitat for thousands of different species. Fungi partner with their roots. Lichens and mosses nestle themselves in the craggy bark. Insects munch on their leaves, attracting birds to the area. Because trees in cemeteries tend to be larger and more decayed than trees found in parks, they offer more excavated cavities for primary and secondary cavity nesters like bats, owls, birds, and pine martens who make their homes in cavities that open as a tree ages. One survey suggested cemetery trees maintain nearly four times as many woodpecker-excavated cavities than do trees in urban parks. In Europe, bird species richness was related to the extent of tree coverage and the age of trees in cemeteries; moreover, several bird species often recognized as urban avoiders could be detected in cemeteries.

"Cemeteries with high structural diversity—including not just trees and shrubs and plant life but also churches and mausoleums and a variety of stone monuments—are especially important for insects. Insects constitute a major source of food for birds, mammals, reptiles, and other taxonomic groups of animals and act as herbivores, scavengers, detritivores, predators, and parasites, making them indispensable in any ecosystem." It goes on to say that in London's expansive Highgate Cemetery, a rare spider species requiring total darkness was found in the sealed vaults, living among the dead. Ten snail species were found in a single Jewish cemetery in Istanbul. An astonishing one hundred and fifty-seven species of bees were identified across nine cemetery sites in Montreal, exceeding the number of bee species found in community gardens and parks. A similar pattern was found in Quebec City and cities across the United Kingdom, a pattern attributed to cemeteries' high floral diversity and abundance.

From there, the chapter describes floral biodiversity, including vascular plants, lichens, and mosses, found in cemeteries and churchyards worldwide. From Bangladesh to the American Midwest, it's common for medicinal and endangered plants to find shelter in these preserved places. In Poland, the tradition of planting ornamental plants is completely absent from the Jewish culture, thus reserving habitat for species native to Eastern Europe. A scant paragraph concerning fungi suggests more research is needed to fully define the diverse species cemeteries harbor. Similarly, most cemeteries that have been studied have been surveyed only once, at one time of year, limiting identification of plants blooming earlier or later, and potentially overlooking animals with no activity in certain parts of the year.

"Consideration of the land on various seasonal and time scales, with special emphasis on the needs of various organisms, is an essential component of holistic management of urban burial places.

"Unlike most Places featured in this book, biodiversity in burial places is tightly interwoven with spirituality. Both faith and traditional ecological knowledge among local populations have a significant defending role of sacred burial sites. Therefore, sustaining and sharing local knowledge can lead to the successful conservation of diverse organisms. Species that people know, use, and respect will be treated with special attention. Emphasizing the significance of sacred sites for maintaining natural and cultural heritage can further create an inclusive brand of conservation that empowers Indigenous peoples and local communities while also protecting biodiversity."

I finish the chapter and close the book feeling unaccountably moved to tears.

*   *   *

On Thursday, three days before Christmas, my mother calls. I thank her for the book.

"You read it already?" she asks. "That was fast."

"I skipped ahead to the chapter on cemeteries—burial places."

"It might be stuff you already know—"

"No!" I insist. "I learned a lot, actually. It made me, I don't know, respect my job—the place itself, where I work and what I do there—it made me love it even more. It feels more important after reading that. Thanks for sending it." I don't want to admit that even I was second-guessing my choices, that it was exactly what I needed, like a balm to soothe raw wounds.

"I'm glad to hear it." When she asks how I'm doing, however, I decide not to beat around the bush.

"Did Liam send you a wedding invitation?" I ask her, monotone.

She takes longer to register the unexpected question than I would have expected. "I don't follow," she admits.

"Remember those photos I showed you?" Of course, she does. "They're engaged, Liam and Fiona."

"It must be some misunderstanding," she insists.

"He called me, Mom. He said he wanted to tell me before they made the official announcement." Whether that announcement has since been made, I cannot say.

On the other end, I can hear my mother fidgeting with something. Her keys, maybe? "I have half a mind to call him, myself," she says, finally. Tersely. She's furious, I can tell. She's always thought of Liam—treated him like a son-in-law, part of the family. "I'm just…I can't…well, just wait till your dad hears about this."

"Hears about what?" Dad asks in the background.

"In a minute, Gordon," Mom says.

"Who is it?" he asks.

"Win's on the phone."

"Hi, honey!" he calls loudly.

"Dad says hi."

"I heard."

"I'll be done here in a minute," my mother says, presumably to my dad.

"Why's Dad home so early?"

"He had a doctor's appointment."

"Everything alright?"

"The doctor put him on Lipitor and now he's getting these awful headaches."

"What? Jesus, mom, why didn't you tell me?"

"Put her on speaker," I hear my dad say.

"Can you hear us?" my mother asks.

"Loud and clear."

"Apparently Liam's engaged," my mother tells him, sweeping any discussion of his health status aside.

"What?!" Dad laughs, as if we've pulled one over on him. Great joke. Briefly, I explain, to which he replies, "I've got half a mind to march over there and sock that boy in the jaw."

"If you want to call and tell him how disappointed you are in his behavior, be my guest, but don't...really and truly, I don't want him back—or whatever—so don't start something, not for my sake," I insist.

"Honey, do you want to come home for a couple days?" my mother asks. I can sense the care implied by the offer.

"I can't leave Clay."

Mom tsks.

"Who now?" Dad asks.

"The cat," my mother explains, exasperated. "Just pour him a few bowls of food. He'll be fine. Cats can take care of themselves."

"He eats wet food, first of all—cats need…it's a common misconception that they can tolerate a dry diet. It's not biologically appropriate for their physiology," I say, parroting the many articles I've absorbed on the subject.

"Oh, for heaven's sake, Winona," she scoffs.

"Plus, I have work."

"Alright, forget I asked," my mother says, put out.

"I'll be there for Christmas," I remind her. "This weekend."

The three of us chat relatively amicably for another few minutes before my mother says she has to go run an errand before the shop closes. Dad stays on the line.

"You'll come pick me up?" I ask.

"You betcha. Mom wants us back by ten to help with lunch and to open presents before everyone arrives."

I wonder if it's going to be another overlarge gathering of unfamiliar guests but decide not to ask. I'll find out in three days.

*   *   *

On Saturday, Christmas Eve, the sun rips open days-old cloud cover, warming the cemetery enough to melt the caps of snow off the headstones. As I go about picking up wet refuse—wreaths and bottles and knickknacks exhumed by the melt—I pass several cars parked along the edges of the lots. Not too far away their drivers stand quietly, sometimes alone, sometimes with a companion or two. I imagine they must be visiting departed friends and relatives for the holidays.

Today, as I often do, I read the names carved in stone as I walk. One monument catches my eye, or rather the goldenrod-yellow speckles clinging to its roughened surfaces, degraded by more than a century of weathering. I move closer. Yellow, turquoise, and sage-colored lichens have made this carved rock their home. As have tender green moss shoots, bedded in the curves of the letters. The moss is feathery and wet and when I kneel for a closer look, my knee touches another pillowy green hummock. The ground moss's growth is so dense that its individual characteristics are indiscernible to my naked eye. Something about the wetness of the day, I think, or maybe just the drab monochrome of everything else—the melting snow, the headstones, the tree bark, the desiccated leaves—makes the colors of these small plants appear especially vibrant.

I touch the little sponge of moss and gently run my finger over the coral reef of the lichen, feeling some regret that I cannot name them, that I do not know them beyond superficial recognition. How peculiar, I think, that I never thought to admire them more closely before now, these little lives being lived out on these craggy surfaces. I take a few quick snapshots, getting the lens on my phone as close as I can without blurring the image. After work I'll go home and identify them. I think of the book, the one my mother gifted to me, and smile.

CHAPTER 17

I'm sitting at my little table, half watching out the window for Dad's car, half flipping through Diversity of Life in Made-Made Places, when an email from Shoko arrives. It reads:

Dear Win-chan,

Merry Christmas to you and your family! I hope you are well. My husband has come down with a bad chest cold, so we are enjoying a quiet winter this year without guests at Michikusa House. We are looking forward to spring when we can once again host visitors and offer new classes in the studio. Recently, our homestay program was featured in a regional magazine, so we have been getting more bookings than ever. The people at the magazine sent me a digital copy. I have attached it to this email. The article starts on page 25. There are plenty of photographs, so do not worry about translating the text. I want to frame the picture they took of my husband and me! It came out well, don't you agree?

I have more good news to share. Recently, I spoke on the phone to Mrs. Nakashima, Jun's mother. This is what she said:

For the past two years, her son has been working in Futaba, one of the towns most badly affected by the 2011 Great East Japan Earthquake. He has been helping farmers somehow. What she said about it, I did not fully understand. When he first arrived, no one was living there; the city was empty. No running water, no electricity. He and others lived outside the city and had to drive very far each day to help with restoration work. That's how she explained it to me. Mrs. Nakashima has been very worried about him, as you can imagine. I think the radiation levels are still very bad and she has tried to convince him to come home many times. She gave me his phone number, but I have not had a chance to call him. When I do, I will let you know.

Best wishes from your friend,

Hanada Shoko

花田 祥子

The confirmation is so complete and so unexpected that I scarcely believe the validity of the information Shoko has been given. I'm so preoccupied rereading the note, interrogating every word as if a falsehood might lie buried beneath their superficial, more obvious meanings, that the sound of the car horn outside fails to penetrate my concentration. Only when Dad calls my phone, telling me he is outside waiting, do I rise. I realize then that my heart is pounding and in a heady rush I work to steady my balance against the table. I've finally found him; I know where Jun is, where he's been all this time.

The revelation feels enormous, too vast to digest in a single morning. Even so, I regret my commitment to this event, wishing for more time alone with Shoko's letter, and a clearer headspace in which to reorganize my thoughts and consider how to proceed from this point forward. But I see Dad sitting out there and pocket my phone, grab the bag of gifts, and the pie pan, say a quick goodbye to Clay, then rush out the door and down the fire escape.

The temperature has dropped again, freezing the snow melt from yesterday. The landscape fairly glistens with ice, which will soon be covered by snow if those clouds coming in from the north are any clue. When I fold myself into the car, the first thing Dad says, in fact, is "Snow's coming. Big lake effect blizzard, Mom said," making it sound like she's the one who decides the course of the weather.

"How were the roads?" I ask, conversationally, feeling the weight of my phone in my pocket. I feel fidgety and anxious, both to reply to Shoko and to determine whether @j.nakashima.j has responded to the last question I sent. Is it possible that he realized he had been chatting with me, Winona Heeley, and vanished again? If he still hasn't responded, should I try gently prodding him with another message? I recall why he disappeared, the phone call he had with Liam, the argument we had afterward, and a flush of shame and regret curses me anew. I wonder whether this separation has hurt him even a fraction as much as it's hurt me…but why disappear to Fukushima? Could pure altruism really have been his motivation to risk his health, permanently?

I cannot focus on what my dad is saying, something about getting the oil changed in the car, and I wonder briefly whether he means to stop now, what with the storm rolling in. But we merge onto I-90 westbound, and I settle back in my seat. I redirect the conversation to the holiday, asking which guests to expect and wondering aloud at how the snowstorm might affect everyone's return journey later that evening. When we segue into how work is going for the both of us, I generalize, describing the categories of tasks I undertake and leave Dodge's ejection completely out of the picture. We decidedly avoid talking about Liam.

Snow starts to swirl and flurry before we exit the highway, and I imagine the drifts I'll have to shovel at the cemetery come morning.

"One of these times you'll have to show me around," Dad says.

"Huh?"

"Mom said you've got a nice place."

"Oh. Sure. But the steps are bad in winter. Maybe after the snow melts." After a beat, I ask, "Do you know if she still talks to Shoko?"

"You know, I'm not sure."

"I heard from her today, is all."

"That right? How is she?"

I tell him about the magazine and what little I know of the development of their own small tourism business.

"I remember when you came back from that place—"

"Michikusa House?"

"Right, right. You came back looking different."

"Like how?"

"You looked stronger. Healthier. Happy, maybe, is the right word."

"Looked? Past tense?"

"Hey, I'm just an old man, but I can still tell when my girls are upset."

"It's just Liam," I say. "I'll get over it." We leave it at that.

By the time we turn into the cul-de-sac, there's already a fresh layer of snow on the ground, gathering swiftly, falling hard and fast like rain. I'm already worrying about the return trip, whether I'll have to call off work tomorrow because I'm stuck on the opposite side of town, or whether I'll have to call

Erin to go over and feed Clay. Before I can calculate the potential consequences of yet undetermined future scenarios, however, my mother appears from the kitchen on a wave of cinnamon- and clove-scented air, taking coats and asking that we take care not to drip on the clean floor before her guests arrive. Dad gives me a wink and we follow her into the kitchen by way of the living room. The house is decorated from floor to ceiling in candles, ribbons, crystal, and boughs of holly and pine. Under the living evergreen tree are dozens of boxes wrapped in white and gold paper containing the gifts she's been making and buying all year. The house smells richly of strong coffee and baking bread.

An hour and a half of brunching and cleanup ensues before the first guests arrive—no time for gift exchanges; that'll have to wait. Dad takes over in the kitchen, doing something with a ham, while Mom shows people where to hang their coats and place their appetizers. Amidst the commotion and faces I only vaguely recognize I slip away unnoticed. This time my old room is unoccupied, so I close myself in, permitting the mental strain that's been building since I left my apartment to claim my full attention.

Again, I reread Shoko's email, homing in on the most significant details:

For the past two years, Jun has been working in Futaba… helping farmers somehow…

Mrs. Nakashima has been very worried about him…radiation levels are still very bad…

She has tried to convince him to come home…

She gave me his phone number…

I feel the pressure around my eyes and across my brow build, forecasting a wellspring of emotions I'm unwilling to tap just now. I found him, after all this time. I've been looking through photos that he took, the places he's been. I shield my eyes to forestall the tears that reside there, unbidden. It's infuriating that Jun still has the power to affect me this way, like a tsunami that began half an ocean away cascading over the shores of my new homeplace. Would I be this disconsolate if Liam and I were still together and happy? But that unrealistic expectation is underpinned by false premises. Liam never needed me, not the way I needed him, and that sort of imbalance cannot function as the support for a stable, wholesome relationship. He knew it, too. We were friends—the best of—but he had others. I did not. Jun and I were more alike in that way; to feel content and heard and valued, we needed only each other. Jun and I achieved a miraculous sort of equilibrium, one that originated from opposite ends of the earth and manifests only once in a lifetime. And I ruined it. I unbalanced the scales by trying to hold onto both of them, risking perfection by clinging to what felt familiar.

I check my face in the mirror. My mascara has bled into my eye shadow. Wetting my finger, I work to smooth out the worst of it, creating a shadowy effect that reminds me of an earlier version of myself. I stopped wearing makeup once I dropped out of college the first time—when I stopped seeing people, had no one to impress. I didn't readopt the habit in Japan—no reflective surfaces in which to gauge my appearance, let alone apply face paint. I don't need it now, either, not at the cemetery. I all but roll out of bed in the morning and head straight to work. In all that time, Liam is the only one for whom I occasionally made an effort to transform my face into a "more attractive" version, occasionally for shifts at the library, as if on a whim. And today, because…well, guests and necessary armor and all that. I laugh at my feeble attempts to disguise myself.

I decide I will wait to reply to Shoko until I can take a proper look through the digital magazine she sent. Holding out hope that I've missed a message announcement from @j.nakashima.j—as if Shoko's message might have prompted activity elsewhere in Japan—I revisit the thread of our conversation. Unsurprisingly, I find nothing new whatsoever.

"Win-chime? You in there?" I hear my mother ask, knocking lightly.

"Yeah."

"Can I come in?"

"Sure."

She opens the door and closes it behind her, coming to sit with me on the bed. "I'm sorry Liam's not here," she says, reading, I suppose, something else in my dour mood.

"I'm not," I say, spitefully.

"I called Meredith."

Liam's mom? "Why?" I ask, suddenly wary. I never got the impression that Meredith Hoxley liked my mother very much. I expect she felt guilty and embarrassed that my family all but adopted her son during her worst drinking years, after her husband died. Plus, it's easy for any woman to feel inferior alongside my mother. I should know.

"I called to wish her a Merry Christmas."

"That's all?" I ask, skeptical.

"I might've said something about missing having Liam around this year."

"What did she say?"

"She said the same about you."

"Really?'

Mom nods, pats my knee.

"Did she mention the engagement?"

"She asked if we'd heard the news. I think she felt embarrassed. She seemed as shocked as we were, actually. It came so suddenly for all of us, that announcement. Liam's not usually like that. He's so calculated and—well, you know—predictable."

Right. Don't I know it.

"She apologized, actually. We all expected the two of you to end up together more permanently. We always thought of him as family. I think she felt the same about you, and of course she doesn't know the first thing about this other girl."

"Sounds more like something Mike would do."

"Meredith said the same thing, actually."

"It's partly my fault. We had that big fight over me dropping out again."

"Partners need to be willing to accept each other as they go through changes in life."

I don't disagree. "We were both in different places. He was way ahead of me, with his job and everything."

"You went through some big changes too. It takes time," she says. I know what she means. After so many years of illness, it took time to heal, start over.

"Plus, Japan." Then I try the same line I tried on Dad, hoping, I guess, for a different response. "I heard from Shoko today."

"Oh, good. I talked to her not that long ago, but I'll have to call her again soon."

"She said Mr. Hanada has a bad cold or something, so they're not taking guests this winter, but she said they'll be back at it in the spring."

"Right. Wait here just a minute. There's something—" Mom says, as she rises, disappears from the room, leaving the door cracked about an inch. Bewildered, I sit tight. When she lets herself back in, she's carrying a flat white envelope, like the kind in which bills and bank statements arrive. "We didn't have time to open gifts earlier but…I think you need this."

She hands the envelope to me. On one side she's written my name in her perfect penmanship. I flip it over and run my thumb under the seal. I can't even begin to guess what it contains. Inside, I find two sheets of paper, folded in thirds. It takes me a moment to process the words printed on it. Cleveland to Tokyo, departing from CLE to ORD to LAX to HND, lines interspersed with travel times and layover durations.

"Are you and Dad going to Japan?" I ask, confused and, honestly, a bit surprised. Hurt, even. They're not the ones who love Japan, not like I do. But they'll be gone a full two weeks, by the look of it. Of course, I shouldn't be jealous since I got to go for a full year, but still.

She laughs and nudges my shoulder. "I thought you and I could go. I already booked two rooms at Shoko's. I hope the dates are okay."

"I'll ask…Curtis," I say, lamely. Then, equally pitifully, add, "Thank you."

"Do you like it?"

As if she couldn't guess how much I've ached to go back ever since I left but find I can't help grinning.

"I'm glad Shoko didn't spoil the surprise in her email," Mom says.

"I had no idea."

"Christmas and birthday," she adds, pointedly.

"Thank you," I say again, noting we will, in fact, be in Japan for my birthday, assuming the itinerary holds. "And thanks again for the book, too. I actually brought it with me, in case I got bored today."

She tsks. "What is it with you?"

"How did you guess, though? That this book would be so—I mean, it talks about exactly the issues I was kind of grappling with, whether this job is right for me, whether it's meaningful enough, you know?"

"Actually," she says, her tone shifting fractionally, "Dean Chowdhury and I got to talking one day. She knew about what was happening, of course." Of course. The night of the Faculty Art Show, at the restaurant, we made a big enough scene of it. "I was having some…ill-conceived preconceptions," my mother admits. "I confessed my misgivings to her, and we chatted for a while. Next thing I know, I find a copy of that book in my mailbox at work. I started reading that same evening."

"Are you convinced now, that I chose well?"

"I'm not thrilled that you gave up on your education, but…I can better appreciate the value of the work you do. I just hope they can spare their best worker for a couple weeks."

*   *   *

The return drive takes twice as long, stop-and-go, averaging thirty on the highway. Snowflakes splatter like paint on the windshield and prevent us seeing more than a car length ahead. Taillights appear hazy. We spot more than one car pulled to the side of the road. If it weren't for the fact I have work in the morning I wouldn't have insisted Dad repeat this process.

"Don't worry about me," he says. "They'll cancel classes tomorrow, I bet you any money." He's teasing me, trying hard to keep the mood lighthearted. Classes don't start up again for another week, at least.

"At this rate you won't get home till next Christmas," I say. "Sorry if you didn't like your gift, by the way. You guys are always hard to buy for." I strongly resent the pressure and expectation of gift-giving holidays. Especially when I have to buy gifts for people like my parents who either have, or can afford to have, anything they want. "Books are the only thing I can ever think to give people, the gift of wisdom, or whatever."

"It's the one thing everyone can always use more of," he agrees. "I'll add them to the top of my reading list."

"That's probably a pretty sizable stack by now."

"My one hope is to get to the bottom of it before I die. Problem is, I keep piling more onto the stack."

"Doesn't sound like a bad problem to have."

"There are certainly worse."

"Thanks for the tickets, by the way."

"Mom's idea. If it was up to me, you'd have ended up with jumper cables for the car you don't have yet but need to buy so that your poor old dad doesn't have to drive back and forth across town like a chauffeur."

"I don't want a car. I prefer walking."

"I know."

"Maybe from now on, now that Liam's not—you and Mom can just visit my side of town more often. Then you wouldn't have to do this back-and-forth business. We could visit the museums or the Botanical Garden, walk around the Oval or the cemetery, eat someplace in Little Italy," I suggest.

"Or have you cook for us. That pie was superb. Besides, Mom keeps telling me I need to keep an eye on my cholesterol."

"Eat more plants," I caution. "And less of everything else."

"Too bad you're not going to end up a nutritionist, like you thought. I could've come to you for advice."

"I dropped out because the advice they wanted us to give sounded like a ploy to administer pharmaceutical shortcuts," I huff. "And people buy it because it's easier to take a pill than deal with underlying issues or develop a meaningful relationship to the food you put in your body. I should know," I add, quietly.

"Mm," is all he says.

"I learned how to eat well, for the first time in my life," I say, with emphasis, "while living on a farm in Japan, working with farmers and chefs, not while copying notes from slides."

"Uh huh," he says, eyes on his mirrors, trying to merge left. "Think you'll like going back there?"

"Yeah," is all I can manage to say. I recall Oita Prefecture in spring, when Mom and I will be traveling. Gathering *sansai* with Shoko, scrambling over riverbeds and up chilly mountain slopes. By the time May rolled around, we had just finished firing the kiln. Then Shoko was away, selling her wares at trade shows. Jun and I, we were finally alone, together.

Will I ever see him again? When I return to Japan, it's not likely we would cross paths. We wouldn't even be on the same island anymore, let alone in the same Prefecture. Heck, we're not even technically on speaking terms. The odds of reuniting with Jun...

"I'll need to find a babysitter for Clay," I add, just for something to fill the space. "Maybe Erin wouldn't mind."

"Who?"

"My friend Erin? My cat Clay?"

"Oh, right. Right."

"How come you're not going with us?"

"It'll be better, just the two of you," Dad says.

He's probably right. No third-wheel business. "Is Mom going to be working with Shoko on another project while we're there?" I'm mining for conversation topics, trying to avoid the silences that my wandering thoughts love to fill.

"You know, I didn't even think to ask," he admits. "I'm selfishly looking forward to the quiet, to work on my memoirs."

"Oh, yeah? Then I expect to find a completed manuscript by the time we get back."

At that moment, Dad suddenly swerves right onto the shoulder. The shock of movement sends me reeling, gripping the door frame. The rear wheels skid out in the snow, losing traction. We narrowly miss the fully stopped vehicle directly in front of us and the concrete barrier separating us from a fifty-foot drop into the Cuyahoga River. The car behind us isn't so lucky. They crash nose first into the rear bumper of the car we had been following. We watch it happen through the driver's side window, the metal crunching and folding as easily as aluminum foil. Dad and I look at each other, knowing that could have been us. Nothing more than a fender bender, nothing too serious, but my hands and heartbeat quiver.

"You alright?" Dad asks.

"Yeah. Looks like, up there, you can probably drive ahead of them and merge back into traffic," I say, eager to be off the road, safe and immobile in my own home.

Dad takes the Chester exit. We drive in silence. I don't feel my nerves settle back into place until we turn onto Euclid. It's well past eleven by the time we reach my apartment. I offer to sleep on the couch so Dad can take the bed, but he declines, preferring a four-hour round trip in a blizzard to roughing it in someone else's house without a travel kit and change of underwear. He waits until he sees I've gotten inside, waving at him from the fire escape, before he pulls a U-turn and slides away down the street. The moment I open the door, I hear Clay leap from the bed, literally hitting the ground running. He cries as if I've been gone a week and left him to starve. I crouch down to scratch his ears, thinking it's nice having someone to come home to.

*   *   *

I'm sitting on the couch midafternoon on Wednesday, tired in a good way from the morning's work. Clay is curled on the opposite end of the sofa, and I've got a steaming mug on the side table. Outside it's sunny—crystalline, glistening like a prism—but the wind is howling mightily, whipping up bursts of snow. I'm about halfway into Diversity of Life in Man-Made Places when Liam calls. To say I'm loath to answer would be a gross understatement, but curiosity wins out, as it so often does.

"Wrong number?" I say in greeting, marking my place in the book.

"Win, come on." I can practically feel his knots tightening. "I just called to ask you something, alright? I don't want to fight."

"Okay. Shoot."

"Alright, so…I don't know what the right thing to do is here, whether or not to invite you to the wedding."

Prick. "Wow. Did you say the same thing to my mother?"

"I knew this was a bad idea. Guess I have my answer."

"Yeah, I guess you do." I consider hanging up but sense he has more to say. Like a pushover, I let him.

"I wish we were on better terms," he begins.

I roll my eyes. This again?

"I mean it, Win. You were my best friend for so many years. It just feels wrong not having you at a—you know, a big life event."

"Jesus, Liam." *Do you even realize how insulting…?* "If you wanted me at your wedding, you could have proposed to me instead." *God, you're such an idiot.* The thought comes unbidden, but I'm not sure which of us—at whom it's directed. "I'm not too keen on celebrating your commitment to another woman, even if we were such great friends for the preceding decade."

"People change. You and I both did. What we wanted changed."

"Look, just—okay, please don't call me anymore. And don't even think about inviting my parents."

This time I really do hang up, my blood pounding in my ears. I want to hurl my phone through the window just to hear the glass shatter. I picture it falling to the ground, landing in a snowbank. I won't be able to focus on reading anymore, I know that much. The only thing I can think to do is walk it off. I do not, however, want to visit the cemetery, like I used to. I don't want to run into anyone I know or work with, be forced to make polite conversation. Instead, bundled and trundled, I head toward campus. Why, I can't say, other than the fact it will likely be empty of students, being Winter Break and all. I take the long way, the quiet backroads and pedestrian paths that wind between and around student dormitories. I turn onto Juniper, passing the painted rock and the Ugly Statue, though I don't think that's its real name. Ahead, the tall glass panels framing the Botanical Garden create angles as sharp as icicles jutting from the snow. Its internal temperature is so warm it fogs the glass. Despite the nearness of my apartment, I've not visited the Botanical Gardens since my childhood, an event too far in the past to recall with any clarity, at least not without the help of my mother's photo albums. Knowing I won't be able to take full advantage of its outdoor landscapes this time of year, I nonetheless check to see whether I brought my wallet—I did—then make the snap decision to go inside.

Being a weekday afternoon, visitors are relatively few. Mothers with toddlers and older couples with expensive cameras, a few international students huddled together in a group. I leave my heaviest layers at the coat check and enter the Madagascar room, a dry environment dominated by succulents and a giant baobab that looks like an inverted tree with its roots sticking out of the ground. When a group of children on a field trip with their daycare ask a docent whether it's real—it does indeed look like cast concrete—she assures them it's very real and lets them touch its rough surface. Then she turns and points out a free-roaming chameleon high up on a branch. I sneak past, winding around the short path, admiring the spiney plants and their contrastingly delicate blooms. Near a tray bearing fruit scraps and leafy greens set out in the gravel, I count three tortoises with rough, bulbous shells marked with yellow lines radiating from the center of each dark plate. I find their unhurried, ungraceful movements utterly endearing and decide to sit on the adjacent rock wall and watch them for a while. Oh, to care for little else than the timely arrival of your next meal; no predators, no hunting, not a care in the world… what a life. Artificial, yes, but attractive in theory. A few students crowd in beside me, pointing, asking their chaperone questions about the tortoises.

"Can they feel anything through their shell?" one asks.

Good question, I think, and wait expectantly for an answer. The docent says that, yes, they have blood vessels and nerve endings in their shells so they can tell when someone touches them.

"It looks like they have elephant feet," another child says.

"They do!" the docent agrees eagerly. "Why do you think they might have big flat feet like that?"

A few suggestions are offered.

"So they can swim?"

"So they can walk on sand?"

Their teacher segues into a discussion about animals' adaptations to their environment, and why it's important to leave animals in their natural habitat. I step aside, thinking back on my own days in school. I distinctly remember never wanting to speak out, never wanting to raise my hand to answer questions, or even ask to go to the bathroom. On field trips, I huddled on the outskirts of the group. Why was that, I wonder? I honestly don't know. It wasn't until I became friends with Liam that I gained any social confidence. Years later, when his company suddenly became unavailable, I lost the anchor that kept me from floating adrift in a sea of grasping individuals, each with their own agenda. Without him, I became unmoored, bashing against the rocky outcroppings that define adult life.

What was it about Liam that gave me structure and solidity where I otherwise had none? Had Jun merely replaced Liam in that capacity? And perhaps more importantly, what did I bring to those relationships? Unlike the "friends" I made during my first failed university stint, I'm certain that both Liam and Jun cared for me beyond use as a mere sex object. But what was it about me, unexceptional and untalented, did they find attractive and interesting? A relationship—a friendship has to go both ways. Liam introduced me to the sciences. With Jun it had been food and cooking. Those were their specialties, fields I found deeply engaging and worthwhile, but not my own. So, what about me? Who am I without them? Guess I have ample time now to figure that out.

Why can't I just have fun for a change, I wonder, thinking of Erin's advice and cursing myself. Stop worrying and calculating for five minutes.

Damning my self-absorption and habitual melancholy, I push through the double doors separating the Madagascar room from the Costa Rican Cloud Forest. It takes my skin a moment to adjust to the change in temperature and humidity. The air is so filled with moisture I drink it in with every breath. Orchids, bromeliads, and bird of paradise flowers add splashes of white and red to an otherwise densely green jungle. Doves coo in the underbrush while exotic butterflies drift lazily overhead, coming delicately to land on nectar feeders or on an outstretched leaf. Leaf-cutter ants, their heavy green burdens held high, climb across a log spanning a precipitous drop into a black pool of water. Again, I circle the room, pausing to watch, listen, and smell. Finally, I take a seat on a bench positioned high in the canopy, overlooking the exuberant vegetation down below.

This place reminds me, unexpectedly, of the cemetery. Gardens, native or kitchen or manicured Victorian or otherwise, have consistently drawn me in with a welcoming embrace. Is that not half the reason I loved Michikusa House? Not the house itself, but the seasonality of the work, the abundant garden, a lifestyle that necessitated time spent outdoors. Ditto for the cemetery. I made my own choice when I interviewed for and accepted a job there, when I gave up a degree to work there, against the wishes of both Liam and my parents. Perhaps my decisions were not entirely self-determined, not consciously at any rate, but rather based on a more instinctual desire to separate myself from the enclosed boxes in which most modern humans spend their time. And hasn't Diversity of Life all but proven that what I do now is valuable? My work directly influences—no, it benefits the community of species, not just humans but myriad forms of life in this tiny corner of the world.

I chose this path. I'm not trailing Liam like a needful puppy seeking approval and attention, nor am I taking instruction from Jun or Shoko, or stepping along the stones my parents have laid out for me. I may feel alone again—lonely, even—but for the first time in memory I'm following a course that I selected, that feels right for me. I'm not manipulating my behavior to be accepted, loved, or admired by anyone.

On the other hand, is it worth the loss? I gave up an education, the respect of my parents, and Liam's commitment to me so that I might make choices without their influence.

Blast it. Who the hell knows? Isn't life a game of give and take? Like it or not, this is where I am now, and from here I'll move forward.

CHAPTER 18

Unexpectedly, it's Kyrone who invites me out for New Year's Eve, a mere two days before the event. He and his girlfriend and a few others are going on a dinner cruise, out on Lake Erie. The price alone sounds prohibitive, but he says one of his buddies bought a ticket and then had to back out, so I could go for free. He promises it will be fun. I tell him I don't have a date, trying to concoct excuses, but he blows it off. No big deal, he says. Come anyway. I tell him I'll have to think about it. And I do. The mere idea of mingling with strangers for an entire night gives me palpitations. Nor am I eager to reenter the dating scene, if indeed it would amount to that, and frankly, when does it not? In the end, I decline politely, but firmly, reminding him I have to work the next morning: we're open every day of the year. The truth is, I offered to work both New Year's Eve and the following day under the assumption I would not be participating in the annual celebrations to which most are accustomed. I always thought it was a fairly ridiculous holiday anyhow, an artificially assigned new beginning. Personally, I would much prefer to honor the winter solstice or the first day of spring. We chat a bit more about work and I ask whether he will return once the weather changes. He thinks so but isn't locked in yet.

On Sunday, the first of January, I head over to the cemetery early, looking forward to an especially quiet morning. I spend a few minutes chatting with Curtis, who says nothing of his nephew, only that we're short staffed. Two of our guys called in sick.

"Hung over's more like it," Curtis says frankly, and I don't disagree.

"Shouldn't be bad today, though. Hasn't snowed in a while."

"Yeah. Check the paths and steps, then you can work on the invasives, if you feel like it," Curtis says. I recognize this is his gift to me, offering me the freedom to work by myself, or rather in the company only of plants.

I load up one of the trucks with salt, a shovel, and the gear I'll need for tackling the buckthorn, even though the paths likely won't need my attention. I check them anyway, then drive over to the reservoir. That was Dodge's last day of work, wasn't it? He and I had been over at the reservoir cutting buckthorn. I work for a couple hours hunched down in the snow then take my lunch break sitting the truck, heat roaring. That's when I notice a familiar car in the rearview pulling up behind me. What on earth?

Liam parks and gets out. When he knocks on my window, I roll it down.

"Hey," he says.

"What are you doing here?" I ask. The only logical question.

"I don't want to end on a fight, Win. That's not what I want. Can we talk? Please?"

"Does Fiona know you're here?"

"She's out with her mom. Wedding stuff," he says, which doesn't answer my question. Or maybe it does.

"How did you know I would be here?"

"I think I know you a little. When you weren't home, I drove over."

"Get in," I say. "You're not dressed for the weather."

He climbs in the passenger's side. I'm reminded of that time, with Jun...

"Okay, hear me out," he says, as if I've done anything other than invite him in. "I've thought about this a lot, and I need to say this: I wasn't good for you, Win."

"Oh, please, Liam. That's just what people say to make the person they dumped feel better."

"Maybe they do, but I mean it. I was keeping you in a cage. I was stagnating you. When we first met, yeah, sure, I helped you come out of your shell. You were so shy you could hardly speak, let alone speak up for yourself."

I roll my eyes, but he presses on.

"I thought going to separate colleges would be the springboard we both needed to grow, you know?" he tries, but I don't have a response to that. "I didn't realize it at the time, but I was relying on you, too. You were still my safe place, and it was easy to retreat to you, end up right back where I started."

I nod. That is what happened.

"Then you went to Japan."

"Right as you were about to come home, back to Ohio."

"Exactly. I had just graduated so I threw myself into work, but I felt like I was just waiting for you to come home. Then when you did you were totally different."

"Yeah," is all I can manage.

"You didn't need me anymore."

"Liam, I don't—" I begin, but he cuts me off.

"That's when I realized, I saw how, all along, what I'd been doing to you. Like it was my fault for keeping you small. It made me so, I don't know...mad? Jealous, maybe? Suddenly you were this confident, self-assured, new person."

"I don't feel that way," I say.

"Only because you're habituated to feeling the opposite. You certainly don't act like it anymore. College, all that shit that happened the first time around, it tore you apart and going to Japan, it put you back together in a way that finally made sense."

That's one way to look at it. "What about Fiona? She seems like the pinnacle of self-assurance. What makes you think she needs you?"

"She doesn't; that's the point. We're both self-determined, self-made."

"Individuals."

"Yes. Exactly. She knows what she wants, a hundred percent, and she's going for it. I respect that about her. A lot. It gives me the freedom to be whoever I want to be. Fiona and I, as a couple, we work in parallel, side by side. Our relationship, you and me, it was never about that. We were too interlocked. We weren't individuals. Does that make sense?"

I lean my head back against the headrest, closing my eyes. "I'm not sure."

"I had this gut feeling, like it was over for you and me, the last time we came here. When we were arguing about your schoolwork. Remember?"

How could I forget? "You were so against—" I sigh loudly— "literally everything I said."

"Yeah, and you bulldozed everything I said. It was like arguing with a battering ram! You never would have done that in high school." He's right, and we both know it. "I think it comes down to our upbringings, honestly."

"You mean because I was born with the silver spoon, and you had to earn yours?"

"That's part of it," he admits, warily. "I guess I wanted to end up more like your parents, but you ended up fighting against that lifestyle, that sort of linear progression. See what I mean?"

"I don't know. Couldn't a relationship just be about friendship?" I try. "About being there, holding hands through thick and thin?"

"That's only part of it, though. Sure, you should be friends with your partner, but it's gotta be more than that when you're with someone—engaged to someone. And that's the thing, I think you knew it too, that I wasn't the right one for you. That's why you fell in love with someone else," he says, and I think I detect a note of sadness there. "Loving someone implies a deeper knowing that only comes from a long-term, really close connection."

"Can't you love two people at once?"

"Probably. But I don't think you loved me anymore after that. Not in the same way."

"Well, for what it's worth, he's gone."

"Right."

"And you have Fiona."

He nods. "She's great. She's what I need right now—"

"—And presumably for the rest of your life."

"I think so, yeah," he says, smiling again, and I feel glad for him, that he's happy. He seems peaceful for a change. Content. "Anyway, that's what I came here to say. You're free now, to do something bigger than…anything either of us would've expected, I think."

"Don't patronize me," I say.

"I mean it, Win. Come here," he says, pulling me across the console, into a hug. It feels awkward, me holding my bento lunchbox on my lap, my side digging into the water bottle nestled in the cup holder.

"I still don't want to come to your wedding," I say, and let go.

"I understand," he says. "It's pretty sudden for me, too."

I don't know what to say to that, other than, "Well, best of luck."

He checks the time, then says, "I should probably get going," which sounds so predictable it's irritating. He is right about one thing though: I don't love him anymore. Care about his well-being? Sure. But I don't feel like I lost him to Fiona. He wasn't meant to be my whole life. Some friends are like that, a lovingly handmade sweater you eventually, through the sheer act of living, outgrow. This time, when he leaves, it's easier saying goodbye.

After he goes, I stay in the truck for a while trying to settle back into what remains of the day. Robins dart from tree branches, collecting berries that dropped onto the snow. A geranium-red cardinal stands sentry, perched on a tree branch. A rabbit scoots from under the brush out into the open, her fawn coloring blending so naturally with her surroundings, the twigs and dry grasses that make up her home, that I keep losing sight of her even when she sits motionless. So, I keep my eyes open. If I rolled down the window, I would hear the chickadees and woodpeckers sounding out the chorus and percussion, respectively, to the wintersong I've grown increasingly accustomed to. Maybe I'll make *nabe* tonight, the perfect winter comfort dish. Sometimes I think it's the craving of nourishment, that inescapable desire for the continuation of life, that keeps any of us going. Though what we long for is fulfillment. To feel satiated, we need connection, somebody to reciprocate our love. If, in all the randomness of living, life graces us with a bond linking us to another being, then we may briefly inhabit the rare, fragile place where joyfulness resides.

Like a reflex, I draw out my phone, opening the @j.nakashima.j account. As always, new photos appear, a new one every day. I take my time scrolling through, imagining Jun among the overgrown weeds and cockeyed homes, scooping up radiated soil.

As if the universe has been waiting for just this moment, a notification springs up at the bottom of the screen, like the first sprouts of spring pushing toward sunlight. My palms shake as I tap on it. It takes me to our original conversation, to which he's replied:

> j.nakashima.j: I came to Futaba because I had to make a big decision in my life. I wanted to make an impact. Since my first love is cooking, I want to know where each ingredient comes from, how it was grown, and who held it before I did. I could have chosen to work in a restaurant, but I wanted to do something that would help people as well as feed them. I became interested in the revival of the soil. If I can help restore the land in this area to good health, I can give people different ways to eat delicious food. That's what I think.

I turn off the screen and lean forward, bracing myself against the steering wheel. Jun, it's me. Don't you remember? My phone buzzes. When I check, I see he has sent a second message. Eagerly, I read:

> j.nakashima.j: For some time, nuclear power has made life more convenient. It was cheap electricity. That's what people said. But when you look at the cost to people and the land, I'm not sure how cheap it is.

Knowing it's essentially social suicide to respond instantly, I nonetheless reply:

Win__chime: You're right. It doesn't seem worth it.

I can't press send, because what I really want to say is, I miss you.

What I want to say is, I'm coming to Japan in five months.

What I want to ask is, how are you, really? How has life changed you? Has it altered you for the better? Do you feel stronger now than ever before? Empowered to do good despite the harrowing, familiar reckoning of catastrophe staring you straight in the eye? Have you been pitched sideways, wrecked and silted with debris, still to find yourself, absurdly, fighting to be hopeful?

Maybe what I really want to know is, who does he run to at night, when his worst fears and self-doubts come crashing in around him.

> Win__chime: You're right. It doesn't seem worth it. Sometimes it seems easier to move to the countryside and grow your own little patch of garden and forget about the fate of the world. That's when I have to remind myself that it's up to people like us, people who really care, to do some good where we can. I work in a cemetery. Even though it's not exactly saving an entire prefecture from contamination, I try to give other species a fighting chance at survival by giving care and attention to the lives being lived out here.

I hit send and shut my eyes. I wonder whether Curtis will find me here, slacking off, but I feel too tired to move. After a few minutes, my phone buzzes again.

> j.nakashima.j: I can see you liking such a job very much. It suits you.

My hand travels involuntarily to my mouth, stifling a small cry. He knows. Of course, he does. He's known this entire time.

Win__chime: I'm actually at work right now. It's a beautiful day, cold but sunny so all the sparrows and cardinals and robins are singing and swooping around me.

I hit send. Suddenly, as if setting off a chain reaction, my phone starts to ring. A number I don't recognize. An international one. He had my phone number at one time; I know he did. I gave it to him so he could forward those photographs I took of the hot springs in Beppu, the ones he never actually sent...of living, pulsating water.

Heartbeat and voice trembling, I answer. "Hello?"

On the other end, clear as day, I hear, "Hey, Win-chan."

AUTHOR'S NOTE

Virginia Woolf once wrote: "Considering how common illness is, how tremendous the spiritual change that it brings, how astonishing, when the lights of health go down, the undiscovered countries that are disclosed…it becomes strange indeed that illness has not taken its place with love and battle and jealousy among the prime themes of literature." It was with such a heart that I began writing about Winona Heeley and her recovery from extreme illness, which took place, in part, at Michikusa House. I did not want to fill the pages of this book with the darkest days of her trauma, however. My desire was to bring some softness to the often excruciating processes of illness and recovery without undermining those important, and often deeply transformative aspects. Neither did I aim to diminish the suffering experienced by those who endure extreme illness. Instead, I hoped to reveal a light at the end of the tunnel and remind readers that healing, in the broadest sense, is possible.

In doing so, I did not aim to trivialize Win's illness, either. That needs to be perfectly clear because the mortality rate of eating disorders is upwards of 10%, the highest of any mental illness. Anorexia is the third most common chronic illness among adolescents, after asthma and obesity, and it is not exclusive to women. Although teenage girls are generally at a higher risk of developing an eating disorder than boys, 1 in 5 teenagers with bulimia nervosa and 1 in 4 teenagers with anorexia nervosa is male. Eating disorders affect all genders, all races, and every ethnic group. Even so, in the United States, eating disorder research is the least funded of all mental illness research. In 2018, the US Department of Health & Human Services spent $38 million researching eating disorders, compared to $213 million researching anxiety disorders and $500 million researching depression.

Eating disorders lead to severe malnutrition that affects nearly every organ in the body. Some of the most common associated issues include: dangerously low heart rate or abnormal heart rhythm; irritability, mood changes and difficulty focusing; stomach and intestines work slower leading to pain, constipation, or bloating; loss of periods in females, which weakens bones; males may develop low levels of testosterone; as well as anemia, poor immune function, and bleeding disorders. Children who haven't started puberty may have delayed puberty or slow growth.

Like addiction, the portrayal of disordered eating in the media is often glamorized. It is important to remember, however, that an eating disorder is not just about weight or food. Eating disorders are complex medical and mental illnesses. It is very common for people with eating disorders to have other mental health disorders, such as depression, anxiety, or obsessive-compulsive disorder.

Although eating disorders can be successfully treated, only 1 in 10 sufferers ever receive treatment. Winona was one of the 10%. Her disordered behavior and recovery, both, mimic my own experience in certain respects, but in the tradition of the Japanese I-novel—in in which writers explore their own actions and thoughts through fictional narratives—I will not reveal where or how our paths cross. In writing this novel I wanted to focus on what comes after illness and the sorts of changes that can take place during the recovery process rather than the more gruesome components that precede it. Call it a sanitized version of reality, but novels often choose how they want to be written, not the other way around.

I also want to emphasize that recovery is a not a final phase one achieves but a process. This, I think, is what Woolf meant when she wrote about the "tremendous spiritual change" illness enables. It forces its sufferers to learn and change, reckon with pain, past and future choices, and the ways in which we choose to live each and every day. Every person's journey through illness is different. Winona's version is not meant to reflect, represent, or guide anyone else's.

I urge anyone suffering with an eating disorder to seek medical help as soon as possible. Below are some resources where you can seek guidance. I wish you wellness and a happy, wholesome heart.

- Eating Disorders: National Eating Disorder Association, call the Eating Disorder Helpline at 800-931-2237, or chat online (see hours online).

- Personal Crisis: Crisis Text Line, text HOME to 741741 to connect with a crisis counselor 24/7

- Suicide: National Suicide Prevention Lifeline, 24 hour hotline: 1-800-273-TALK (8255)

RESOURCES

1. "April 2018: Eating Disorders in Adolescents." US Department of Health and Human Services.

2. Baldock KCR, Goddard MA, Hicks DM, et al. *A systems approach reveals urban pollinator hotspots and conservation opportunities.* Nat Ecol Evol. 2019;3(3):363-373. doi:10.1038/s41559-018-0769-y

3. Bovyn, R., Lordon, M., Grecco, A., Leeper, A., LaMontagne, J. Tree cavity availability in urban cemeteries and city parks, *Journal of Urban Ecology,* Volume 5, Issue 1, 2019 <https://doi.org/10.1093/jue/juy030>

4. Davidson, H., Wahlquist, C. Australian dig finds evidence of Aboriginal habitation up to 80,000 years ago. *The Guardian.* 19 July, 2017. Web <https://www.theguardian.com/australia-news/2017/jul/19/dig-finds-evidence-of-aboriginal-habitation-up-to-80000-years-ago>

5. Deák, B., Tóthmérész, B., Valkó, O., Sudnik-Wójcikowska, B., Bragina, T.-M., Moysiyenko, I., Apostolova, I., Bykov, N., Dembicz, I. & Török, P. 2016. Cultural monuments and nature conservation: The role of kurgans in maintaining steppe vegetation. Biodiversity & Conservation 25: 2473-2490.

6. Eating Disorder Statistics. "National Association of Anorexia Nervosa and Associated Disorders." National Association of Anorexia Nervosa and Associated Disorders anad.org/education-and-awareness/about-eating-disorders/eating-disorders-statistics/

7."Estimates of Funding for Various Research, Condition, and Disease Categories (RCDC)." US Department of Health and Human Services. https://report.nih.gov/categorical_spending.aspx. Accessed Feb. 20, 2020.

8.Ferriera, Dan. *Dealing with the fallout in Fukushima - Part 1. Soils Matter, Get the Scoop!.* Soil Science Society of America. 1 March, 2019. <https://soilsmatter.wordpress.com/2019/03/01/dealing-with-the-fallout-in-fukushima-part-1/>

9.Ferriera, *Dan. Dealing with the fallout in Fukushima - Part 2. Soils Matter, Get the Scoop!.* Soil Science Society of America. 15 March, 2019. <https://soilsmatter.wordpress.com/2019/03/15/dealing-with-the-fallout-in-fukushima-part-2/>

10.Korn, Larry. *One Straw Revolutionary: The Philosophy and Work of Masanobu Fukuoka.* Chelsea Green Publishing. 2015

11.Löki, V., Schmotzer, A., Takács, A., Süveges, K., Lovas-Kiss, Á., Lukács, B. A., Tökölyi, J., & Molnár V, A. (2020). The protected flora of long-established cemeteries in Hungary: Using historical maps in biodiversity conservation. Ecology and evolution, 10(14), 7497–7508. https://doi.org/10.1002/ece3.6476

12.Lonsdorf, Kat. Fukushima has turned these grandparents into avid radiation testers. NPR. 11 Sept, 2020. Web <https://www.npr.org/2020/09/11/907881531/fukushima-has-turned-these-grandparents-into-avid-radiation-testers>

13.MaMing, R., Lee, L., Yang, X., Buzzard, P. Vultures and sky burials on the Qinghai-Tibet Plateau. Vulture News, 71. Nov 2016. Web <file:///C:/Users/14405/

Downloads/168874-Article%20Text-434342-1-10-20180329.
pdf>

14.McLeod, Fiona. Bears Ears. Sacred Land Film Project. 8
Aug, 2019. Web <https://sacredland.org/bears-ears/>

15.Merculieff, Illarion. Out of the Head, Into the Heart:
The Way of the Human Being. Humans and Nature.
16 June, 2017. Web < https://humansandnature.org/
out-of-the-head-into-the-heart-the-way-of-the-human-being>

16.Mukai H, Hirose A, Motai S et al. Cesium adsorption/de-
sorption behavior of clay minerals considering actual contamination conditions in Fukushima. Sci Rep 2016;6:21543.

17.Nakanishi TM, Tanoi K (eds). Agricultural implications of
Fukushima Nuclear Accident – the first three years. Springer,
2016.

18.Nakanishi TM, Tanoi K (eds). Agricultural implications of
Fukushima Nuclear Accident. Springer, 2013.

19.Normandin É, Vereecken NJ, Buddle CM, Fournier V.
2017. *Taxonomic and functional trait diversity of wild bees in
different urban settings.* PeerJ 5:e3051 https://doi.org/10.7717/
peerj.3051

20. Provenza, Fred. *Nourishment.* Chelsea Green Publishing.
2018

21.Rare spider species found in Highgate Cemetery
vaults. BBC. 20 Jan, 2013. <https://www.bbc.com/news/
uk-england-london-21107807>

22.Thornton, Katie. Why cemeteries are a surprising
source of life. *National Geographic.* 16 Oct, 2019. Web

<https://www.nationalgeographic.com/animals/2019/10/cemeteries-home-to-diverse-plants-animals/#close>

23.Van der Kolk, Besser. *The Body Keeps the Score: Brain, Mind, and Body in the Healing of Trauma*. Penguin Books. 2015

ACKNOWLEDGMENTS

A book does not come into the world on its own; it must first pass between many caring hands. This book was made possible thanks to Homebound Publication's Landmark Prize, which celebrates "titles that focus on a return to simplicity and balance, connection to the earth and to each other, and a search for meaning and authenticity." I want to thank Connor Wolfe for seeing these admirable qualities in *Michikusa House* and for ushering the manuscript, start to finish, through the publication process. Your guidance, wisdom, and careful tending of its release is deeply appreciated.

I also am indebted to the fellow writers, readers, and lovers of words who were willing to dedicate hours of their time to sift through early versions of this work to help it become the best version of itself. Susan Zupancic for her enthusiasm and support from my earliest writing ventures up until my first publication and beyond. Alex Austen for sharing his wisdom and experience and a much-needed critical eye. Josh Walker for taking a chance on this one and for spending time talking through trouble spots and, importantly, highlighting strengths. Andrew Shafer for being my first, last, and most dedicated reader, and for investing in this story and its characters as much as I did.

Any book is incomplete without a cover that reveals something of its inner magic. I am thrilled and full of gratitude for the work of Stephanie Shafer, whose gorgeous cover design represents so much of what I want potential readers to discover within this book, but especially that sense of calm and connection.

Finally, I want to thank my parents, Rob and Carol Grandy, for their unwavering support through all my trials and failings, and for their encouragement every step of the way. I also want to thank my partner, Andrew Shafer. I am a kinder, healthier, and far happier person thanks to you and without those qualities this book would not have been possible.